IMPOSSIBLE

DARCY BURKE

Zealous Quill Press

IMPOSSIBLE

Society's most exclusive invitation...

Welcome to the Phoenix Club, where London's most audacious, disreputable, and intriguing ladies and gentlemen find scandal, redemption, and second chances.

Ada Treadway has been in love before, and it brought nothing but heartache. Still, she retains her cheerful optimism and is fiercely protective of the independence and respect she's earned as bookkeeper of the Phoenix Club. When the owner enlists her help to organize his friend's estate ledgers, she's eager to prove her expertise and her worth. But his friend turns out to be a disagreeable, unpleasant beast, and Ada works to find the warm-hearted gentleman she's sure lurks beneath.

Maximillian Hunt, the Viscount Warfield doesn't care if he lives to see tomorrow, and he certainly doesn't want to recall yesterday. The arrival of the meddlesome and effusively positive woman who will put his accounts in order not only reminds him of the past he's desperate to forget, she sparks something within him he thought dead. Tempted by a future he never imagined, he must do the impossible: convince her that he's worth risking her heart a second time.

Don't miss the rest of *The Phoenix Club*!

Do you want to hear all the latest about me and my books? Sign up at <u>Reader Club newsletter</u> for members-only bonus content, advance notice of pre-orders, insider scoop, as well as contests and giveaways!

Care to share your love for my books with like-minded readers? Want to hang with me and see pictures of my cats (who doesn't!)? Then don't miss my exclusive Facebook groups!

Darcy's Duchesses for historical readers
Burke's Book Lovers for contemporary readers

Want more historical romance? Do you like your historical romance filled with passion and red hot chemistry? Join me and my author friends in the Facebook group, Historical Harlots, for exclusive giveaways, chat with amazing HistRom authors, and more!

CHAPTER 1

June 1815

*H*undreds of years ago, Stonehill had been a castle. Now, it was a large country house built within the last hundred years with a Palladian front. The façade was beautiful, but Ada Treadway would have preferred the castle.

Dark storm clouds hovered in the south, as if she needed to be reminded that this errand could be fraught with turmoil. *Could be?* Ada suspected nothing less from the Viscount Warfield.

The coach, which belonged to her employer, Lord Lucien Westbrook, rumbled to a stop in front of the entrance to the house. The coachman opened the door, and Ada stepped out into the early evening. A brisk wind whipped the ribbons of her hat beneath her chin. It seemed the storm was coming quickly. There was no avoiding it now.

"I'll fetch your case, Miss Treadway," the coachman said.

Thanking him, Ada started toward the house. The door did not magically open when she arrived at the threshold. So she knocked.

The coachman arrived beside her. "No one's come to greet you?"

"Not yet." Ada knocked again, this time with more vigor.

Another moment passed and still nothing. Frowning, the coachman looked about. "Perhaps I should take the coach to the stable and find someone there."

"There must be someone in the house," Ada reasoned, knocking a third time.

At last, there seemed to be a sound beyond the door —footsteps.

The door swung open to reveal a small red-faced woman with graying brown hair and weary chestnut eyes. "Begging your pardon, miss. My son—that is, the footman—is busy at the moment, and I'm afraid I was belowstairs." She summoned a smile, but it was hard-fought, or so it seemed to Ada.

"Good evening," Ada said warmly. "I'm here to help Lord Warfield with his ledgers."

"Yes, I received a letter from Lord Lucien about your arrival. Do come in. I'm Mrs. Bundle, the housekeeper." She stepped aside, holding the door. Looking to the coachman, she said, "If you'll leave her case here in the hall, my son will fetch it shortly. I know you need to tend the horses."

"Thank you." The coachman inclined his head before setting Ada's traveling case just inside the doorway. He nodded at Ada before departing for the stable.

Ada doubted she would see him again before he left in the morning. He'd be back in a fortnight to fetch her back to London. "Thank you, Jackson," she called after him.

Returning her attention to Mrs. Bundle, Ada clasped her

hands before her. "I can carry my own case upstairs—I don't mind. If you'll just show me the way to my room?"

A tall, rather lean young man hurried into the hall just then. His brown eyes were the same color as his mother's and held the same weariness. No, not quite the same, for his mother possessed many more years of experience that made her gaze heavier.

"Here is Timothy now," Mrs. Bundle said, brightening at the arrival of her son. "He'll show you to the Primrose Room. Dinner is at seven." She gestured to the left. "The dining room is through there—you'll find it."

"Should I expect to meet with Lord Warfield before dinner?" Ada asked.

Mrs. Bundle blanched. Ada hadn't expected to be welcomed enthusiastically by her host—she was well versed on the viscount's surly demeanor. However, she hadn't expected this…strangeness from his retainers.

"No, I shouldn't think so," Mrs. Bundle said, an apologetic glimmer in her expression. "I doubt he'll join you for dinner either. I will remind him that you've come."

Ada suddenly recalled that the housekeeper had said she'd received a letter from Lucien about her arrival. Lucien had seen fit to write directly to the housekeeper. Was the viscount even aware that she was coming? It seemed he must have been at some point if Mrs. Bundle was going to remind him.

Ah well, Ada had known this would be a challenging assignment. Warfield was angry, wounded inside and out, and completely uninterested in help from anyone. These were things she'd learned from Lucien, who was one of Warfield's closest friends, if the viscount truly had any of those anymore. She'd also heard them from Warfield's half sister, who happened to be Ada's closest friend, Prudence

Lancaster. No, Prudence St. James since she had recently wed the Viscount Glastonbury.

By all accounts, Warfield was a nasty fellow with no desire to improve his demeanor. As a former governess, Ada had decided to view him as an unruly child. She had plenty of experience with those.

She gave Mrs. Bundle what she hoped was a supportive smile. "I understand his lordship possesses a difficult nature. Do not worry for me. I am up to the task at hand, which is to organize his ledgers and determine how he might make improvements. Not that I am versed in running an estate, but I understand numbers and will report my findings to Lord Lucien, who will help his lordship make the necessary changes."

Mrs. Bundle stared at her as if Ada had suddenly sprouted a second head. "You and Lord Lucien are awfully confident." Her tone was rife with skepticism.

"We are hopeful," Ada said. It was also her hope that she'd be able to accomplish her mission with very little interaction with his lordship. She planned to stay out of his way as much as possible. So, it was really quite fine if he didn't join her for dinner. In truth, all she really needed was access to his ledgers. He could stay wherever he was hiding.

"Bless you, Miss Treadway. Timothy will show you to the Primrose Room now." Mrs. Bundle inclined her head toward her son before leaving the hall.

Ada offered the lad—he looked younger than her twenty-five years—an encouraging smile, for he seemed a trifle nervous. Perhaps that was what happened when you worked in a house with an excessively disagreeable employer. "The Primrose Room sounds quite charming."

Without a word, he picked up her case and gestured straight through the entry hall.

They moved into a large staircase hall, with the stairs

climbing from the center to the back wall and then splitting up either side to a gallery on the first floor. Ada preceded him up the stairs. "Have you and your mother been here a long time?" she asked.

"Yes." The word was so quiet, Ada had to strain to hear it. She glanced back at him to see him staring past her, his features taut.

She very much wanted to put him at ease. "Well, I am here to help if I can. I look forward to my time here."

He said nothing, and at the top of the stairs merely pointed again, this time to the left. If he hadn't answered her question a moment ago, she might have begun to wonder whether he could speak.

They moved along the gallery, and she would have kept on going if he hadn't said, "Here."

Stopping, she turned back to see him standing in front of a door, which he opened for her.

"Thank you," she said with a smile, still hoping he might relax a bit—she hated that he might feel nervous around her. Moving into the chamber, she wondered why it was called the Primrose Room, for there was nary a primrose about. "Is it called Primrose because of the yellow?" Bright, cheerful yellow dominated the color scheme of the room. Ada's favorite primroses were that color yellow.

Timothy's only answer was to shrug. He set her case down. "Do you need anything else?" His voice was rather small, and it seemed an effort to say so much.

"No, thank you. Very much," she added with a great deal of warmth and another smile.

He inclined his head, then took himself off. Ada found that she had tensed in his presence—because she'd been unsettled by his nervousness. She hoped she hadn't upset him somehow. But how could she have?

Ada shook her head. She sometimes worried far too

much what others thought or took responsibility for making sure everyone around her felt happy. Or that they were at least positive rather than sad or troubled.

Bother, it *wasn't* her responsibility. Still, she couldn't seem to help herself. Perhaps she'd ask Mrs. Bundle about her son. But then Mrs. Bundle had also seemed beleaguered. Had Warfield cast a pall over his entire household? It seemed possible, if not likely, given all she knew of him.

"Do not assume he has kind qualities or a hidden desire to be happy," Prudence had warned, though she couldn't know that for certain because she'd only met him the one time. It was more that she was cautioning Ada not to treat him as she did others, that he wasn't a typical person who had a bad day now and again. Lucien had made it clear the viscount was disagreeable and surly *every* day. Or at least every time Lucien made the journey to visit his friend.

Ada realized she was hoping Warfield might be different around her. She did bring out the best in people, or tried to anyway. Her optimism refused to believe she wouldn't be able to manage it.

She poked around the room, feeling slightly out of place. She supposed she'd expected a room on the servants' floor, but when Mrs. Bundle had said "Primrose Room," she'd realized that would not be the case. Still, she hadn't expected a room of this size, with a beautiful seating area, large four-poster bed with hangings, and a separate dressing chamber where a maid could prepare her garments. As if she had a maid. Ada giggled.

She no more required a maid than she did a husband. Independence suited her quite wonderfully. She'd been on her own for nearly ten years, since a fever had taken her mother, just a few months after her sister had died. And she'd lost her father five years before that. That she retained such a positive outlook after tragedy surprised everyone, but to

Ada, it was simply survival. What good would it be to wallow?

Not that she hadn't spent time wallowing... She pushed those thoughts away. Better to focus on her love of independence, for that was what would keep her strong and happy.

And she was going to need that to get through the next fortnight.

~

*A*fter a solitary dinner served by a silent Timothy, Ada found the library. At the back of the house in the center, it seemed an addition to the original structure. The library's domed ceiling soared well past the first floor. It was almost cathedral-like with high windows, some of which were stained glass. They were flowers, she realized—a rose, a lily, a dahlia, and even a primrose. She was now curious about the meaning of flowers at Stonehill.

Her curiosity was perhaps second only to her positivity—and perhaps not even that—and it drove Ada through one of the doorways leading from the library. At once, she knew she'd found the viscount's study.

The scent of leather, paper, and brandy enveloped her as she stepped inside. Meager light from the hearth provided more shadows than illumination, but Ada made out the rich blue draperies cloaking the tall windows that presumably looked out at the rear garden and parkland beyond. Presumably, she thought, because it was now dark, and she couldn't see anything past the panes of glass.

The remnants of the fire prompted her to wonder if his lordship had been there earlier. A cozy blue, gold, and brown patterned chair sat near the fireplace, providing the perfect place to sit and read or simply contemplate. Ada liked to think, and she could see herself enjoying that spot for just that purpose.

Alas, this was not her place, and she should go. But the same curiosity that had beckoned her inside now pushed her to the desk. Perhaps she could get an early start on the ledgers. She wasn't terribly tired, despite the day's journey.

Fetching a spill from the mantel, she borrowed some fire from the hearth to light the lamp on the desk. Finding it still warm, she wondered if Warfield had only recently left.

"What are you doing in here?"

The bellow from the doorway made her jump, and she dropped the spill before lighting the lamp. Muttering a curse, she plucked up a leather-bound volume and slapped it on the smoking spill before it could catch something on fire.

"Are you trying to set my bloody house ablaze?" The large figure moved into the room, but it was too dark to make out his features. She could, however, see that he was quite tall and rather broad across the shoulders.

"No. I was lighting a lamp."

"*Failing* to light it and starting a fire in the meantime."

She lifted the book and took the spill from beneath it to return it to the mantel. "I did not."

He moved to the desk, his body angled away from her so that she could only see his right side. Even so, she still couldn't discern his face, just the strong jut of his square jaw.

Moving the book she'd used to extinguish the spill to the other side of the desk, he grunted. "You aren't supposed to be in here. You're to keep to your chamber or the dining room."

"Those are the only places I may go?" Ada snorted. "I'm going to be here a fortnight. I shall need more than my chamber and the dining room to escape boredom."

"Why? You're here to look at my ledgers. You may take them to your room. The Primrose Room has a fine desk, and

I'll make sure the lamp is lit in the evenings, since you can't seem to accomplish that feat."

"That was your fault," she said with disdain, forgetting that she preferred to be good-natured. Ada took a deep breath and forced herself to find magnanimity. "You startled me."

"You're trespassing where you shouldn't be."

Though he was being a dolt about it, she acknowledged that he was right. She was overly inquisitive, and she knew it. "My apologies. I only meant to see if I could get started on my work." That was, inquisitiveness aside, the primary reason she'd wanted to look at his desk.

"Or to see what you could find out about me while I wasn't here to stop you." His low growl stole over her like a shadow, making her shiver.

Not in fear, but awareness. And it roused her ire. "You might be able to frighten everyone," she said, thinking of Timothy. "However, I will not be cowed by your outrage. I've no patience for such theatrics. I came here to do a job, and I'd like to do it."

His jaw clenched. "Mrs. Bundle was supposed to tell you we would meet in the morning."

"Even if she had, I would have still come in here. I like to be busy, and I wasn't tired."

He grunted. "Then read a book. The library is next door."

"Yes, I was just in there. It's a stunning room. Was it added to the house after it was built?"

Silence reigned for a moment, and she could almost feel his derision. So much for making chitchat.

She gave up on conversation. "If you'd like to hand me one of your ledgers, I can take it up to my room and get started. Though, I'd rather have a different place to work. Perhaps the libr—"

He slammed his palm on the desk. "Enough! Get out

before I toss you from the estate entirely. I never should have let Lucien talk me into letting you come."

"He is rather persuasive."

His head turned toward her for the briefest moment, and his eyes—completely shadowed—met hers. "Get. Out."

Ada inhaled slowly and counted to five in her head. "My lord, I am not someone you can order about. You are not my employer—Lucien is the one I am serving during my stay here. The sooner you accept that I've come to help, the better you will feel." She went back to the desk and picked up the book she'd inadvertently almost caught on fire. "I'll start with this. Good evening, Lord Warfield."

He turned his head toward hers again, and because she was closer, she could actually make out part of his features beyond the shape of his chin. His nose was long and aquiline, and his brow wide, with a lock of blond hair falling across it. But it was the scar, rather scars, she glimpsed running over the left side of his face that caught her attention.

He snatched the book from her grasp and walked into the shadows, turning his back to her. "Go."

Ada pivoted and returned to the library before finding her way to the Primrose Room.

This was going to be a very long fortnight.

CHAPTER 2

*M*aximillian Hunt, the extremely reluctant Viscount Warfield, glowered at the lamp on his desk and fervently hoped it would soon cease reminding him of his unwelcome houseguest. Perhaps she would do as he'd said and leave today. Last night had been too late to depart, of course. Not even he was so beastly as to demand she venture out into the darkness.

But today was pleasant and plenty light enough. If she were smart, she'd leave as soon as she broke her fast.

At that precise moment, Mrs. Bundle came in bearing his breakfast tray, as she did every morning around this time. She brought the tray to his desk and removed the cover to reveal the usual plate: toast, eggs, kippers, and turnips.

"Where would you like to meet with Miss Treadway after breakfast?" she asked perfunctorily.

"Nowhere. I'd like you to get her to leave."

"I feel certain you'll be able to do that without my assistance," she said with a touch of heat, which she hadn't done with him in some time.

Chewing a bite of toast, he slid her a glower.

She glared right back at him. "Meet her in the library. With your ledgers. She's here to help, and you need it."

He growled before taking another bite of toast, masticating it as if it were meat instead of bread, and that he was the beast everyone described him to be.

Because he was.

Mrs. Bundle put her hands on her hips and fixed him with maternal disdain. It was one of the few things that could still provoke discomfort—the kind he felt when he knew he ought to do better and thought, perhaps, that he should.

"We can't keep on as we are." She glanced toward the window that looked out to the overgrown gardens. "Stonehill requires a much larger staff to care for the house, let alone the grounds. Your tenants need support, or they'll move on. Are you truly content to allow Stonehill to fall into disrepair?"

Max shrugged. "What do I care? I don't plan to wed or have children, and I am not aware of any heirs to the title. Does it really matter what happens to the estate?"

The housekeeper's brown eyes sparked with anger. "Only to the tenants. One of these days, you're going to drive me to leave. And Timothy will come with me. Where will you be then?"

He speared a whole kipper on his fork and fixed her with a dark stare. "I'll be right here, surveying the view of my dilapidated gardens." Stuffing the fish into his mouth, he champed it harshly, grinding his teeth in the process.

She gave a disgusted snort. "And who will bring your breakfast?"

"One of the scullery maids."

"There is *only* one, and she's only here in the afternoons. You could ask Mrs. Debley, I suppose, but she's worked to the bone, not that she would say so or that you would care.

What's worse is that she'll do it until she's in her grave. Anything for her 'dearest boy.'" Mrs. Bundle rolled her eyes.

Max suffered a moment's self-recrimination. Mrs. Debley had been the cook at Stonehill since before he was born. She and Og in the stables were the only retainers left who had known him as a boy. She'd also known his father, his brother, and, of course, his beloved mother. If she—or Og—left, he might truly break.

If he wasn't already broken.

He pulled himself back to the situation at hand—his aggrieved housekeeper. "If you want to leave, you should."

"Who will be here to clean up after you and ensure you don't waste away?"

Max shrugged again. "Perhaps I want to. Waste away, that is."

She groaned, her frustration palpable. "Please go to the library to meet Miss Treadway when you're finished. She's quite charming and seems capable. Just give her what she needs and stay out of her way. Perhaps she can set things right." Mrs. Bundle turned, her shoulders sagging as she retreated from the study.

Another pang of self-loathing dashed through him. Mrs. Bundle *should* leave—she'd be better off. No one could set things right, not his hardworking housekeeper, and certainly not some meddlesome chit from Lucien's silly London club.

Lowering his gaze to his plate, Max pushed the food around. As usual, he'd started his meal with gusto only to lose his appetite rather quickly. It was too bad, for Mrs. Debley was an exceptionally fine cook. Even with a dearth of help in the kitchen.

He set his utensils down and reached for the coffee, taking too much into his mouth and scalding his tongue. Swallowing, he set the cup back down with a muttered curse.

Things were fine as they were. Mrs. Debley clearly didn't

need help in the kitchen, and Mrs. Bundle was managing things just fine. She was only provoking him because she was *worried*. How he loathed that word. If he never heard it again the rest of his life, it would be too soon. Everyone had been nothing *but* worried since he'd returned from Spain.

There was nothing to worry about. The estate wasn't in shambles, and the tenants wouldn't leave because he didn't raise the rent. Indeed, perhaps he'd lower their rent to compensate for his poor management. Yes, that was a capital idea. Then Mrs. Bundle could stop worrying about that at least.

Pushing the tray away, he leaned back in his chair and looked at the portrait hanging over the mantel. His mother's loving smile didn't ease his pain, but it quieted the noise, at least for a few moments.

How had it been nearly twenty years since her passing? He could still feel her comforting embrace, smell her rose-and-peony soap, hear her warm laugh. But recalling things had never been his problem. In fact, memories were what kept him immersed in suffering.

And that was precisely what he deserved.

Fuck it.

He abruptly stood, sweeping up his coffee cup so it nearly sloshed over the rim. Just what he needed, a burn on his hand to go with the one on his tongue. What was one more wound?

Max stalked into the library and immediately caught sight of a blue skirt swaying far above eye level on the other side of the room. His unwelcome guest teetered on one of the very old, very rickety ladders used to access the books on the highest shelves. They were in need of replacement or repair, but he never used them.

"Oh!"

The rung on which she perched gave out. Max dropped

his coffee cup and sprinted across the library, catching his thigh on a piece of furniture in his haste. Pain shot through him, but he didn't slow. She dangled from the ladder by one hand, her feet swinging as she sought purchase.

"Help!" The plea leapt from her lips as she lost her grip and fell.

~

*S*trong arms caught Ada, and she gasped. Her rescuer grunted, his arms holding her tightly against his hard, broad chest.

She looked up into his face, seeing it for the first time in the light of day. His handsome, chiseled, and terribly scarred face. Framed with too-long but neatly combed blond hair. The night before, it had been untidy, falling across his forehead in a rather dashing manner.

"Thank you," she managed, sounding rather breathless.

He narrowed his hazel eyes at her. They were more green at the center, becoming increasingly brown toward the outside. "You're quite a little fool, aren't you?"

"I'm not the one who allowed the ladder in my library to fall into disrepair."

Satisfaction glimmered in his gaze. "You recognized its failure was imminent, yet chose to climb it anyway?"

"That's not at all what I said. I recognized its *imminent failure* when it was too late to climb down. My goodness, but you are incredibly disagreeable. I thought I was prepared for your boorishness, but I can see I underestimated your lack of amiability. It isn't just lacking; it's nonexistent."

He released her with a grunt, ensuring her feet had found the floor before he stepped back. "Then we are well suited, for I must say you suffer from a severe paucity of charm."

She gaped at him, wounded to the quick. "Everyone finds

me charming, or at least amenable and pleasant to be around. You bring out the worst in me, clearly."

"It's one of my finest skills."

Was he bragging about his ability to provoke others' worst natures? Who would do such a thing? "Is that your intent? To make everyone else as miserable as you are?"

His features shuttered, making his expression completely inscrutable. "That would be impossible."

"Then you admit you're miserable." That was a start at least. But a start to what? Did she really think she'd be able to cure whatever ailed him during her fortnight here? What if it wasn't a curable ailment? Just because he'd been vastly different—according to both Lucien, who'd known him very well, and Prudence's mother, who'd known the viscount's father well—before he'd gone to war didn't mean he could go back to being that way. Perhaps he was permanently damaged.

No, Ada refused to think that. Everyone could come back from the abyss. She had.

His jaw worked, as though he clenched his teeth. "I admitted nothing. You are an insulting chit."

"I'm insulting?" She crossed her arms over her chest and gave him a benign smile. "You're only trying to provoke me to leave. Don't bother. I'm here to complete my task." She narrowed one eye. "What are you so afraid of?"

"I'm not afraid," he snapped. "I simply want to be left alone. You're intruding on my privacy."

"Heaven forbid! I am more than happy to leave you alone. I require your ledgers, not you. I'll write up any questions I have, and you can respond in writing. We needn't even see each other again." Except then she couldn't try to coax forth the kinder, more pleasant gentleman buried beneath the beast before her. Assuming that gentleman could be found.

He seemed to mull what she offered, his lips pressing together, and his gaze focused beyond her.

She didn't believe him about not being afraid. Something was keeping him locked inside his misery. What was preventing him from being the man he once was? And how was she to determine answers without spending time with him? Bother!

She'd see what Mrs. Bundle would reveal. Or other retainers, perhaps. Not Timothy, obviously, since he barely spoke. There had to be a maid. Didn't there? Not that Ada had seen one yet. There most definitely was a cook. Dinner and breakfast had been delicious, and Ada doubted Mrs. Bundle could accomplish the feat of preparing both while attending to her other duties. Especially if there wasn't a maid. Goodness, what if Mrs. Bundle made all the beds and laid the fires and cleaned and did the laundry and…Ada was suddenly feeling exhausted.

No, there had to be other retainers. Surely there were groomsmen in the stables. Unless Warfield didn't have any livestock. How could that be? Except, he never went anywhere, so it was entirely possible. Did he expect Mrs. Bundle to venture out to purchase things for the household without a cart at least? Perhaps someone from the village delivered what they required. Including the delicious pheasant that she'd devoured the night before? There must be a gamekeeper. Yes, there had to be people she could speak to about his lordship so she could fully conduct her investigation.

An *investigation*. That was precisely what was required. There were far too many questions about the viscount, his household, and his estate. Reviewing the ledgers would likely only prompt more questions.

She realized the beast was staring at her, his hazel eyes

focused squarely on her face. She wondered what had caused the scars on his cheek and temple.

"Are you finished?" he asked.

Ada blinked at him. "With what?" He couldn't be asking about her investigation. She'd only just decided that was what she must do. And she certainly wasn't going to tell *him* her plan.

"Thinking. You were doing it so loudly that I nearly covered my ears."

A laugh tumbled from her. Wit was the last thing she'd expected.

His eyes flickered with surprise, as if he too were astonished by what he'd said. But no, he was reacting to her laughter, for now he was glowering at her once more. Ah well, it was nice while it lasted.

Pivoting, he stamped back to his study, and Ada feared she'd ruined everything. Only how could she ruin something that was already a mess?

Perhaps she ought to follow him, to persuade him that he needed her. Or at least remind him that he was stuck with her for the full fortnight since Lucien's coach wouldn't return to fetch her until then. And if Warfield truly didn't have any livestock, she was most certainly stranded.

Stranded with a beast. This had all the makings of a gothic novel.

Just when she was about to stalk after him into his study, he reappeared, his arms laden with books as he moved across the library to a table near the windows. He dropped the stack of volumes onto the top and turned to face her.

Ada hurried to join him, pushing aside her shock that he'd actually fetched the bloody ledgers. "I hope these are the ledgers," she said, voicing her next thought.

"The past five years."

Back to before his father had died, when presumably

things were in better order. But perhaps they hadn't been. It was possible the beast had inherited a failing estate. Was that why he was this way? Had his father been a poor viscount and somehow driven his son to become this angry ogre? Ada shook her head. If she wasn't careful, her overactive mind was going to write this gothic novel in her head before she puzzled out the truth.

She looked out the windows and gasped. What should have been stunning gardens were laid out but horribly overgrown. There were also a great many dead things. It was an abysmal sight. "What on earth is going on out there?"

"Never mind," he growled. "Focus on your task."

"The gardens *are* my task. They are part of Stonehill."

"They aren't necessary to running a profitable estate. Isn't that why you're here?"

That was why Lucien had sent her, but that was no longer her only purpose. She had an investigation to conduct and a man to rehabilitate. "Yes, that is why I'm here," she said evenly. "Your *friend*, Lord Lucien, wants to ensure Stonehill is profitable and that you can maintain it that way."

His lip curled as his gaze moved to the windows. "I don't care if it's profitable. I'd be just fine letting it rot."

She pursed her lips. "I'd say the garden is well on its way. Were you always this selfish? I've been led to believe you were once far more amiable."

He turned his frigid gaze on her, but said nothing.

"I understand the war wounded you, changed you, but does everyone around you need to suffer because of that? What of your retainers? Your tenants?"

"Goddammit, woman!" he thundered, startling Ada. But she refused to flinch, even if she did feel a trifle frightened by his reaction. He leaned toward her, his features menacing. "You push too far."

She imagined he was a fearful sight on the battlefield. It

was no wonder he was a decorated war hero. Gentling her tone, she stood her ground and said, "What if I can find a steward to run the estate for you? Then you wouldn't have to concern yourself with any of it."

"I had a steward," he clipped.

She knew that, of course, but not why he didn't have one anymore. "What happened to him?"

"He left."

She probably oughtn't press him, but the investigation was afoot. "Why?"

Stony silence was his response.

"Did he find another position elsewhere?" She waited for him to answer, but he did not. "Did you stop paying him?" She held her breath, praying he would respond. Still nothing. It seemed goading was the only thing he reacted to—or could be guaranteed to react to. How she hated to poke at a wounded animal. In her sunniest tone, she offered, "Perhaps he simply found you impossible to work with."

His nostrils flared, and he growled. At last, he spoke. "You have one week, not a fortnight. I'm not agreeing to anything beyond that. I would be grateful if you could complete your work even faster." He stepped closer, towering over her with his height and bulk. "If you question me or speak to me in that manner again, I'll toss you out, regardless of the time of day. Or the weather."

Spinning about, he tramped back to his study and slammed the door.

Well. That hadn't gone *too* badly. But if he thought he could get rid of her before the fortnight was through, he was quite mistaken. When she sent him her first note, she'd remind him that Lucien's coach wouldn't return to fetch her until then.

In the meantime, she'd better find out whether he actually had any livestock.

~

*M*ax had managed to get through an entire day without suffering the presence of his unwanted guest. Still, he'd been deeply aware of her in the library. Why hadn't he thought to situate her far from his study instead of immediately adjacent?

As he finished his toilet, he worked to breathe and think of inane things. When he went to pick up his coat, he cleared his mind completely. For whatever reason, the simple act of donning this garment so often took him back to Spain. To that horrible day…

It was perhaps the best argument to hire a valet, but he still couldn't bring himself to do so. He'd managed quite well on his own, and allowing someone that close to him wasn't something he wished to do. Furthermore, he wasn't even supposed to be a viscount or live this bloody life. By all accounts, he should be dead. Instead, his father and brother were, and here he was.

Pleased that he'd successfully avoided the unwanted memories, he made his way downstairs to his study. Was Miss Treadway already at work in the library? She had been yesterday morning. Apparently, she was a very early riser since she'd been up before Max, and he rose with the sun—or before it, depending on how or if he slept. That she'd beat him downstairs also annoyed him. Everything about her annoyed him.

She was too damned pleasant. And she was obviously thinking constantly. No, not just thinking, *plotting*. She was organizing some scheme or even a series of schemes. Perhaps he was being paranoid. Mrs. Bundle would say so.

Upon arriving in his study, he repeated what he'd done yesterday—he went to the door leading to the library and gently pried it open a few inches. He peered through the small opening toward the table near the windows. There she was again, her dark hair piled neatly atop her head, the column of her throat arcing as she bent over her work.

She'd beat him again. Yes, he should have stationed her in the sitting room upstairs at the front of the house. Then she would have been on an entirely different floor. Perhaps he'd move her there today. When she took a break from her work, he'd have Timothy carry her things upstairs. Unless she didn't take any breaks. That would be just like her to be annoyingly committed to her work.

Closing the door, he retreated to his desk, then froze. A folded piece of parchment sat in the center. His name was written in beautiful strokes across the paper. There was no question who had put it there.

With a scowl, he snatched it up and opened it. She'd written out a series of questions. Did he have any vacant cottages? Any vacant farms? Did he personally collect the quarterly rents, and if not, who did? It went on and on, with a dozen or more queries. The last asked whether he had livestock, and if so, how many and what kind?

He read the closing twice, astonished by her brazenness.

I would be delighted if you would respond in person; however, if you would prefer to do so in writing, I have left space so that you may record your answers on this paper. I do appreciate your time.

 Most sincerely,
 Miss Treadway

Was she angling to become his steward? No, she already had a job at Lucien's infernal club in London, which Lucien kept trying to persuade Max to join. The thought of mingling with people, socially or otherwise, made Max's lip curl. That was why he'd mostly stayed away from the House of Lords, though he ought to attend. He'd been a few times, and on each occasion had beaten as hasty a retreat as possible.

It was the way people looked at him—with warmth and pride as they thanked him for his heroism. If they only knew the truth, they would revile him instead. He'd be banned from the Lords, his title stripped, probably. Not that he cared about any of that. His brother should have inherited the title, but fate had stolen him too. Everyone whom Max cared about met the same end. Well, most everyone. Hence, he now cared for no one.

He returned his mind to the need for a steward. He'd driven poor Acton away by refusing to allow him to spend money on improvements and by being generally obnoxious. Max had declined to meet with him, nor did he read the man's reports. Frustrated, Acton had taken another position, which was precisely what Max had hoped. Indeed, he'd been satisfied when most of the retainers at Stonehill had taken themselves off. The fewer people around him, the better.

He grudgingly admitted that Miss Treadway was slightly impressive, at least in her zeal. In one day, she'd invested more time into his estate than he did in a month. He flinched, his shoulders twitching.

Going back to the library door, he pried it open again and looked in.

"My lord?"

Startled, he pulled the door shut more loudly than he would have preferred. He turned to see Mrs. Bundle setting his breakfast tray on the desk. "Just leave it there," he said grumpily.

The housekeeper's dark brows arched briefly. "Are you going to eat?"

"Of course." But he made no move toward the desk.

Mrs. Bundle pursed her lips before turning and leaving. Exhaling, Max carefully opened the door again, half expecting to find Miss Treadway right there in response to hearing the door shut. But she wasn't. She was still seated at her table, her attention wholly focused on her task.

Max clenched her missive in his grasp and walked toward her. She was incredibly engaged in her work, for she didn't look up at all as he approached. He noted the little pleats between her brows as she read the book laid open on the table beneath her gaze. She was rather attractive, in an adorable, endearing way. Which was asinine because there was nothing he found adorable nor endearing.

He scowled just as she looked up, a brilliant smile lighting her face. She instantly went from adorable to captivating. He hated that his body responded with a mild heat.

"You ask too many damned questions."

She nodded, unperturbed by his sourness. "I do. It's a personality trait that some find aggravating, I admit. But I can't help my curiosity." She smiled again. "In this case, my questions are quite necessary. Will you answer them?" She sounded both hopeful and doubtful at the same time.

"My steward collected the rents until he left last year."

"And who has collected them since?"

"Og."

She cocked her head to the side. "Is that a person?"

"Ogden, the stable master."

She wrote down his name on a parchment to the side of her book, where she'd written a great deal in her lovely, sweeping hand. "How did he know what to collect?"

"He had a list."

"I see. And he recorded the payments? I can't seem to find a record of payments since Mr. Acton left last spring."

"Og must have marked them on the list."

"He reads, then?" she asked cautiously.

"Er...probably?" Og was over sixty and had worked in the Stonehill stables most of his life. When would he have learned to read and why? Max hated that he felt stupid, especially in front of Miss Treadway. Which was irritating since she was the one making him feel stupid with her endless questions.

That he ought to know the answers to.

But he didn't. He had no desire to manage this estate. Did it matter if the rents were collected? He didn't need the money.

"I'll speak to Og," she said with another perturbing smile. "Care to answer any other questions?"

"There is one vacant farm."

"Oh, thank you." She scribbled the information down. "I wasn't quite sure. There's an indication that a lease terminated last fall, but no record if they left or perhaps entered into another lease."

The farmer had requested to meet with Max, but he'd declined—not that Max would tell her that. Then Og had informed him that the farm had been vacated after the harvest.

"Are there any potential tenants?" she asked expectantly, her blue-gray eyes fixed on him with that bloody curiosity she'd mentioned. She was beyond curious—she was *meddlesome*.

"Not that I'm aware of." Hell, he really did need a steward, even if he didn't plan to maintain the estate for future generations. He just needed to hire someone who understood that. Perhaps that was how he could get her to leave him alone. "If I promise to hire a steward, will you return to London?"

"Hiring a steward is an excellent idea!" she exclaimed brightly. "But no, I can't return to London until the end of the fortnight when Lucien's coach returns to fetch me. I'm afraid you have to suffer my presence." She didn't sound the least bit apologetic.

He leveled her with his sternest stare. "I can send you back in my coach."

"You do have livestock, then? And a coach?" She snatched up her pencil once more. "How many horses? And how many of them are for riding as opposed to coaching?"

Did she never stop? "What does any of that have to do with the estate?"

She wrote "one coach" on the paper. "Livestock are an expense—their care and whether you need to replace them anytime soon."

"There is a coach and a cart and some other vehicles." He shrugged. "You can ask Og when you speak with him." Shit, now he was encouraging her to speak with his retainers? Og was the only person who might be surlier than him, so it was entirely possible that the stable master wouldn't spare even a moment for her.

Max ought to warn her about that. He did not.

"What about the horses you ride?" she pressed.

Tension gripped his frame, and he clenched his teeth. "I don't ride."

Her gaze widened with surprise. "I see. Actually, no, I don't see. You're a viscount. I thought it was a requirement that noblemen gad about the countryside on horseback. How do you even hunt?"

"I don't ride, and I don't hunt." And he didn't explain. "If I promise to hire a steward, you'll leave in my coach?"

"No, because I'm not sure I trust you to hire someone. Anyway, you *can't* hire a steward within my allotted fortnight. I suppose I could always extend my—"

"*No.*"

"Visit, *but*—what I was going to say before you rudely interrupted—you obviously won't allow that." She gave him a scolding look. "Furthermore, I've only just begun, and I promised Lucien a thorough review. I keep my promises, my lord."

She didn't say that he didn't keep his, but she'd just admitted to not trusting him, which was nearly the same thing.

"I've begun reading about estate management." She inclined her head toward the open book on the table. "I'd love to speak with your tenants, and I imagine that will take at least the fortnight—"

"That is not what you are here to do. I don't know what constitutes your 'thorough review,' but it isn't interviewing my tenants. You're here to look at my ledgers. You've already far overstepped. I should return you to London immediately."

"You said *should*, which leads me to believe you will not." Her lips spread in a brief satisfied smile. "What harm am I doing, exactly, Lord Warfield?"

She was aggravating the hell out of him.

"I think you must realize this is important," she continued. "To ensure your ledgers are updated and accurate, I need information. I'm sure you'll agree, however, that accuracy isn't enough. Your estate must be profitable, and I suspect it's not." A faint grimace pulled at her alluring pink lips.

Wait. She was saying Stonehill was failing. Anger coiled within him.

Except he didn't care if the estate failed. He had no reason to make it profitable. There was enough money for him to live out his life, however long he was cursed to endure it.

The urge to toss her in his coach and have Og drive her to London was overwhelming. But he knew Lucien would only come back and harass him again. The next time Lucien visited, Max feared they would come to blows. Again. Perhaps this time, they wouldn't stop.

Exhaling, he ran his hand through his hair. She was staring at him. Specifically, at the scarred left side of his face. He'd been intrigued by the fact that she hadn't seemed to notice his disfigurement, but clearly she had. Just as she didn't want him to know that it bothered her, as evidenced by her rapid blinking and refocusing on the other side of his face. The handsome side. Sometimes he wished it was scarred too.

"If you stay, can you stop annoying me?" he asked.

She frowned, and the little pleats between her brows that he'd noticed while she was reading returned. "I confess I find it difficult to understand why you find me annoying. In general, people find me quite amiable and often seek my company. I try very hard to improve the moods of those around me. If someone is having a bad day, I do my best to make it better." She pinned him with a frank stare. "You seem to have perpetual bad days, and so far, nothing I do improves a thing. I've tried to stay out of your way. That's why I left you a note instead of bothering you in person."

Yes, she had done that. He hadn't even spoken to her yesterday, and the only reason he'd seen her was because he'd spied on her. "I do appreciate that."

She was also right that every single day was bad. So perhaps it wasn't that she was annoying at all. The problem, which he very much knew, was his.

Except she *was* annoying, and it was precisely because she was charming and exuberant and sought to cheer him. He didn't want to let go of any of the bitterness that made him the nasty beast he'd become and that everyone avoided. If he allowed her to break through his defenses even the slightest bit, his war could very well be lost.

"Would you like to answer the rest of my questions now?" she asked hopefully.

"In writing." He'd had enough of her for the moment.

"Just do your work and leave me alone. And don't bother anyone unless you ask me first."

"How am I to do that and leave you alone at the same time? Shall I request to meet with people in writing and wait for your approval? That seems rather inefficient."

He growled low in his throat.

"That wasn't a response. Or if it was, I can't translate it. I'm afraid I don't speak Angry Gentleman." She leaned toward him slightly. "Is there a guide that would help me?"

Now she was just poking fun. Trying to improve his mood. He refused to be amused.

He glowered at her. "You're annoying me again."

"My apologies. I will send you a list of the people I wish to see. Is there someone who can drive me around the estate in your coach? Or do you perhaps have a cart so that I can see things without having to peer through a window?"

She acted as if she were some sort of expert on estates. "What on earth would you even be looking for?"

Shrugging, she waved her hand. "Everything. I'm a keen observer. And an excellent listener."

"I find that hard to believe since you're almost always talking," he muttered.

"Would it further annoy you for me to say that you are also being annoying?" she asked sweetly.

She nearly provoked him to laugh. Nearly. He gritted his teeth.

Her eyes lit. "Was that a faint smile?"

"No. I had a pain in my gut. It's a result of my present company. I must excuse myself."

"I'll have a list for you by this evening." She returned her attention to the book on the table. "And I'll look forward to reading your responses."

He felt dismissed, which annoyed him even more. Before he could say something else, which would only prolong this irritating conversation, he stalked back to his office. He slapped her missive with its interminable list of queries onto the desk.

Sitting down, he took the cover from his breakfast and wondered how he would endure the next twelve days.

CHAPTER 3

*A*da stepped from the bright sunlight into the cool dimness of the stable. A horse whinnied, and she looked toward the sound. It was too shadowy to see which animal had greeted her.

"What do you want?"

The loud barking question startled her, but Ada recovered quickly, smiling at the older man striding toward her. Tall and grizzled, with a wide-brimmed hat, he wore a deep frown.

"Are you Og?" she asked pleasantly, refusing to be deterred by his rudeness.

"Who's asking?"

"I'm Miss Treadway—Lord Warfield's guest. I'm a bookkeeper, and I've come to, ah, organize his ledgers."

He put his hands on his hips, which made him seem wider. Did he do that to compensate for his thinness? Perhaps he felt as though he had to make himself look more substantial. "What in the devil are you doing here, then?"

She held a partially filled ledger, the one the former steward had used and which should contain information from the estate for the past year but didn't. "I understand you've been collecting the rents, and I wanted to see your accounting."

He stared at her. "What?"

"Surely you have a ledger where you recorded who paid how much and when you collected it?"

"I wrote it down on a piece of parchment. What I could remember anyway."

Ada resisted the urge to explain why this was a poor system because she still needed more information. "I don't suppose you have these records?"

He shrugged. "I probably gave them to his lordship." He rubbed his hand down his cheek. "Or they're around here somewhere. Why does it matter?"

Clinging to her patience by a thread, Ada smiled benignly. "As I said, I'm organizing his ledgers. All receipts and records matter. If you find them, please bring them to the house. I would deeply appreciate it." In the meantime, she'd move on to her next objective. "I'm also here to take an inventory of the stables."

He twisted his mouth into a rather surly frown. "That's my job."

"I assumed so," she responded sunnily in an effort to keep him from stamping away in irritation. "You can help me, and I'll be on my way."

"Don't have time for that."

"I understand." She did not. "I'll just see myself around."

"The hell you will." He practically growled, and she began to think there was a local dialect for exceedingly grumpy men.

She took the pencil from her pocket and opened the ledger, balancing it on her left hand against her chest. "I'd be happy to record your inventory. How many horses and what kind?"

He swore, and Ada scowled at him. "There's no call to be offensive. You can either help me in this endeavor or allow me to continue on my errand without interruption. I assure you that his lordship understands the need for me to gather this information."

His expression soured, which she would not have thought possible since it was already quite harassed. "You can have a quarter hour to poke your nose about, but I'll be following you."

Or you could just tell me what I want to know and save both of us the aggravation. Ada wondered what had happened to make Og so disagreeable. With his lordship, she knew it was the war. At least, she assumed it was. Perhaps she oughtn't assume. It was only that she'd been told he was quite pleasant before going to war. Logically, she deduced that the war had changed him. And why wouldn't it?

"Were you in the army, Og?"

He grunted. "No."

She supposed it was possible that the viscount's poor demeanor had worn off on Og. It had certainly cast a pallor over the entire household. While Mrs. Bundle and Timothy weren't surly, they were overworked and seemingly unhappy, even disgruntled. That Ada had met only the two retainers was alarming—both because she ought to have at least seen more and because she was fairly certain that meant there weren't any others.

"I'll start over here," she said to Og, moving into the shadows where she'd heard the horse.

Ada met him—or her—a beautiful brown animal with warm, intelligent eyes. She'd always found horses captivating, but she didn't necessarily want to ride one. Feeding and stroking them, however, had been one of her favorite things to do as a child, on the rare occasion she'd been able to do so, for her family hadn't owned any. Later, when she'd worked as a governess, she'd had the luxury of visiting with the family's horses now and again.

"Is this horse for riding or pulling equipment?" Ada hoped Og would answer her, but prepared herself for another grunt or growl in lieu of words.

"Ride. Her and the one next to her."

Smiling, Ada pet the horse, who nickered softly. "What's her name?"

"Topaz."

"Well, hello, Topaz," she said. "Aren't you a pretty girl?"

This provoked a grunt from Og. "You can't ride her," he said brusquely.

"I wouldn't want to. I don't know how. But I can still visit and perhaps give her an apple. Would you like that, Topaz?"

"Never mind that nonsense. You aren't coming back into my stables. Hurry with your business now."

Ada tossed him a frown over her shoulder, then whispered to Topaz that she would definitely be back. After making notes about the horses in the ledger, she asked, "Who rides Topaz? I understand his lordship does not ride."

"Me."

Unable to contain her curiosity, she surrendered to it. "Why does he not ride? I find that so unusual for a viscount. I would think he would have ridden in the army."

Another growl. "Mind yourself."

Sighing, Ada knew it had been too much to hope for answers to her questions. She continued through the stable, recording the animals and equipment. The building was in decent repair and clean enough—for a stable.

"Is it just you here?" she asked finally, hoping he would at least answer that.

"There's a lad who helps in the afternoons after he finishes his chores at home."

"Where does he live?"

"On the estate."

She barely lifted her lips into a fatigued smile. "How... vague." She made notes in the ledger, then snapped it closed and stashed the pencil in her pocket.

Og crossed his arms over his chest. "Anything else, or will you get out of here now?"

"One last thing, though I'm not sure why I'm asking," she added in a frustrated mutter. "I need to tour the estate and hoped you would take me around in the cart."

"I don't have time for that."

"Of course you don't. What if his lordship insisted?"

This earned her a scoff that was almost a derisive laugh. "He wouldn't."

No, he probably wouldn't. Still, she'd ask him to. "Thank you so much for your time and...assistance, Og. Have a nice day!"

Squinting as she strode out into the bright morning, she gritted her teeth in frustration. But only for a moment. There was no benefit in succumbing to anger or allowing Og to ruin her day or her mood.

She went into the house and decided it was time to find the kitchen so she could see how many people worked there. Then she'd definitely learn how many retainers were employed in the household. These were crucial details in her investigation.

Making her way to the breakfast room, she went through the servants' door and down the backstairs. Instead of noise and bustle, as one might expect from a kitchen in a house of this size, Ada was greeted with silence.

She passed a few doors before reaching the kitchen, a large, open room with a long table in the center. Standing on the other side near the middle was a squat woman with a cap mostly covering her blonde hair—and Mrs. Bundle, who leaned her hip against the table.

"Good morning," Ada said, appearing to startle them as Mrs. Bundle jerked and stood straight. The cook—for Ada presumed the other woman was the cook since she'd been slicing carrots—dropped her knife.

"Good heavens, you silly chit, I nearly cut my finger off," the cook said.

"You didn't either," Mrs. Bundle admonished. She gave Ada an apologetic smile. "You surprised us, Miss Treadway. Is there something you need?"

"Many things, actually. I just came from the stable. Why is Og so very disagreeable?"

The cook waved her hand. "He's always been that way. He's been here nearly as long as I have, and in all that time— near forty years—I've never once seen him smile."

Perhaps it was he who'd influenced the viscount to be surly.

Forty years! The cook and Og would have such wonderful information to share, not that Ada expected Og would do so. She only hoped the cook would be more amenable.

"What a long history you have here," Ada said, moving to the table to stand opposite them. "I imagine you've seen a great many things."

"That I have," she said with a twinkle in her blue eyes. She picked up the knife and began slicing carrots again.

"This is Mrs. Debley," Mrs. Bundle said. "You've probably deduced that she is the cook."

"And a wonderful one at that," Ada remarked with a smile. "Your bread is especially delicious. As are your biscuits. And last night's meat pie was divine. Everything I've eaten since arriving has been sublime."

Mrs. Debley paused in her work, her face flushing slightly as she smiled. "I thank you. It's pleasing to cook for someone who appreciates it." She rushed to add, "Not that his lordship doesn't. His appetite just isn't the same since he came back from war, the poor thing."

Proof that he was changed, at least when it came to food. "I understand the viscount was rather different before—more cheerful, perhaps."

"War will damage anyone, I imagine," Mrs. Debley noted sadly.

Ada didn't disagree, but couldn't help but think of Lucien who had fought alongside Warfield yet managed to be one of the kindest, most charming, and altogether pleasant people she'd ever met. As much as she wanted to know about Warfield and why he was so angry—and whether it was to do with that nasty scarring on his face—she had to focus on the matter at hand, which was the estate.

"It's so quiet down here, Mrs. Debley. Where are your assistants, your scullery maids?"

The cook exchanged a look with Mrs. Bundle and gave her head a slight but brisk shake. "I've a girl who comes in the afternoons to help me prepare food. I don't need much with only his lordship to cook for."

"But you also cook for the retainers. Surely that is a good amount of work."

"Not at all. We eat the same as his lordship, so I'm only preparing one meal."

That was certainly odd. But efficient in a household of this size, Ada supposed.

"There are very few of us," Mrs. Bundle said, sounding weary as she often did. "But I suspect you know that. I also suspect you want to know exactly how many there are."

"I need to know for my report." Ada offered a gentle smile. "I have the impression you are all overworked and would benefit from assistance. It seems several retainers have left over the past few years, and it doesn't appear as though they've been replaced."

"We're doing all right," Mrs. Debley said, her brow furrowing. She went back to her task, her hand moving quickly and accurately as she cut small disks of carrot and moved on to the next one. "Don't you go bothering his lordship. He's doing the best he can."

Mrs. Bundle cast a glance toward the cook. "We *could* use more help, especially you."

"Bah. I'm fine." Mrs. Debley looked up from her slicing and fixed Ada with a direct stare. "Don't make trouble where it isn't needed."

"I have no wish to do that," Ada assured her gently. "I seek the truth so that I may communicate it to Lord Lucien. As his lordship's closest friend, he only wants to support Lord Warfield."

"He can do that by minding his own business," Mrs. Debley said pertly. She finished cutting the last carrot, then moved away from the table to fetch a pot.

Mrs. Bundle met Ada's gaze and inclined her head toward the doorway. Ada left the table and went into the corridor. The housekeeper met her there and gestured for them to walk back toward the stairs.

"Mrs. Debley is incredibly fond—and protective—of his lordship," Mrs. Bundle said quietly.

"So I gathered. That seems appropriate since she's known him his entire life." Ada couldn't find fault with people who were loyal, not when her own family had turned their backs on her. It made her wonder if the viscount realized the support and love he had.

"To satisfy your curiosity about the retainers—in the kitchen, there is just Mrs. Debley and Molly Tallent, the girl who comes in the afternoons. There is also Og in the stable, and my son is the sole footman."

"Og mentioned there's a boy who comes to help there too."

"That's Molly's brother, Archie. They live fairly close. Mrs. Tallent is a widow—her husband died last year, but she's meeting the obligations of the lease."

"His lordship is allowing her to stay?" Or was he even aware that Mr. Tallent had died?

"You must think he's horrible—and he can be—but underneath his bluster, there's a kind and caring gentleman. At least there was once," she added softly. "He wouldn't turn anyone out."

Perhaps not, but he also wouldn't invite anyone in, as evidenced by his refusal to give his half sister a job when she'd come asking. Granted, Prudence hadn't told him they were related, but it shouldn't have mattered. She was more than qualified to do any number of things, and it was clear he needed help and had for some time.

But Ada wouldn't get into any of that with Mrs. Bundle. If she wanted to find some grace in her employer, Ada wouldn't try to persuade her otherwise. Even if the truth was that he had none.

"I'm glad to hear of your confidence in his lordship," Ada said. "He is not being very helpful to me in my endeavors. I would like to tour the estate, but he refuses to take me. He suggested Og would do so, but Og has just informed me that he doesn't have time. I suppose I can just walk about and talk with people."

Mrs. Bundle's brow furrowed. "You can't walk the estate every day. That would take you far longer than the fortnight you are here."

"Well, I don't ride, and I can't drive either, so I'm afraid I don't have any other options."

Mrs. Bundle nodded. "Archie Tallent could drive you. I'll speak with him and make sure Og doesn't get in the way. When would you like to go?"

Ada felt a surge of excitement and gratitude. "Tomorrow would be excellent. Thank you, Mrs. Bundle."

"I believe we want the same thing, Miss Treadway," the housekeeper said with a smile. "His lordship just needs a push to get back to where he needs to be."

"And you need help," Ada said pointedly. "I mean to make sure you get it."

"I suspect if anyone can do that, it's you." She winked at Ada. "I'll inform you when tomorrow's arrangements are complete."

"Thank you, truly." Ada practically skipped off to the library.

She stopped short just over the threshold when she saw the viscount standing next to her worktable, a book in his hand. "How unexpected to find you here," she said loudly so he wouldn't be surprised by her arrival.

He pivoted toward her, a scowl etched into his features along with the scars. She realized the disfigurement made him look permanently fierce. Did that intensify his expressions so that he appeared more irritable or angry than he actually was?

People likely reacted poorly upon seeing him. Surely that contributed to his overall surliness. She imagined that would be frustrating or wearisome. Or even depressing.

"I see you've been reading this drivel instead of working on my ledgers," he said sternly. "If you can't do what you were sent here to do, I'll send you back to London."

Ada opened her mouth to deliver a well-deserved setdown, but she realized he was provoking her and still hoping there was a way to get rid of her.

She wasn't going anywhere.

∽

*M*iss Treadway set one of the estate ledgers on the table. "As you can see, I was just working on your ledgers." She inclined her head toward the book in his grasp. "Do you expect me to work during every moment I'm awake? I read that book last night to relax. I happen to enjoy love stories. What do *you* do to relax?" She stared at him expectantly and crossed her arms over her chest.

She wore a simple day gown of dark blue that covered her up to her neck. But the way she held her arms drew his gaze to her breasts, which were larger than he might have expected of a woman of her diminutive size.

He jerked his attention to her face. "This isn't about me. This is about you squandering your time."

She rolled her eyes and unfolded her arms, dropping them to her sides, where her hands curled into fists. Good, he'd irritated her.

"I'm not squandering anything. I wake early, and I work after dinner. You will not berate me for relaxing before bed, nor will you criticize what I read. Romance is not drivel. Everyone should be so fortunate as to experience love and find a happy relationship. Why denigrate that?"

"Everyone should be so fortunate as to *keep* a relationship like that." He swore under his breath, hating himself for saying that out loud. He tossed the novel onto the table. "Just make sure you're doing what you came here to do."

She took a deep breath, and her hands flexed at her sides. "If you read my updates—I left another in your study last night—you would know that I am working hard. I'd be happy to apprise you of my progress."

Hell, he'd walked right into that. He didn't want to engage her on this, but the truth was that he did want to know where she'd been with one of the ledgers. "Where were you?"

"At the stables. I spoke with Og. He makes you look like a veritable romance novel hero."

The side of Max's mouth ticked up before he could stop it. He did, however, manage not to fully grin. Damn, that was the second time she'd provoked that response from him.

She took a step toward him, her gaze fixing on his mouth. "Why did you keep from smiling? You never let yourself smile. Why?"

"Has anyone ever told you that you're intrusive?"

"Many times. Because I am." She cocked her head slightly. "Why won't you smile?"

"Intrusive, impertinent, and uselessly persistent." He glowered at her, recovering his ill humor. "Mind your own business."

"You are utterly infuriating. I've never met anyone so committed to their own misery. You need to relax—perhaps read a romantic novel." Her expression lit, and now she smiled, and the answering flip of his stomach made him want to growl. Hopefully with irritation. "You should join me tonight. Read something for pleasure. You may find yourself smiling."

"Not a chance."

"What would the harm be?" She looked at him so guilelessly, as if she were completely unaware of the demon inside him. But of course she was, as she had to be.

The harm would be to her. He was not someone she should spend time with.

"You're considering it," she said wrongly. "That's all I can hope for, I suppose."

He didn't wish to pursue that line of conversation a moment longer, so he glanced toward the ledger she'd set on the table. "What did you do in the stable?"

"Besides find Og annoying? I pet one of your horses. She was lovely. I recorded the animals and vehicles as well as other items. Though, I'm not at all sure what most of it is. I am woefully uneducated when it comes to anything to do with a stable."

"You've always lived in London, I take it."

"No, I'm from Devon actually."

He should have realized her accent wasn't London. "You lived in a city there, then."

She nodded. "Plymouth. My father was a fisherman. I can sail a boat, but I can't ride a horse."

"That's not a very useful skill for a bookkeeper," he said.

"It is not, but while I *can* sail a boat, I don't. The sea took my father, and I am now unable to get into or onto water."

The mention of her loss reminded him that he was supposed to keep himself apart, to ensure his darkest nature stayed buried. He shouldn't be making idle chatter with her.

"Then you are precisely where you should be," he said. "Just avoid the small lake near the southeast corner of the estate."

"I will do that," she replied. "Now let me tell you what I *didn't* do at the stable—obtain a copy of Og's records for rent collection. He says he wrote it on a parchment and that you might have it here. I don't suppose you do?" she asked hopefully.

"No, and before you ask me to look for it, Og never gave it to me." That he could remember. It was more likely Og mentioned it, and Max hadn't bothered to even look at it, let alone bring it here.

She pursed her lips in disappointment. Before she could respond further, he turned and stalked from the library, intent on taking a walk to clear Miss Treadway from his mind. On his way out, he encountered Mrs. Bundle.

She hesitated, and he could tell she wanted to say something, so he paused too. "I'm arranging for Archie to drive

Miss Treadway around the estate tomorrow since neither you nor Og can be bothered."

He knew Mrs. Bundle wanted him to change his mind about that. "I don't see why it's necessary. Her presence here is a nuisance."

"It's also nearly half-over. She arrived five days ago." Mrs. Bundle's expression softened, and he tensed for the coming assault on his sentiment—as if he had any left. "She's only trying to help. What harm could there be?"

Had she and Miss Treadway planned this? Their words were too similar. "She put you up to this, didn't she?"

"Not at all." Mrs. Bundle frowned at him. "You are too quick to believe the worst in people. Not that the two of us working together to help you and the estate would be the worst, only that *you* think it is."

He decided to repeat his own words. "Mind your own business."

Her shoulder twitched, and her expression turned to frustration, her eyes sparking. "I work on this estate for you, so this *is* my business as far as I can tell. Furthermore, if no one meddled in your business, nothing would get done because *you* don't mind *your* business."

A pang of guilt smacked him in the chest. Exhaling, as if doing so would rid him of the emotion, he asked, "What would you have me do?"

She took a moment to respond, and he realized he'd surprised her. "To start, you should listen to Miss Treadway. And you should be the one to take her around the estate."

"I'm sorry to disappoint you, but I won't do either of those things." He actually was sorry to disappoint her, but neither could he bring himself to change his manner. Perhaps he could satisfy her, at least in a small way. "I am, however, considering hiring a new steward."

Surprise arrested her gaze with perhaps a dash of relief.

"That would be a good start." She sounded as if she didn't quite believe it. "I only want the best for you, my lord. That's why I haven't left yet," she added softly.

"I don't ever want you to think you must stay." He wasn't actually hoping she might leave, as he'd done with the steward. Which, in hindsight, might have been foolish. He hadn't thought he needed the man, but perhaps he did.

She shook her head. "Someone has to take care of you. I'd best get on." She continued on her way.

Max watched her go, thinking no one should have to take care of him. Indeed, he should have died in Spain. He'd certainly done his best to try to achieve that end. That he hadn't was a miracle.

No, it was a curse.

CHAPTER 4

*L*edger in hand, Ada walked to the stable yard at midmorning, eager to meet Archie. She saw the cart drawn by a single horse and wondered if the boy might even teach her how to drive. That would be a very useful skill for an independent young woman like herself.

A head popped up from the back of the cart, and she nearly tripped. There was no mistaking the brooding expression even with a hat pulled low over his brow. She'd always found hats attractive, and in this case, it gave Lord Warfield a dashing air.

And dashing was not a word she ever would have used to describe him. Cantankerous. Unhelpful. Antagonistic. Also enigmatic and alluring. Did she only think so because she was burdened with overactive curiosity? She decided it didn't matter why she thought that.

"Good morning," she called as she approached the cart. "Did you come to see me off?"

"No."

Of course he hadn't. That would be so out of what she knew of his character that she was surprised she'd even asked. "You're driving me to London, aren't you? Well, I won't go."

He stared at her a moment. "I said you could stay the fortnight provided you didn't annoy me."

"I was all but certain I'd continued to be a thorn in your side."

"My side, my neck, my eye, my bloody arse." He grunted.

"My apologies. I didn't mean to be crude."

Now he was apologizing? "What's wrong with you?" she asked.

"Nothing. I thought I would drive you around the estate, but perhaps that's a bad idea since it seems you are—"

"No, no," she interrupted, not at all interested in hearing what he thought she was. Beyond annoying, she was sure. "I'm thrilled you'll be driving me today." Indeed, she couldn't keep the smile from her face. "Who better to tell me everything I need to know?" Except he probably didn't know everything she needed to know. Not if he'd been as uninvolved in his estate as it seemed.

From what she could piece together from the former steward's notes, the viscount's father had died about the time his lordship had left Spain to return home due to his injuries. The new viscount, his lordship's older brother, had soon followed, dying only days before Warfield arrived.

The new *new* viscount had spent months recovering from his wounds, and had, understandably, taken little interest in the estate. However, that hadn't changed as he'd recovered. As far as Ada could tell, the current viscount had never completely assumed his new position.

She had to assume he didn't want it. How she longed to ask.

As expected, he didn't respond to her rhetorical question. With a faint growl, he offered her his hand to help her into the cart.

Her gaze fell upon his appendage, covered in black leather. His hand was large, the fingers long. He looked as if he could break something quite easily.

Yet, when she put her hand in his, he helped her into the cart with a gentle strength that said he wouldn't harm her. Not that she was afraid he would. He was grumpy and beastly, but she wasn't frightened of him.

When she was seated, he went around and climbed in beside her. Without a word, he drove them from the stable yard and out to the front of the house.

"I understand Stonehill was once a castle," she said, hoping he might finally engage in cordial conversation.

"Yes."

She'd take a one-word answer over his signature grunts. It was a good start, anyway. "Do you know which of your ancestors built it?"

"None of them. The first Lord Warfield was given the property by Charles the Second after his restoration. My ancestor was elevated to the peerage and awarded this estate for his loyalty to the crown. The castle was in ruins by then. The first Lord Warfield tore the remainder down and built a new house, which my great-grandfather almost completely demolished and rebuilt. That's the house that stands today. Some of the castle stone was used for the cornerstones."

She bit her tongue before noting that might be the most he'd ever said to her. And without irritation. "How fascinating. Does the house sit where the castle did?"

"No. The castle was up on the rise south of the current house. It wasn't terribly large—just a small keep and the surrounding walls. There are a few stones still there. If you look hard enough and use some imagination, you can see some of the wall."

A thrill of anticipation shot through her. "I'd love to see it. I have plenty of imagination."

"That has absolutely nothing to do with your errand here." There was his disagreeability. She knew it had to emerge sometime.

"No, but do you really expect me to work all day, every day?" That was precisely what she'd done, even yesterday on Sunday. "I don't do that at my regular position."

They left the drive, and he steered them onto a dirt track. The day was warm with a light breeze, and the scent of wildflowers was in the air.

"Where are we going first?" she asked.

"Ah, there's a farm just up ahead."

She suspected he didn't know the names of who lived there. "What do they grow?" She waved her hand, anticipating that he didn't know that either. "Never mind. I'll pester them with my questions instead of you. What else do you know of Stonehill Castle?"

"Nothing. I've shared the extent of my knowledge."

"Aren't you interested to learn more?"

"Not particularly." He slid her a glance. "You seem quite fascinated by the past."

"I love history. There's something comforting about knowing that your family has roots in a particular place, that the land is part of your ancestry—your blood, even."

"It's not, no matter how it may seem with entailments. Stonehill Castle didn't belong to my family. I have no connection to it whatsoever. Honestly, I feel no connection to the current estate either."

Ada held her breath. She'd never imagined he'd share such sentiments! She wanted to ask why, but feared he wouldn't answer, even if he'd been more loquacious this morning than in any of their previous encounters. So she'd ask him something he could answer the way he preferred—with one word. "Is that because you didn't expect to inherit?"

There was a beat of silence—save the birdsong coming

from their right—in which she felt the air shift. Had he drawn in a breath?

"Yes."

"Yes, you didn't expect to inherit?" she clarified.

"My brother should have been the viscount. I'm a soldier, not a landowner." He grunted. "At least, I was."

"I'm sorry about your brother," she said softly. "And your father. My father died when I was ten."

"That can't have been easy."

"No. My older brother went to sea then, leaving my mother and me with my three younger sisters." She glanced at him, seated on her right so that the scarred left side of his face was completely exposed to her. She noticed he wore his hat at a slight angle, as if he could shade that side and prevent people from seeing his disfigurement. What would he say if she told him she wanted to touch it, to feel the ripples in his flesh? It looked as though he'd sustained a burn, but what kind?

"You seem to have come out all right," he said gruffly.

"So far." But the path hadn't been easy. She'd been foolish and paid a price. Still, she'd survived, and that was more than she could say for her mother and one of her sisters. The terrible old guilt threatened to grip her, but she held it at bay. No good would ever come of that.

Pushing the dark thoughts away, she lifted her face to the sky, closing her eyes as she inhaled. "I love summer, don't you?"

"No. I prefer the cold and rain."

"I don't mind those either. I like snow the most, I think."

He snorted. "I'm beginning to think you like everything. Is there nothing that peeves you?"

"Grumpy viscounts with disdain for romance novels." She laughed softly.

He shook his head and drove from the track onto a narrower lane. "If I peeve you, it can't be for long."

"Life is too fleeting to harbor ill will. Besides, feeling angry or upset isn't pleasant. I'd much rather be happy."

He brought the cart to a stop in front of a small stone cottage and several outbuildings. His gaze met hers, and her breath stalled at the intensity in his expression. "You can simply decide to feel happy whenever you want?"

"It's not always simple, but I do try."

He got down and came around to help her out. By the time they moved back to the other side of the cart, a woman had emerged from the cottage. Of medium height with a tidy cap atop her gray hair, she wiped her hands on her apron.

"Good morning," she called out as they approached.

When the viscount said nothing, Ada moved swiftly toward the woman. "Good morning. I'm Miss Treadway, ah, secretary to Lord Warfield. And this is his lordship." She swiveled her body to see where he'd ended up.

He stood a few feet away, looking distinctly uncomfortable.

"My goodness," the woman said softly, but not so softly that Ada couldn't hear. She dropped into a curtsey. "What an honor to receive you at our humble farm, my lord."

Warfield said nothing, but he at least inclined his head. Couldn't he say good morning? He didn't have to smile, though that would have been nice.

Ada turned back to the woman and smiled on his behalf. "He's delighted to be here. You are Mrs. Spratt?" She guessed one of the names she recalled from the estate ledgers.

"Yes, indeed," she said warmly. "Would you care to come inside? I just took some bread from the oven."

At that precise moment, Ada got a noseful of the scent of fresh bread. Her stomach grumbled in response. "That would be lovely." She looked back to the viscount and inclined her head toward the cottage.

Warfield appeared tense, his jaw tight as the muscles in his neck worked. Still, he walked toward the cottage, and when Mrs. Spratt stood to the side at the door, he went inside.

Ada followed their hostess into the small but neat main room. The kitchen area was in the corner, and the bread sat on a table where she clearly prepared food.

"Mr. Spratt should be here any time. He's just finishing his morning chores. There's so much to do, and it's just the two of us."

Opening her ledger, Ada took the pencil from her pocket and recorded the couple's names as well as the information she'd already gathered. Then she asked a series of questions about the farm while Mrs. Spratt cut the bread. The woman answered as she slathered butter on the bread, then brought a piece to each of them—first to Warfield.

Ada held her breath, but he took it from the woman with a slight nod. He did not, however, immediately eat it. Ada had no such patience. She could hardly wait to take a bite. It smelled delicious, and she told Mrs. Spratt so.

"Nothing like fresh bread," Mrs. Spratt said with a grin. "Ah, here's Mr. Spratt."

The door had opened and in walked the woman's husband, a tall, rather fit man past middle age. Ada would guess them to be in their late fifties. Mr. Spratt removed his hat and clutched it in his hands.

"John, you'll never guess who's here," Mrs. Spratt said, handing Ada her slice of bread. Ada snapped her ledger closed, clasping it and the pencil in one hand while she accepted the bread with the other.

"I can see it's his lordship. What an honor to have you in my house, my lord."

"The pleasure is his," Ada responded before waiting to see if Warfield would respond.

"Yes, it's my pleasure," Warfield said, surprising Ada as she took a bite of bread and accidentally bit her cheek. "This is Miss Treadway. If you have any issues that require my attention, please convey them to her."

Mr. Spratt looked at Ada in disbelief. "Is she the new steward?"

"No, she's the secretary," Mrs. Spratt answered. "She's just making notes in that book."

Ada hurriedly worked to finish her bread, both because it was the best bread she'd ever eaten and so she could get back to writing. Mr. Spratt still looked skeptical.

"Tell his lordship about the roof of the cowshed," Mrs. Spratt urged her husband.

Mr. Spratt glanced toward the viscount. "Bah. I can fix it. I won't bother him with that."

Ada swallowed her next-to-last bite of bread. "Please, if you don't mind, we'd like to hear about it." She popped the last corner into her mouth and reopened the ledger.

"Mr. Spratt is also in need of some new equipment," Mrs. Spratt said, looking to Ada, who made a note in the ledger.

"What equipment is that?" Ada wanted to record precisely what he needed.

"I can get by," Mr. Spratt said, sending a slight scowl toward his wife. "We don't need to bother his lordship."

"It isn't a bother," Ada said cheerfully. "In fact, it's his responsibility, and he'd be delighted to help however he can."

All three of them stared at her, conveying that no one present believed the viscount would be delighted by anything. It seemed his tenants were aware of his demeanor. Was that due to gossip, or had he demonstrated his lack of... delight in front of them?

"Just tell us what equipment needs to be replaced," Lord

Warfield said, sounding either weary or perturbed. Or perhaps both.

"Yes, sir," Mr. Spratt responded. Then he itemized a handful of tools, which Ada quickly documented. He glanced toward the viscount, appearing nervous suddenly. "I can show you the items, so you can determine if they really ought to be replaced."

"I believe you, Mr. Spratt." Warfield's voice was deep and firm.

The farmer nodded. "I appreciate that, sir."

"We should be moving on," Warfield said.

"Thank you for your kind hospitality, and especially for the bread." Ada closed the ledger.

"It's our honor to have you here." Mrs. Spratt went to the door and opened it for them.

Warfield gestured for Ada to leave before him. Then he followed her to the cart where he helped her onto the seat.

Mr. Spratt came out into the yard and thanked them for visiting. "I don't need anything right away," he said.

With a nod, Warfield climbed onto the seat and drove away from the farm.

"Have you never visited them before?" Ada asked.

"Once. Before my steward left, I toured the estate with him." He sent her a curious look. "How did you know their name?"

"Utter luck—I'd read the names in the ledgers, but I'd no idea *they* were the Spratts. I was quite amused by that, actually. Don't tell me the names of the next tenants either. Perhaps I'll get that one correct too."

"I couldn't tell you anyway. You know I am completely uninvolved in the management of this estate. I don't know anyone's names, what they farm, what they pay in rent, or when their leases are up." He spoke matter-of-factly, without a hint of remorse.

"It doesn't sound as if you care either."

When he didn't respond, she sat in silence for several minutes, enjoying the pastoral view as she wondered how this man existed. What did he do all day? What motivated him to even get out of bed in the morning?

"Did you eat your bread?" she asked rather absurdly, recalling that she hadn't seen him actually eat it.

"No. I set it on a table. You were too busy gobbling yours down."

"I'm so disappointed," she said, shaking her head. "You could have given your piece to *me*. It was really good bread."

He made a sound like a snort. But it might have been a grunt because he was him. She really hoped it was a snort—the kind that was akin to a laugh.

They fell quiet again, and she thought back, trying to determine when he'd abandoned that lovely, lovely slice of bread. "You didn't say much," she said.

"You seemed to have things well in hand. Besides, you're the one who wanted to make these visits, not me."

She exhaled. "I suppose. Still, you could be more amenable. Perhaps you can try at our next stop."

"What would you have me say?"

Ada lowered her voice to a deep rasp. "Good morning, I'm Lord Warfield and this is my secretary, Miss Treadway."

"You are *not* my secretary."

She grunted in response, mimicking the way he did it. "This is my annoying houseguest, Miss Treadway. She's going to open her annoying little book and ask several annoying questions. Then she'll scribble in her book and perchance ask you even more annoying questions. She will also eat all your bread."

Ada watched him as she imitated his low, grumbly tone. The barest of smiles flashed across his lips. She nearly leapt from her seat with a delighted cry.

His scowl moved back into place. "Don't say a word, or I'll never do it again."

She clapped her hand over her mouth and swallowed her giggle with great effort. There was a happier gentleman underneath his brusque exterior—she just knew it. If she could glimpse him by being silly, perhaps she could find a way to coax him free.

He steered the cart onto the drive of the next farm. This one was larger than the Spratts', with a two-story cottage and a large barn not far from it. "They have sheep," Warfield said.

"That's helpful to know." Ada tried to remember who had sheep and what the farmers' names were.

As they neared the cottage, two small children ran outside and headed for them.

"What the bloody hell?" Warfield brought the horse to a swift halt. "They're going to get themselves killed behaving like that."

They both, no more than five years of age, ran right up to the cart—on Warfield's side. Ada's breath stalled in her chest, and everything seemed to move in slow motion. She squeezed her eyes shut, unable to watch.

The cart stopped. There was no screaming or awful sound of wheels going over a small body. Surely Ada would have felt that. Carefully, she opened her eyes and saw the children standing next to the cart, their gazes fixed on the viscount. Thank God.

Drawing deep breaths to calm the frantic racing of her heart, Ada didn't wait for Warfield's assistance to climb down from the cart. She moved quickly to greet the children. The older one was a girl, and the younger was a boy. Both had dark hair and wide brown eyes.

"Good morning," Ada said a bit more shakily than she would have liked. She realized it was surely afternoon by now, not that the children would notice. "I'm Miss Treadway and this is Lord Warfield." Their eyes grew even wider as they looked at the viscount, who still sat in the cart, his gaze dark and unreadable as he stared at Ada—not the children. She hoped he hadn't noticed her panicked reaction to the children.

Ada crouched down in front of the children to draw their attention from Warfield. "What are your names?"

The girl pointed to her chest. "I'm Daisy, and this is Jem."

Ada smiled at them both, noting that Jem was still looking at Warfield, his expression a mix of curiosity and apprehension. "I'm pleased to meet you."

"He looks angry," Daisy said, pointing at the viscount.

"Because I am," Warfield answered, climbing down from his seat. Both children moved back. "You shouldn't have run toward the cart. You could have scared the horse and caused an accident injuring us or yourselves. Don't you know any better?"

Though he sounded frightening, Ada was glad he'd said it. They *could* have caused injury. Ada closed her eyes against the distant memory.

"Papa did say not to bother horses," Daisy answered somewhat sullenly. "We didn't mean to be naughty."

Ada exhaled, her pulse finally returning to normal. "You weren't naughty. But you must be safe. We've come to speak with your parents. Are they about?"

"Mama's inside with the baby. They're sick. Papa is with the sheep."

"I'm sorry to hear they're sick." Ada wondered how ill they were. It was no wonder these children were running about. Plus, they were *children*. They tended to run about.

"Perhaps we should come back another time," Warfield murmured.

Ada turned to him and spoke in a low tone. "I want to

check on their mother to see if she needs any help. I'd like to know how sick they are."

And who would help them if they needed it? It wasn't as if Ada could send someone from the house. There was no one to be spared. Perhaps they could hire someone from the village. If not, she was tempted to come herself. The thought of these children putting themselves in harm's way was untenable.

"Don't bombard her with questions," he said sternly.

"You can't think I'd do that," she said with a touch of incredulity. "I'm glad you thought to caution me, however." That indicated he wasn't completely incapable of recognizing appropriate behavior. "I'll be as brief as possible."

Ada looked to Daisy. "Will you take me to meet your mother?"

Daisy skipped toward the house, and her brother followed as if tied to her by a string. Inside, Daisy led Ada to a room at the back—the kitchen, where her mother stood holding a sleeping babe who appeared to be nearing a year. The woman's dark hair was lank, her face pale. She looked exhausted. Her eyes widened upon seeing Ada.

"This lady came here with a lord," Daisy said.

Ada didn't think the woman's pallor could worsen, but it did. Any remaining color in her face completely drained away. "Yes, I'm here with the viscount," Ada said brightly. "We're visiting tenants." She realized she hadn't brought her ledger, but then she wasn't going to query her. She'd make notes about the family when she returned to the cart.

The woman appeared relieved. "Oh. As you can see, we aren't fit for visitors at the moment. The babe's got a fever."

"So do you, Mama," Daisy said helpfully.

Her mother cast her a beleaguered stare. "Will you take your brother outside, please?"

Turning, Daisy skipped out of the kitchen, her brother trailing after.

"Have you been ill long?" Ada asked gently.

"Nearly a week."

Ada took in the unwashed dishes and general chaos of the kitchen. "Looks like you could use some help while you and the babe recover. Do you need medicine?"

The woman shrugged. "Haven't seen a doctor."

"Then I'll make sure one visits. Today." Ada recalled the names of the farmers who kept sheep. "You're Mrs. Niven?"

"No, the Nivens are on the other side of the estate. I'm Mrs. Kempton."

"Ah yes, thank you for correcting me. You've three children? I ask because I want to hire someone to come help until you're well. I just need to know what sort of person to hire. Or if you perhaps need more than one helper."

Mrs. Kempton's dark eyes narrowed slightly, and she adjusted the baby in her arms. "I can't afford any help."

Ada gave her a reassuring smile. "You needn't worry about that. His lordship will pay for it."

Surprise followed by skepticism flashed across Mrs. Kempton's weary features. "Are you certain of that?"

"Yes." Ada would pay for it herself if she had to. Or get Lucien to—he'd be horrified to learn that Warfield wasn't taking care of his tenants. "Don't doubt it. I promise."

"Pardon me for saying so, but his lordship has been absent since coming into the title. The old viscount—his father—was attentive. He was a good landlord. I don't have much faith that this one will pay for medicine, let alone someone to help us."

Ada wanted to rail at Warfield. These people depended on him, and he was letting them down. How could he not realize that? Well, she'd make sure he knew it now—and that things had to change.

"You can trust me," Ada said firmly. "I'll pay the doctor before he even comes here today. Will that ease your concern?"

Mrs. Kempton nodded. "Thank you. Truly." She kissed her baby's head, and Ada felt a pang of loss that made her breath stutter.

Ada walked outside into the bright day and took a long breath. This one visit was threatening to steal every bit of positivity she had. Her gaze found the viscount standing away from the cart, his attention on the ground.

Moving toward him, Ada frowned, as she meant to admonish him for his treatment—or general ignorance—of his tenants. But the closer she got to him, the more she realized something was amiss. He was wholly fixated on the ground and didn't even seem to register her approach.

She followed his gaze and saw a bright red ribbon lying in the dirt. Hadn't that been in Daisy's hair? "Where's the girl?" she asked as the bottom of her stomach seemed to drop away.

He didn't respond, and Ada looked up, glancing around the yard. There she was—not too far distant, crouched down with her brother investigating something. Ada exhaled with relief. She wasn't sure what she thought had happened, but something about Warfield's demeanor was off.

"Are you all right?" she asked.

It took a moment before he finally turned his head toward her. His eyes were glassy, his skin pale. His full lips had seemed to thin. "Let's go."

He turned and strode toward the cart, moving quickly so that Ada had to practically dash after him. She stopped short. "Wait." Pivoting, she went back to fetch the ribbon, then took it to Daisy.

"Thank you," the girl said in astonishment, clearly

unaware she'd lost the ribbon. "Mama would have been upset that I lost it."

Ada made a mental note to bring more ribbon for them. "Here." Ada tied it back into the girl's hair. "All fixed."

Daisy smiled widely, then twirled around, her skirt billowing. Her brother did the same, but of course he had no skirt to make his movements look elegant. Or perhaps it was because he immediately got dizzy and fell down. Chuckling, Ada helped him up. "All right?"

He nodded, but didn't speak. Then he smiled at her. "Pretty."

"He's only two," Daisy said as if that explained everything.

"Thank you, Jem. You take care of your sister now, all right?" Ada ruffled his hair, then gave Daisy a pat before hurrying to the cart. Thankfully, Warfield hadn't left without her.

"I said we needed to go." He didn't sound like his typical irritated self. There was a hollow, worrisome quality to his tone. Ada didn't like it. She also wasn't about to take him to task for not paying attention to his tenants. She'd have to do that later.

She climbed into the cart on her own since he was already seated. She was barely situated before he started driving.

Casting sidelong glances in his direction, she tried to read his expression. That was impossible since he didn't have one. He looked as if he were carved out of stone, a statue. But who would create a statue with such a flawed face?

That thought made her angry. Why not create a statue with a scar? He was a war hero, was he not?

"Did something happen?" she finally asked, his tension swirling around her until her shoulders felt tight.

"No."

She realized they were driving back to the stables. "We're finished with our visits?"

"Yes."

"Why?" She tried to stifle her disappointment and failed.

"Because I never wanted to make them in the first place. You've been nothing but an irritation since you arrived. I want you to—no, I *need* you to—leave me the hell alone. Stop trying to make me smile, stop trying to trick me into engaging with the estate, and for the love of fuck, stop being so bloody *nice*." He stopped the cart abruptly and turned toward her. "I am not a good man, Miss Treadway. I've done things that would make you scream in terror. I don't want your kindness or your help. Just make your damn notes and leave me alone."

All while he'd spoken, a low, horrible fury burned in his voice. His eyes flashed with anger, but something else too—pain. He hid it quickly, kept his features schooled into an impenetrable mask of disdain.

He started driving again at a slightly faster clip. Ada fought to keep still, clasping her hands together lest she try to touch him in comfort. He wouldn't want that, even if he probably needed it.

Mrs. Bundle had told her there was a different man beneath his façade. Ada was certain she'd just glimpsed him.

And there was no way she was leaving him alone.

CHAPTER 5

*H*e'd behaved horribly.

Which wasn't different from any other day, except that it was. That afternoon, Max had let his anger and self-loathing run rampant, and he'd frightened Miss Treadway in the process.

Because of a red ribbon.

Everything about that long-ago day was burned into his mind for all time. A warm summer afternoon with a light breeze. The scent of dirt and grass. Birdsong. Dark hair. Red ribbon.

No. White ribbon stained with blood.

Max squeezed his eyes shut and clenched his hands into fists. He wouldn't go back to Spain, to that horrible day. Except he couldn't escape it.

Exhaling slowly, he pushed the tension from his shoulders down his arms and flexed his hands. He might not be able to run from it, but he could hide. Or try to, anyway. What else did he have to do?

Opening his eyes, he regarded himself in the mirror. His

face looked weary, with lines etched around his eyes and mouth. Even his scars, wrinkled and pinkish, had lines.

You should apologize to her.

He owed her that much, at least. He turned to fetch his coat and drew it on, straightening the garment over his waistcoat. He feared his garments were out of fashion—and they were too large since he'd lost weight and hadn't bothered to gain it back—but he didn't care. Whom did he need to impress?

He went downstairs and made his way to the dining room, hoping he wasn't too late. As he entered, he realized Timothy was just serving the soup. The footman clattered the spoon against the tureen as his gaze landed on Max.

Damn, he hadn't meant to startle the poor lad. But then Timothy was easily spooked.

"Will you set a place for me, Timothy?" Max asked, walking to the head of the table. He noted that Miss Treadway was seated near the middle.

"Right away, my lord." Timothy bustled to set Max's place.

"What a surprise," Miss Treadway said evenly. "I'm delighted you'll be joining me."

He might have thought she was jesting, but delight seemed to be one of her natural moods. "Were you always this cheerful?"

"Yes. And before you ask, yes, it was also occasionally annoying to my family, particularly my father when he wasn't satisfied with the number of fish he'd caught that day. He preferred if everyone shared his disappointment. But I eventually won him over."

"How did you manage that?"

Her blue-gray eyes glimmered in the candlelight. There was mischief in their depths, along with glee. What he wouldn't give to feel either of those things. "By acting silly or telling him a story or making up a song."

Timothy had finished the setting, and Max took his seat. The footman then served his soup. Max had almost forgotten what this was like.

"You made up songs?" he prompted, as much out of a sense of awkwardness as curiosity. He imagined she was a precocious child.

"Yes, typically about mermaids or fish, although I suppose mermaids *are* fish." She laughed softly, and he didn't find it irritating.

Timothy poured wine, and Max took a sip, eyeing Miss Treadway over the rim as she ate her soup. "Why are you sitting there?" he asked, putting his glass down.

"I sit in a different chair every night. That way, I can see the room from different perspectives."

He stared at her, thinking she couldn't be that charming. Or that he was surprised to find he was being charmed by her. But his defenses were low. Today had been rough.

"I want to apologize for what I said earlier." He focused on his soup so he wouldn't have to look at her.

"Thank you," she said softly. "I certainly didn't expect to see you here tonight. Would you mind if I moved closer?" She was already standing, and Timothy rushed to help her. Then he transported her place setting next to Max. To his left. Dammit.

"I, ah, perhaps you wouldn't mind sitting there." He inclined his head toward the empty chair on his right.

She bent slightly and whispered, "I sat on your left in the cart earlier. Your scars don't bother me. Indeed, without them, you'd look far too perfect."

He looked up at her and wanted to argue, but words froze on his tongue. At this proximity, he smelled apples and spice, a deliciously alluring scent. And her eyes sparkled with her excess of charm and wit. They were framed with the most magnificently long, dark lashes and capped by elegantly seductive brows. She was the one who looked perfect.

Before he could muster speech, she motioned for Timothy to set the place on Max's right.

When she was seated once more, Max murmured. "Thank you." He grimaced. "Hell, I should have stood that entire time. My manners are in bad shape, I'm afraid."

"You needn't worry about impressing me."

He nearly laughed at that, recalling what he'd been thinking before coming downstairs.

They finished their soup, and Timothy laid the next course.

Max feared he wouldn't be able to make it to the third course. "It's been a while since I ate a dinner like this."

"You don't eat the same meal in your study?"

"Not in courses like this. I, ah, don't eat very much."

"That's a shame since Mrs. Debley is such a fine cook."

He spent a few minutes sampling the delicious meal and decided it was a terrible shame indeed.

Miss Treadway forked a carrot, her gaze glinting with that mischief again. "I mean to find a way to persuade her to tell me stories about you as a boy."

"She'll tell you I stole biscuits from the kitchen like every other boy. Except my brother. He stole cheese."

"Oh, I would have liked your brother," she said, chuckling. "There is nothing better than cheese."

Max arched a brow. "Except biscuits."

She grinned. "Shall we duel over it?"

"No." Her casual jest about violence reminded him that he was perilously close to forgetting that he oughtn't be sitting here enjoying her company.

"Is that how you got the scar?" she asked, sounding quite sober now, her voice low and even tentative, which he found surprising.

"It's from the war. I suppose battles are a series of duels. Only there are no rules, and no one behaves like a gentleman." And there went his appetite. Dammit. The beef was delicious, as was the potato pudding.

"It looks as though you were burned." She watched him as if she expected him to turn his head so she could inspect the scars.

"I was." That day returned once more. The summer breeze. The bloodied ribbon. Later, the sharp, blinding pain of his flesh scalding. And so very much more.

Max seized and drained his wineglass. Timothy quickly refilled it, much to Max's appreciation.

"Thank you," Max murmured. Then he turned his head slightly so he could look Miss Treadway in the eye. "I'd rather not discuss the injury in detail. I hope you can respect my wishes, particularly given your nosiness."

She stared at him a moment, then her face lit as she smiled broadly. "Thank you for that. Teasing me, I mean. I deserve it. I told you, I'm horribly inquisitive. I just like to know *everything*. Especially when I find things interesting."

"You think I'm interesting?"

"Positively fascinating." She ate a few peas she'd managed to spear on her fork, contemplating him as she chewed. After she swallowed, she added, "You are vastly disagreeable, and yet underneath your surly exterior, there hides a wealth of secrets. I hear you were actually a very likable person once. Lucien insists you're one of his dearest friends, and for that to be true, you can't be the man you show to the world."

He was in real danger of letting her breach his defenses. "Perhaps Lucien is a poor judge of character."

She looked affronted. "He helped me when I needed it, so I take that as an offense, sir."

Time to deflect the conversation to her. "How did he help you?"

"I needed employment." For the first time, she seemed uncomfortable, or at least not her usual sunny self. No, not the first time. That afternoon, before his own mental crash, she'd seemed troubled. It had been when the children had run toward the cart. He'd sensed something from her that he hadn't before: fear.

"He hired you as the bookkeeper of his club? You must have had excellent references."

Her eyes met his. "Just one, but it was enough to matter. I don't think he regrets the decision. I'm very good at what I do."

"I can see that. You're incredibly organized and detailed. If you weren't already employed, I might have to consider hiring you as my steward." Except he couldn't have her here. Look at the damage she was doing, and it hadn't even been a week. "If you weren't so annoying, that is."

She laughed, but she was also swallowing, so she coughed. Then she reached for her wine and took a drink. She coughed again.

"I didn't mean to cause you discomfort," he said.

She waved her hand as she took another sip. "I'm fine. You're rather charming this evening. I'm glad you decided to have dinner with me." She looked at him with a bright intensity that made him feel better than he had in a very long time.

He put his attention on his plate and forced himself to eat, though he was long past feeling hungry.

She didn't let the silence gather too long. "I sent the doctor from the village to call on Mrs. Kempton this afternoon. She didn't want me to because of the expense, but I paid for the visit and the medicine he left for her and the baby."

Max put his utensils down. There would be no more

eating. Shame and self-loathing tore through him. "I should pay for that."

"Yes, you should, but I know you don't like to part with money." There was a frost to her tone.

"Because I don't spend money on the estate?"

"That and...other things. I was inclined to believe you weren't interested in helping people."

He narrowed his eyes at her. "Are you referring to something specific?"

"Yes, but we needn't discuss it. I'm glad to hear that you are going to pay for the doctor." She blinked. "Are you going to pay for the doctor, or were you merely acknowledging the fact that you should?"

He'd done an excellent job of ensuring everyone believed the worst of him. He ought to feel satisfied, but instead felt queasy. "I'll reimburse you."

"Thank you. You should also know that Mrs. Kempton needs temporary help while she recovers. She can't take care of a sick baby and two small children. Her husband is busy with the farm, of course. I want to hire someone from the village."

"I'll pay for that too," he said. "But...can you take care of the hiring?"

"Certainly."

Every day she showed him how she could run Stonehill better than he could. He could blame the fact that his father hadn't really educated him on how to do it—why would he when his brother was meant to be the next viscount? Only, Max had spent the past two years doing everything possible to avoid learning anything. To avoid doing anything.

To avoid *feeling* anything. Except anger and despair. He was quite accomplished at feeling those.

The people at Stonehill—his retainers and the tenants—depended on the viscount. He had a responsibility to them, albeit one he didn't want. Dammit, he never should have inherited this. Why wasn't there a bloody cousin he could turn this over to? Someone else ought to be the viscount. Someone worthy.

"I'll go to the village tomorrow morning," she said, setting her utensils down. "How far a walk is it?"

Timothy cleared their plates and went about setting the next course, which Max didn't want.

"Three miles." Max didn't doubt she could easily do it, but her time was valuable. "I'll have...Archie drive you." He realized he didn't even have a bloody groom or coachman to drive her. He could instruct Og to do it, but he now found he didn't want to subject her to the ornery stable master.

He needed more than a steward. He needed people in the stables, in the house, in the overgrown gardens. He needed a damn butler. He didn't *want* any of it.

She broke into his thoughts. "Thank you, I appreciate your help with this. I confess I'm surprised I didn't have to convince you this was necessary."

"I am too." He exhaled. "It seems I must take a more active role, beginning with hiring a steward." That way, Max could turn everything over to him. He'd make sure whoever he hired understood that Max didn't want to be involved.

"Will you manage that?" she asked tentatively.

"I'd rather not." He leaned back in his chair. "I don't suppose I can expect you to take that on too. No, of course not. Perhaps Lucien will help me."

"He'd be delighted to." She couldn't contain her smile, and he envied her that buoyant, uncontrollable emotion. He'd almost forgotten what that felt like.

As soon as he let it in, a searing pain would crush the sensation. He wasn't able to feel joy anymore, and watching her was a grim reminder.

Max stood. "Please excuse me."

"I'm glad you came to dinner," she said. "I look forward to helping you get back to work with the estate. You'll be happy to be involved, I promise. It will be wonderful—for everyone."

He wouldn't be happy, and it wouldn't be wonderful, not for him. But it was necessary, and Max had always done the hard, seemingly impossible things.

Someone had to.

~

*A*da was delighted to meet Archie Tallent the next morning. He was waiting for her with the cart when she walked into the stable yard. Though just fourteen, he was exceedingly tall. His face was still quite boyish, his cheeks full, and his smile easy. His dark hair curled against his forehead beneath his hat.

"Good morning, Archie," she greeted him. "I'm so pleased to meet you. If you don't mind, I'd like our first stop to be your house so that I can meet your mother. I'm doing my best to tour the estate while I'm here, and for the next week, I believe, you will be my driver."

He nodded. "I'm at your command, Miss Treadway. At least that's what my mother told me to be," he added with a smile.

Ada laughed. "I think I'm going to like your mother."

Archie offered to help her into the cart, and Ada took his hand. They left a moment later, and Ada caught sight of Og standing in the doorway of the stables, his disgruntled expression trained on them.

Ada tried to imagine the pleasant young man beside her working with Og on a daily basis. "I hope Og didn't give you any trouble about driving me."

"He doesn't give me anything else." Archie didn't sound

the least bit bothered by it, however. "I know he means well. He just has a rough disposition. My mother always tells me to treat others with kindness because we never know what path they've walked."

Ada was definitely going to like his mother. "Do you happen to know what path Og has traveled?" Not that she really needed to know. Sometimes her curiosity really was a curse.

"My mother says his wife and daughter died of fever a long time ago."

"Well, that would make anyone despondent and would likely be difficult to recover from."

"Can I tell you a secret?" Archie asked in a whisper as if anyone were around to hear them.

"Certainly."

"I sometimes wonder if he and his lordship have a pact to help each other remain grumpy."

Ada clapped her hand over her mouth before she laughed. She didn't know if Archie was making a jest. "Are you serious?"

Archie shrugged. "They're both so consistently in bad moods. If I did that, my mother would banish me to bed without supper."

"Perhaps that's what they need." Although after watching Warfield eat last night—or not eat, really—Ada suspected missing supper wouldn't have much effect on him.

They arrived shortly at Archie's house, a neat cottage with flowers blooming in tidy beds out front. A dog ran toward them as Archie set the brake. He bounded out to greet the animal, a black-and-white collie. Archie ruffled the dog's fur, and the dog let out a few happy barks.

Ada climbed down from the cart, clasping her ledger in her left hand. "What's his name?"

Archie glanced up at her from where he crouched.

"Happy. Because he makes us all happy. Plus, just look at his face. He's always happy. Aren't you, boy?" The love between boy and animal was so strong, Ada felt a thickening in her chest.

"He looks like a very happy boy."

Suddenly Archie sent her a distressed look. He stood. "I should have helped you from the cart. I beg your pardon."

"It's all right." Ada waved her hand. "I wouldn't want to come between a boy and his dog." She went to Happy and patted his head.

"Archie, what are you doing back here?" A woman's voice drew Ada's attention to the house. Mrs. Tallent stood on the stoop, her hand shading her eyes as she gazed into the yard toward her son.

Ada strode toward her, eager to make the woman's acquaintance. "Good morning, Mrs. Tallent, I'm Miss Ada Treadway. I asked Archie to bring me here first. I hope it's all right and that you have time to meet with me. I'd like to ask you about your farm and see if there is anything you might need."

Mrs. Tallent sized her up, her gaze moving from Ada's straw bonnet to her sturdy boots. Ada returned the scrutiny, taking in the woman's dark, curly hair and sharp green eyes. Like her son, she was tall, towering several inches over Ada. The woman appeared to be in her early thirties. "Come in." She looked over Ada's head to the yard. "Archie, feed the goats while you're here, please."

"Yes, Mama."

Ada turned her head to see him and Happy take off. "I've hardly spent any time with your son, but he's a lovely boy. You must be so proud of him."

"I am. He has a good heart. Can I get you anything?"

Ada shook her head. "No, thank you. Do you want to sit?"

"For a few minutes, then I must get on. This is a busy time of day for me, especially since Archie isn't here to help."

Ada grimaced. "Oh, I've stolen your help." Ada didn't want the woman to spend the next week working overly hard to satisfy Ada's need to travel about the estate.

Mrs. Tallent took a chair near the hearth and gestured for Ada to sit on the worn settee. "I've told Og he can't have him this week. He's paid for half days at Stonehill, and that's what they can have."

"I could ask his lordship to pay him for full days this week if that would help you." Ada hadn't realized their jaunts would be only half the day, but that was just as well so that she had time to make notes and plans.

"Not as much as having Archie here. I wish his lordship would hire proper grooms. I'd prefer Archie were here all day. He needs to focus more time on his studies as well as learn the farm since it will be his to manage."

"I'm working on that," Ada said with determination. "The grooms, I mean. Just last night, his lordship agreed to hire a steward, so I hope grooms are not far off, along with maids and perhaps even a butler."

Mrs. Tallent gaped at her. "You've been here, what, a week?"

"Yes." Based on Mrs. Tallent's reaction and Mrs. Kempton's attitude toward Warfield yesterday, Ada gathered that his tenants didn't hold him in the highest opinion and seized the moment to further her investigation. "What do you know of his lordship?"

"What do you want to know?" Mrs. Tallent sounded somewhat guarded.

"I admit I'm curious about him. I'm employed by one of his closest friends—that's how I came to be on this assignment. Which is to organize his ledgers." Ada vaguely worried that she ought not share so much, but these people had a right to know about things that would affect their livelihood. And hopefully Ada's efforts would do that, for the better.

"I didn't realize he still had friends," Mrs. Tallent said wryly. "I've lived on this estate since I married fifteen years ago. His lordship was away at school then. When he finished, he spent a few years sowing his wild oats before his father purchased him a commission in the army. Then he was mostly absent over the next several years."

Sowing his wild oats? Ada had difficulty imagining Warfield enjoying anything. But of course he did, and she'd seen glimpses of it yesterday. Perhaps the first step in rehabilitating him was believing it could be done.

"Was he a rake?" Ada asked, still trying to see the viscount as a carefree young man. Without scars, both inside and out. With his face, he probably *was* a rake.

"I don't know about that, just that his father called him home and made him choose between an army commission and a living as a vicar."

If thinking of him as a rake was challenging, Ada had even less success imagining him as a vicar. "Do you know if there was anything he liked to do? Besides sow his wild oats."

"He was an excellent rider. He rode all over the estate, apparently from when he was a very young lad. But when he came home after being wounded, he sold most of the horses at Stonehill, including his, which had gone with him to Spain."

That sounded rather sad. "Do you know why?"

Mrs. Tallent lifted a shoulder. "No one does. The speculation is that he was wounded on horseback and perhaps that's why he doesn't care to ride anymore."

"Only it doesn't sound like his horse was wounded." Furthermore, he'd suffered burns. How did that happen while riding? Before Ada went completely down the rabbit hole of her curiosity and thoroughly wasted Mrs. Tallent's precious time, she reined herself in. "I suppose selling off horses made him think he didn't need as many grooms working in the stables?"

"I believe that was the case. He's also quite accomplished at driving people away with his surly behavior. The steward had suffered enough, which was too bad because he was excellent."

"I don't suppose he'd come back?" Ada asked.

"I highly doubt it. He went to work for an earl in Staffordshire. Unless he's unhappy there. But he was unhappy here, and I suspect nothing could lure him back."

That was a shame. Still, it might be best for everyone, especially Warfield, to start anew with someone who wasn't aware of his disagreeability.

Except Ada suspected his reputation was probably well known.

She exhaled, committed to improving things. Just because something was difficult didn't mean it shouldn't be done. Difficult things were often those that were most worth doing.

Ada went back to the matter of the stable. "Is that how Archie came to work in the stable? When the grooms left?"

"Not long after. And Molly's been working in the kitchens for about six months now. Mrs. Debley is in desperate need of help. Molly is exhausted when she gets home. At least they pay her well. Otherwise, I wouldn't let her do it."

Having the necessary funds wasn't the issue, and yet the viscount wouldn't hire more help. Anger curled through Ada as she recalled her best friend, Prudence, and how she'd needed money from him recently—for a dowry so she could marry her destitute husband—and he'd refused. She suddenly wanted to turn around and go back to Stonehill, where she would demand an explanation from him for why he'd treated Prudence so badly. There wouldn't be a good one, and she'd bloody well shame him for it. How could he not realize how he was affecting those around him?

"You must need Molly here at home too," Ada said.

"I'd prefer it. The farm is a great deal of work. But at least his lordship allowed us to stay after my husband died last year."

This was what confused Ada so much. Why was Warfield kind about some things and ruthlessly horrid about others? "I have a hard time understanding his lordship."

"We all do," Mrs. Tallent said wearily. "You must know that tenants have left when their lease expired. Others plan to do the same."

The awful truth was that Ada didn't think he cared. But he should. "I would think he'd want to preserve this for the next viscount, that it's his responsibility to do so."

Mrs. Tallent flicked something from her skirt. "I don't think he has any plans to have an heir. He barely leaves the house and certainly doesn't do anything social."

"Perhaps he's still recovering from his wounds?"

"If his wounds include a broken heart, then yes."

Ada's curiosity forced her forward in her chair, eager to know more. "Why would you say that?"

"He was quite different before he went to Spain. He was charming, even flirtatious. He seems to have recovered from his wounds—he had a pronounced limp when he first came home but doesn't any longer—however, he is a completely changed man, a hollow shell, really." There was no mistaking the pity in her voice.

"You think his heart was broken?"

"I think it's possible that whatever happened to him in Spain goes beyond a battle that damaged his body."

That certainly seemed likely, given his demeanor. Ada

already knew his angry façade hid the real man. Or was that man gone forever?

He couldn't be. People could recover from horrible things. Ada had. More than once.

She could show him how to find himself again, to experience joy. Except that wasn't her objective in coming here. Lucien had asked her to organize his ledgers, not bring back the man they all remembered.

Even so, wouldn't Lucien want her to do that? He missed his friend and was frustrated by this beastly version who refused friendship and family. He could have a half sister, but preferred his isolation.

"I'm taking up too much of your time, Mrs. Tallent." Ada opened her ledger and made a few notes. "Before I go, would you mind telling me about your farm and whether you need any improvements?"

"Certainly."

Over the next quarter hour, Mrs. Tallent gave Ada a thorough accounting of their farm, even showing her the farm's ledgers. Ada was thoroughly impressed by the woman and decided she would make an excellent steward if she wasn't already a farmer.

"Do you like farming?" Ada asked.

Mrs. Tallent shrugged. "It's all we have. I worry that things are changing, that it will be harder for Archie. I would have liked for him to go to school."

"Perhaps he still can," Ada said, her mind working. "Molly too, if you wanted her to."

"I don't know how any of that would be possible," Mrs. Tallent responded, sounding bemused.

Ada set the farm's ledger on a table between her and Mrs. Tallent. "I mentioned that his lordship will be hiring a steward, and I'm going to suggest he consider you."

Mrs. Tallent gaped at her. "You can't."

"Why not?"

"I wouldn't want that job. He's awful to work for." Her shoulders twitched. "I'd like to get my children *away* from his household."

"I understand why you would feel that way, but what if he were different, more like the man he used to be?"

Mrs. Tallent scoffed. "Then I would think about it. However, he isn't different, and the man he used to be is long gone."

Yes, he was, but Ada now hoped with great conviction that she could bring him back. "I have one more week," she said with a confidence she didn't entirely feel. "Hopefully, I can get you to change your mind."

"The fact that he's even considering making changes is a huge step forward. It seems you may be just what he needs." Mrs. Tallent stood. "Still, I'm not going to hold my breath. I've a farm to tend."

"You do indeed." Ada clutched her ledger as she got to her feet. "Thank you again for your time and for your son's time. I will do my best to effect positive change at Stonehill."

"That would be wonderful," Mrs. Tallent said. "But promise me you won't be disappointed if you fail. It won't be your fault."

"I promise." It was an easy one to make, because Ada wasn't going to fail.

CHAPTER 6

*T*he hair ribbon was still bothering him.

Max hadn't thought about that specific detail in a very long time, likely because he tried to block everything about that day and night from his memory. But yesterday, that girl's scarlet ribbon had taken him back, and while he'd done a fair job of keeping himself from recalling what had happened, he couldn't stop the wave of fury and despair. It wasn't the memory itself, it was the memory of the emotions. News of the battle won in Waterloo added to his unease even though Napoleon had been defeated.

God, he felt so weak.

He finished another glass of whisky and was about to get up to pour another when there was a light knock on the door. No one bothered him here at this time of night. Mrs. Bundle had long ago cleared away his half-eaten dinner.

And it wasn't the library door, so he didn't think it would be Miss Treadway. He'd successfully avoided her all day too, which he'd considered a victory. She either annoyed him or somehow coaxed him to agree to things he'd refused to consider. She'd even somehow managed to get him to drive her around the damned estate. But he was through succumbing to her magnetic charm.

The knock came again, and Max pushed himself up. He ambled to the door and opened it just wide enough to see who the hell was intruding on his solitude. It *was* her.

Dressed in a tidy, pale yellow gown, she looked fresh and lovely. That included the strands of dark hair that grazed her neck. Rebel hair that refused to remain neatly pinned. Of course she would have that.

"Good evening, my lord," she said with her usual buoyant tone and easy smile. "I missed you at dinner."

"I can't imagine why you would have expected to see me. Last night was an anomaly."

"I hoped it wasn't. May I come in for a few minutes?"

"I was about to retire," he fibbed.

"I shan't take long." She pushed inward, and he had no choice but to step back unless he wanted to be a complete brute. He wasn't that far gone. Not yet.

Her gaze fell on his empty glass beside the chair he'd been sitting in by the hearth. "What are you drinking?"

"Whisky."

"Irish or Scotch?"

"Scotch. My father was rather fond of it." He used to have a friend who smuggled it south. "This has been in the cupboard for nearly twenty years, I think."

"Is it good?" she asked.

"I like it."

She put a hand on her hip. "Are you going to offer me any, or do I have to ask?"

Max blew out an irritated breath. "I told you I was going to retire."

"You did, but our conversation will be much more pleasant if we have a nightcap to go with it."

"Please tell me you aren't delivering bad news," he said with exasperation. "Or going out of your way to annoy me?"

"No bad news, and I didn't think I had to try to annoy you. You made it seem as though my simple existence was enough."

"Saucy chit," he muttered as he went to pour her a glass of whisky. After handing it to her, he refilled his glass and set the bottle back on the cabinet beside bottles of port and brandy.

She perched on a small chair situated near the hearth, but thankfully not too close to his. "Did you post the letter to Lucien this morning that I left on your desk?"

"Yes. When did you do that?" He looked at her intently. "It wasn't here when I left last night."

"I get up rather early, and especially so today, since I was touring the estate with Archie. Are you going to ask me what the letter was about?"

"No." He sipped his drink.

"I informed him you are hiring a steward and asked for his assistance. I hope he'll send some names. That was before I discovered a potential candidate." She took a sip and immediately coughed. A deep grimace lined her face, and she put her fingers to her lips. "Good lord, this is quite strong."

Max stared at her mouth and the hand covering it. She had long, delicate fingers, he realized, fingers that ought to play the pianoforte. Or... His mind was suddenly overcome with lewd images of things her lovely fingers could do.

He jerked his attention to the hearth. "Would you prefer port or brandy?"

"No, this is good. After a few more sips, I'll be used to it."

"You've experience drinking whisky?" He dared look at her again, and thankfully, her hand was in her lap while the other still held the glass.

"From working at the Phoenix Club, yes. If Lord Wexford

is around, there's a debate as to which is superior—Irish or Scotch. Because he's Irish."

"What's your opinion?" He both hated and loved that he found her so interesting.

"In truth, I prefer the Irish, but I don't ever say. It's better to be noncommittal." She winked at him before taking another sip. This time, she barely winced.

"You actually drink with the gentlemen?"

"Certainly. I probably would anyway, given my position in the club, but on Tuesdays, women may enter the gentlemen's side of the club. It's probably the busiest night of the week. When we aren't hosting assemblies most Fridays during the Season, that is."

Max stared at her. "Lucien allows women into the club?"

"Did you not realize that?" She laughed softly. "There's a ladies' side and a gentlemen's side. The men are never allowed on our side—save our half of the ballroom during assemblies. But we're given access to theirs on Tuesdays. It's deliciously rewarding."

There was a seductive quality to the rich glee in her tone that stirred something inside him, something he wanted to keep buried. He didn't like spending time with her.

Because he did.

She gave him a pointed look. "I think Lucien is hoping you will accept his invitation for membership."

"I'm rarely in London."

"It would be a good reason to come." She seemed to want to say more, but didn't.

He grunted. "I don't like social gatherings."

"You could find a quiet corner at the club. The library is a nice place to enjoy peace and solitude. And the whisky is unparalleled." She lifted her glass in a silent toast.

He met her gaze and narrowed his. "Are you maligning my whisky?"

"Not at all. But if you're fond of it, you could sample many different kinds."

"You're not talking me into joining that club. You've persuaded me to do enough as it is."

"All necessary and important things, I assure you," she said cheerfully. "I was able to hire someone in the village today to help Mrs. Kempton for the next fortnight. The young woman was grateful for the work. In fact, she'd make a wonderful addition to your household, perhaps as a maid. Mrs. Bundle could certainly use the help."

He glowered at her, knowing she was right and hating that she was making this look so bloody easy. "I see what you're trying to do."

"Good. I'm certainly not trying to be secretive. You can't keep employing Mrs. Tallent's children. She needs them on her farm. Mrs. Debley requires additional kitchen staff, Og needs help in the stables, and Mrs. Bundle needs maids. You could also use a butler and a valet."

"I don't need either of those. Butlers are for people who have guests."

"Am I not a guest?"

"You are an aberration."

She rolled her eyes, not in the least insulted, not that he expected her to be. "I'm still a guest. A butler will keep your household in order so that you don't have to. If you truly want to retreat into yourself and live an isolated existence, you must rely on others to maintain Stonehill."

"I'm already doing that."

She exhaled in exasperation. "You're asking a handful of people to do the work of many more. Surely you know that. I can only conclude that you don't care about these people—or the estate."

"I definitely don't care about the estate. It can rot into the ground as far as I care."

"What of your heirs?"

"I don't have any bloody heirs, nor do I plan to," he said, gritting his teeth as his anger began to escalate.

She didn't seem surprised. "Then think of the people around you—the retainers and the tenants. You're going to lose them if you don't change things, and then where will you be?"

"Right where I want to be."

Her mouth rounded briefly before she snapped it closed. There was the surprise. "That can't be true."

"It is, and I can't change that."

"You mean won't. You didn't used to be like this, as far as I can tell. Why can't you go back to being the man you once were?"

He leapt out of the chair and grasped the arms of hers, leaning over her. "That man is gone. Just as you're going to be. Get out of the chair and my house." He bared his teeth at her.

She plastered her shoulders to the chair and lifted her chin. "No."

Fury raged inside him. He leaned closer, his face a few inches from hers. "I will pick you up and toss you out."

Her gaze frosted. "Is that what you did to my friend Prudence when she came looking for a job?"

What the hell was she talking about? "Who is Prudence?"

"Prudence Lancaster. Actually, she's the Viscountess Glastonbury now."

Recognition lit his brain. He knew that name. Lucien had come pleading for a dowry for her. But Miss Treadway wasn't talking about that. "She didn't come here for a job or anything else."

"Actually, she did. It was some time ago now, and thankfully, Lucien was here to rescue her from destitution by helping her find a job as a paid companion. How a wonderful man like him remains friendly or continues to believe in someone like you is beyond me, but that's just who Lucien is."

Every word she said struck his chest like a knife blade, slicing into him with painful precision. His anger remained, but she'd taken the acid from it. "I don't know why he does that either. I've told him not to." He let go of her chair and backed away, disgusted with himself for menacing her like that.

She smoothed her hand across her forehead and relaxed her shoulders, showing she'd been far more tense—and perhaps even afraid—than he'd realized. Then she took her longest drink of whisky yet. "This is no way to live, Warfield. Do you truly like feeling grumpy and being alone?"

"Yes." The word creaked from his throat like an old, unused door hinge.

"I don't believe you. I think you've simply forgotten how to feel anything else."

"I've good reason," he mumbled before taking another drink.

"Because some bad things have happened to you. Bad things happen to everyone, and we find a way to carry on."

He growled, curling his lip. "You've no idea."

"I've survived a number of bad things."

"Such as what?"

"My father died, my mother died…my sister also died." She swallowed, her gaze moving to the wall behind him. "And other things."

Curiosity about those other things burned in his mind, but he didn't ask. "My parents and my brother also died. I have no family left."

Her eyes narrowed at him. "Except your half sister. Remember Prudence?"

"Of course I remember. I just didn't recall her name. Her

existence dredges up more bad things—that my father was completely unfaithful to my mother and was a lying scoundrel. There's a special pain in learning your hero was a fraud." He finished his whisky and immediately refilled his tumbler.

She was silent a moment as she sipped her drink. At last, she said, "I'm sorry. But that isn't Prudence's fault. She didn't get to choose the circumstances of her birth. Why wouldn't you give her a dowry? I'm fairly certain you can afford it."

He cast his head back and looked at the ceiling. Shadows waved here and there with the flickering candlelight. "I preferred to pretend she didn't exist. It was rather childish of me."

"I'm glad you recognize that, but she's a real person. A lovely one too. You'd like her."

"I don't like anyone."

"Perhaps you should. I thought for a brief moment last night that you might like me."

He lowered his gaze to hers and found her watching him intently. Yes, he'd thought that too. He ought to tell her he didn't, that he never would, that he was biding his time until she was gone—they were halfway there.

But the words wouldn't come. He'd been nothing but an absolute blackguard since he'd come back from Spain. Did he really want to spend the rest of his life in this misery?

The problem was that he didn't know how to escape it. But he had to admit that having her here ensured he was at least thinking of something else part of the time.

He ignored what she said and went back to his half sister. "It sounds as if you know Prudence well."

"She's my best friend."

He snorted. What were the fucking odds that this slip of a woman who'd turned his life upside down in a week was best friend to the half sister he never wanted?

Actually, given his luck, the odds were quite good.

"You *are* an aberration," he murmured before sipping his whisky. The amount of alcohol he'd consumed suddenly caught up with him, making his head spin. This was not a good place to be. This was the state where his emotions were unpredictable, where he was in real danger.

He stood, and the floor wavered beneath his feet.

"Can I move forward with hiring people?"

"No." He shook his head and immediately regretted the motion as the room continued to spin long after he stilled.

"But you need them," she said with determination. "Will you at least let me hire Teresa when she's finished helping Mrs. Kempton?"

"You won't be here then." He made his way to the door, still carrying his whisky, though he didn't plan to drink anymore. He'd had enough to settle into oblivion, where red ribbons and nagging bookkeepers wouldn't trouble him.

"I can do it now," she called after him.

He didn't respond. The sooner he lost himself to darkness, the better everything would be.

$\approx$

*A*da woke, her eyes shooting open as if she'd been startled by a sound. But there hadn't been a sound. Rolling to her side, she stared into the darkness, wondering how long she'd been asleep. She'd tossed and turned interminably before finally succumbing to exhaustion.

But now her mind was working, as it had when sleep had been elusive. She was thinking of Warfield again and was still unsettled at how their evening had ended. Or perhaps she was disappointed in herself for the way she'd talked to him about Prudence and Lucien. She shouldn't have compared them.

What was she even doing? She was supposed to be tidying his ledgers and determining the state of his affairs. Lucien had given her a simple assignment, and she'd turned it into an *investigation* because of her infernal curiosity.

Yet here she was, and she couldn't un-know what she'd learned. Warfield was trapped by something, and she'd wager anything that he wanted to be free, even if he didn't realize it yet.

Guilt was a horrible thing. Ada knew that better than most. It had ruined her life for two long years in which she'd inhabited the darkest spaces before pulling herself from despair.

Then she'd spent two more long years reinventing herself and trying to leave the past behind. She'd done a fair job of it too, until she'd made yet another mistake. She hoped she wasn't bungling things now by sticking her nose where it didn't belong.

Not that she could seem to help herself.

Agitated, Ada threw the covers aside and slid from the bed. There was a chill in the air, so she grabbed her dressing gown and pulled it over her night rail before shoving her feet into slippers. She went to the hearth and stirred the coals, adding fuel to the fire until flames began to lick the air.

Now she was warm. And still restless.

Perhaps a walk would help. Did she need a candle? She went to the door and opened it, peering into the gallery that ran the length of the first floor. A few sconces lit the way, banishing the need for a candle, thank goodness.

Slipping from her chamber, she closed the door and wandered along the gallery. There wasn't enough light to study the paintings along the way, except for the ones next to the sconces.

She stopped at the first such portrait and wondered if this was one of Warfield's relatives. The man stared back at her with blue eyes and a round face tinged with mirth. There was absolutely no resemblance.

Moving on, she meandered back and forth across the gallery, stopping at the next sconce, where a haughty young woman gazed at her from probably the midseventeenth century. The portrait had to predate the current house, unless it had been painted decades later than the time it seemed to portray. There was a fullness to the woman's lips that reminded her of Warfield. He had an incredibly sensual mouth for a man. She longed to see what it did when he smiled, a slow, lazy, thoroughly seductive smile that would melt anyone who beheld it. She imagined him doing that during his younger years, when he'd left school and gone to sow his wild oats. She hoped she'd get a chance to ask him about that period of his life.

As she neared the other end of the gallery, a distant sound drew her attention. She continued until she found herself in a sitting room. The sound came again, much louder this time —a horrible keening that nearly pulled her heart from her chest.

Rushing forward, she hesitated when the moaning stopped. She stood just outside the door, her pulse roaring. Then it started once more, and she jumped in reaction.

It was an awful, gut-wrenching sound. She couldn't ignore it.

Then he screamed.

Ada pushed into the chamber, heedless of what she might find, only knowing that she had to help whoever was making that terrible noise.

As if she didn't know.

The chamber was nearly dark, with only the coals in the hearth for light. The keening had stopped, but the figure in the bed thrashed. Then went suddenly quiet.

She crept to the side of the bed and made out his form.

He lay on his back, his arm cast over his eyes as his chest heaved. Was he awake?

"Warfield," she whispered. The covers were pushed away, and he was nearly nude, garbed in only small clothes covering his groin. A nasty scar, far angrier than the ones on his face, marred his thigh. Letting her gaze rove upward, she saw more scars on his chest—a small round disk on his right shoulder, a long, thin arc across his chest, another burn on his left side between his shoulder and collarbone.

He cried out again, startling her once more. "Warfield," she said more loudly, reaching for him. The moment she touched his arm, she realized she'd miscalculated.

He vaulted up and grasped her, turning her so that he pinned her to the bed. Then his hands wrapped around her throat, his eyes open but sightless as he stared down at her.

"No!" she managed to shout.

His hands fell away. "Oh God." He collapsed beside her and drew her against himself. "I'm so sorry, my love. Forgive me. I would never hurt you. I thought you were someone else." He brushed the hair that had come loose from her braid away from her face. "It doesn't matter," he whispered. "You're here." He stroked her back as his lips found hers.

Ada went stiff with shock, but only for a moment. Her body decided she didn't mind his touch or his kiss, and she found herself clasping his shoulders.

His tongue drove deep into her mouth, stirring a sultry desire she'd hoped was buried. Alas, it roared to life, stoked by his caresses.

She clung to him, gripping the back of his neck as he moved over her, pressing her into the mattress. He was hot and hard, and his weight upon her was delicious. Lust pulsed in her sex, making her mindless and desperate.

He skimmed his hand to her breast, stroking her through

her clothing and bringing her nipple to a tight peak. She arched up, kissing him with hungry abandon.

He murmured something she didn't understand, a foreign language perhaps, as he licked along her jawline. This was wrong. She didn't think he knew who she was. Perhaps he didn't even know where or when he was.

But then he rolled to his side and went silent and still. Ada stared at the bed hangings above her, unable to move. Her heart raced and her skin tingled. She felt him next to her, his arm against hers.

He twitched, then made a sound that was part gasp and part grunt. Then he was gone, pushing away from her. "What…?"

She turned her head to see him staring at her in horror. "I thought you were having a nightmare."

"I was, I think." He sounded breathless. Glancing down at himself, he swore. Her gaze followed his, but she knew what she'd see—his erection, because she'd felt it between her legs, pressing against her in the most glorious way.

Ada sat up as he leapt from the bed and grabbed a dressing gown. He wrapped it around himself and fastened it closed before turning to face her.

"Why are you here?"

"I shouldn't have come, but I heard you and I was concerned. I wanted to help. Is there anything I can do?"

"No," he croaked before running a hand through his already tousled blond hair.

She chose her next words carefully. Curiosity was going to kill her, but she refused to submit. She really did just want to help. "Would you like me to sit with you for a bit? Just sit here. Together."

He didn't answer for a long moment, his head slightly cocked as he stared at her. "I suppose." Slowly, he returned to the bed and sat beside her, but not close enough to touch.

"I used to have nightmares," she said, closing her eyes briefly and taking a long, deep breath to calm her racing heart.

"About your parents who died?"

"No, it was about my sister, Clara. She was younger than me by eight years."

"She's the sister who died?"

Ada clasped her hands together as sweat prickled her neck. "Yes. It was my fault," she whispered. "Our mother was already sick, and as the eldest daughter—I was fifteen—I had to take care of everyone. I took her with me to fetch my mother's medicine. There was a kitten, not that I saw it. Clara squealed that she saw one." Ada's limbs began to tremble, and she became very cold. She hadn't told this story in a long time. "I told her to keep up, that we needed to get home. But she ran after the kitten into the street. There was a coach." The next words clogged her throat, and she couldn't speak.

His warmth was against her, his thigh pressed to hers as he put his hand over hers. "The children at the farm," he said softly. "You were upset when they ran toward the cart. I thought there was something the matter. I should have said something."

Ada swallowed, then coughed slightly to clear her throat. "Why would you? You aren't meddlesome like I am." She let out a hollow laugh.

"You aren't always meddlesome. You're helpful. Anyway, I should at least have acknowledged another person's distress. You do it with me." He hesitated, his thumb stroking her hand. "Why?"

She shrugged. "I can't seem to help myself. I suppose it's my curiosity, but I just...I care."

"Why would you care about me?"

"I care about everyone." Especially those in pain, which he most definitely was.

"I'm so sorry about your sister," he said. "You blame yourself for that?"

"I do. So did my mother. She died a few months later. I don't think she ever forgave me. She didn't tell me so, anyway."

His hand tightened around hers. "You shouldn't have to carry that."

"I've learned not to—most of the time." She shook her shoulders out. "It wasn't easy. You asked me why I'm happy. Because I choose to be. It's better than the alternative. My brother drove me out after our mother died, insisting my sister Agatha, who was just a year younger than I, could do everything I was doing, only better—meaning she wouldn't get our other younger sister killed."

"That's awful," he whispered. "Your sisters didn't defend you?"

"No." How that had hurt too. "They went along with our brother. My youngest sister was devastated. She blamed me more than the others did, and that was quite a great deal."

"I'm so sorry."

"I spent a long time alone, sad and blaming myself." She'd barely existed, begging for food and eventually selling the only thing she could to survive. But just once. "I let myself fall to the lowest level of despair and then I said, *no more.*"

"What did you do?" He sounded enthralled, as if his next breath depended on her answer.

She turned her head to look at him and could just make out the tension in his face. "I knew in that moment, after I'd done the unthinkable of selling my body to simply exist, that I wanted to live. I left Plymouth and went to Cornwall, where I started over. I worked my way to becoming a governess. After a few years, I decided I didn't want to do that anymore and I came to London. Every day, I choose to be happy, to *live*."

Had she said too much? She'd only ever shared that with one other person—her dear friend Evie, who'd brought her to London and introduced her to Lucien. "I'm not trying to persuade you to do anything. I'm truly just answering your question."

"You're incredibly brave." There was awe in his voice, and it made her uncomfortable.

"I don't know if that's true. I was afraid of what I'd become, of where I was going, where I would end up."

"Leaving that and choosing the light over the dark, that's bravery. Don't let anyone tell you otherwise."

She rotated her hand so she could clasp his and allowed herself to smile. "Thank you."

"Thank *you* for sharing your story."

"I don't usually do that." She let out an uneven laugh. "I know you think I talk too much, but that's not something I tell people." Yet she'd told him rather easily. What's more, she felt good about doing so. Indeed, she felt a lightness, as if he'd somehow taken a piece of her burden. "Guilt is a terrible thing. It will eat at you until there's nothing left."

He let go of her hand, and she immediately knew she'd gone a trifle too far. The wall was back up.

He stood. "What were you doing on this side of the house anyway?"

"I couldn't sleep," she said, also rising. She smoothed the wrinkles from her dressing gown. "I was walking along the gallery when I heard you call out." She wasn't going to describe what she'd actually heard. He didn't need to know what he'd sounded like—a horribly wounded animal.

"I hope I didn't frighten you." His gaze met hers briefly.

"No." Perhaps for a moment, but she wouldn't tell him that either. He didn't need even a speck more guilt.

She longed to touch him, to tell him she was there for him, that he could share his story with her if he wanted. But his defenses were back in place, and she didn't want to push him to anger. She knew how easily she annoyed him.

Unless by kissing her, he could become somehow immune to that? No, she wouldn't be that naïve. Still, she couldn't deny that she was drawn to him, that she had been almost since the moment she'd arrived.

"You should return to your chamber." He didn't look at her.

"Yes. Good night." She turned to go on suddenly quivering legs.

"Good night."

She made it out of his chamber, closing the door behind her, before her shoulders drooped and she clapped her hand over her mouth. This couldn't happen again. She wouldn't allow it.

All she needed was another Jonathan—another mistake—to remind her that the only way she found happiness was on her bloody own.

CHAPTER 7

*S*omehow, Max had been able to find sleep again after Miss Treadway had left. "Miss Treadway." That was an awfully formal way to think of someone he'd kissed so thoroughly and desperately.

Or so he thought. He'd kissed *someone*—it had been too real to be a dream. Except his dreams, or more accurately, his nightmares always felt disturbingly real.

But she'd been there, in his bed, so he had to believe he'd kissed her. His body had certainly been aroused as if he had.

He wasn't going to ask her for confirmation. Better to just pretend it hadn't happened or at least that he didn't remember it happening.

He had to admit that made him feel a little cowardly. Or something unsettling.

Finishing with his cravat, he looked at himself in the mirror. Unfortunately, he still didn't like what he saw and doubted he ever would. He turned to grab his coat and hesitated, his fingers brushing the sleeve. Then he gritted his teeth and pulled it on, along with the guilt and sadness that accompanied the daily act.

Putting on a coat. Riding a horse. Eating a meal. Simple things he should be able to do, but couldn't without suffering.

Ada's words from the night before lingered in his mind: *Guilt is a terrible thing. It will eat at you until there's nothing left.*

He wondered if he was getting close to that end.

Then he thought of everything else she'd revealed to him. She was a woman of amazing courage and strength. To think of her at fifteen, overwhelmed with guilt and grief, and driven away by the only family she had left made him want to take her in his arms and hold her until every last remnant of those terrible emotions washed away. But he feared they couldn't. He didn't expect *his* guilt or grief ever would.

Perhaps things could improve for him, however. *She'd* managed it. She'd dragged herself from the darkness and forged a path forward. Not just to a peaceable existence, but to actual happiness. He saw real joy in her. That she could experience that after all she'd been through made him wonder what the hell was wrong with him.

She was likely just stronger than him. If he were lucky, he could learn something from her.

Too bad he wasn't lucky.

Max went downstairs to the breakfast room, a place he hadn't been to in years. Not since before he'd returned from Spain.

The room was empty, unfortunately, but the food was covered on the sideboard. Perhaps Miss Treadway hadn't come down yet.

He filled his plate with more food than he could ever eat and sat down at the small round table where he'd had years of breakfasts with his parents and his brother, Alexander. He and Alec would compete over who could eat more kippers.

"Good morning!" Miss Treadway's cheerful greeting startled him, which she seemed to realize. "My apologies, I didn't mean to surprise you." She sailed to the sideboard and dished up her food before joining him at the table.

"Good morning," he said gruffly, not entirely certain how he ought to behave with her after last night.

They ate in silence for a moment, but he'd come to know her well enough that he recognized she wanted to say something. He decided to help her for once. "I hope you slept well."

"I did, thank you. I must apologize for last night. I shouldn't have come to your room, and I should not have shared so much. It's a bad habit, I'm afraid." Bright color swathed her cheeks, and she took a bite of eggs.

"What's a bad habit?" he asked, wondering if she meant invading his room or oversharing.

"Trusting people too easily." She lifted a shoulder. "I look for connection with people when there sometimes isn't any. Or shouldn't be," she muttered.

He wanted to ask what she meant, but didn't. She'd just said she was trying not to trust people too easily. Perhaps she meant him, particularly since she was apologizing.

She waved her fork. "I'm hopelessly doomed to try to make friends with everyone."

"That doesn't sound like a bad thing," he said, wondering if he could try that. Well, perhaps not that exactly, but something like it. She'd talked about living instead of existing. That appealed to him, even if he didn't quite know how to go about doing so.

He supposed he could start by taking notice of those around him, by caring for his retainers and his tenants. "You can hire people for the household—maids for the kitchen and Mrs. Bundle."

She stared at him, her fork frozen above her plate. "Can I?"

"No valet. I'll consider a butler, but he has to be just right. And I'll speak to Og about the grooms."

"Thank goodness. I'd rather not have to manage that aspect. Speaking to Og, I mean. Would you like me to see about hiring grooms after you do so?"

"Yes, please. I doubt Og would do it even if I asked."

"I'm so thrilled." Her enthusiasm nearly made him smile. She stood and went to pour herself a cup of tea, glancing at him over her shoulder. "Would you like a cup?"

"I prefer coffee in the morning."

Nodding, she found the coffee, poured him some, then returned to the table with both.

"To new beginnings," she said, lifting her tea toward him.

"Er, yes." He raised his coffee awkwardly, and she tapped her cup against his.

After swallowing, she said, "You won't regret this."

He didn't think he would. In fact, he felt a tad lighter already. After a few more bites and another drink of coffee, he set his napkin on the table.

"You're finished?" she asked.

"I thought I'd go and speak with Og now."

"Why do you never finish eating?" she blurted.

He tensed. The Max he'd been would have told her to mind her own business, and he would have stamped from the room. Instead, he took a steadying breath. "I lose my appetite."

She almost looked surprised that he'd answered. "Why?"

The urge to glower at her and simply walk away was overwhelming. While he didn't want to do that, he wasn't sure he wanted to give her an honest answer either. He wavered on whether to politely decline to answer or—and this made him queasy—respond with the truth.

"My meal was interrupted once, and I haven't been able to finish one since." He didn't give her the details, but they rose in his mind. The summer evening, the boy running to tell him that he'd seen soldiers coming from where Lucia had been cleaning clothes, the terror that erupted inside him as he ran to find out what had happened. The bloody ribbon...

"Does that frustrate you? Not being able to finish meals, I mean." She leaned toward him slightly in what appeared to be genuine concern.

"I haven't thought too deeply about it, but I suppose it does, particularly since Mrs. Debley is such a fine cook."

"Hmmm. I will ponder this."

Max realized that she saw him as something to fix. While she wasn't wrong, he didn't like being the subject of such scrutiny. Though, he suspected that was precisely what had been happening since she'd arrived. She was, rather openly and unapologetically, a very inquisitive and managing person.

"You needn't bother." He stood. "I'm not your assignment, Miss Treadway, as much as you'd like me to be." She *had* provoked him to make a few changes, but that would be the extent of it.

She pursed her lips before he turned to take his leave. Max didn't look back.

He made his way directly to the stables, finding Og with Topaz. "Good morning, Og."

Og looked up from brushing the horse. "'Good morning'? You look like his lordship, but you can't be him."

"Have I never said good morning to you?"

"Not in a long while." Og grunted. "I hope that chit isn't charming you."

"She's doing her damnedest." Max nearly smiled, and that would certainly set Og off. "I came to talk to you about hiring grooms."

"Bah, I don't need anyone. Don't bother."

"We can't keep relying on Archie. His mother needs him at her farm."

Og frowned, then spat into the corner of the stall. "He's a good helper."

"I'm going to hire at least one groom. You aren't as spry as you once were, Og. You ought to take things easier."

"Don't you put me out to pasture yet," Og said grumpily.

"I will never do that." Max felt a particular kinship to this man and to Mrs. Debley. They'd known him his entire life. He thought about Miss Treadway and how she had no one like that. At least, it seemed she didn't if her family had pushed her out, and she now lived so far from where she'd been born and raised.

"What's prompted this?" Og asked. "Is it the chit?"

"She has—correctly—pointed out that several people on the estate are overworked."

"I'm not." He sounded offended at the insinuation.

"Perhaps, but as I said, you can't keep using Archie, so we will hire someone." Max noted the usually tense set of Og's jaw and the general air of irritation he carried. Was that how Max looked? "Do you ever tire of being angry and gruff all the time?" he asked somewhat quietly, his attention moving to Topaz.

Og grunted again. "I don't think of myself that way. I don't think the animals would say I'm grumpy, would you, girl?" He stroked Topaz's neck, and his expression actually softened.

Perhaps animals would help Max. For the first time in ages, he thought of his beloved horse, Arrow, whom he'd sold upon returning from Spain. He wouldn't even have brought him back to England, but Max had been in no condition to manage anything, and someone had seen fit to return Arrow along with him.

Max felt a pang of remorse over the loss of his horse.

Poor Arrow. He hadn't done anything wrong. In fact, he'd been a noble and tireless friend and partner. Without him, Max would not have found vengeance.

And that was why he'd had to let him go. Just the thought of riding a horse, let alone Arrow, took Max back to that day and night. Could he really never ride a horse again? He realized in that moment that he was afraid to try.

Pivoting slightly, Max tentatively touched Topaz's forelock. "You are a good girl, aren't you?" She nudged his hand, and he stroked her in earnest. Something within him relaxed. Perhaps Og had found a secret with caring for the animals.

"You thinking of riding?" Og asked, as if he'd been privy to Max's thoughts.

"Perhaps." But not yet. Maybe never. But he *was* thinking about it, and that was a change.

He seemed to be taking small steps forward. He just prayed he didn't fall.

~

*A*da's hand moved quickly across the parchment as she recorded notes from her day. She'd spent the morning touring the estate with Archie, and the afternoon reviewing very old estate ledgers to see how it was run more than fifty years ago. Some things were different, and yet much was the same. Warfield's grandfather had been very involved in the management.

In fact, one of the tenants she'd met that day had gone on and on about how wonderful the man had been. That was what had prompted Ada to dig up these ledgers. That particular tenant, Mr. Hardy, was in his sixties, and he was not happy with the current state of things. He needed new equipment, his cottage was in desperate need of repair, and his requests for assistance had gone unanswered. His lease would be up next year, but at his age, he didn't want to leave. Ada had reassured him that she would ensure his needs were met—and not at some indeterminate time in the future. She'd address them posthaste.

Mr. Hardy had also been informative about a number of things. Shockingly, he'd shared that Warfield had been a rake. Mr. Hardy had indicated that nearly every woman on the estate had swooned over him and his older brother when they'd ridden about as young men. It was "bloody aggravating" because they were distracting.

Ada had stifled a laugh. She tried to imagine a handsome, grinning Warfield galloping across the estate with his probably equally handsome brother while every woman fell madly in love with them. She could see it quite easily. He'd already somehow wiggled his way into her sentiments—she cared about him more than she ever expected to. But it was more than that. She was drawn to him like a bee to honey. She wanted to know everything about him. And she wanted to touch him. Everywhere.

Work, Ada!

She could hear Prudence now, telling her she was far too romantic for her own good. It was true. Ada often wondered if the circumstances of her split from her family had driven her to constantly crave connection and love.

She shook her head. *Never mind that now.*

Her thoughts went back to Mr. Hardy. He'd told Ada that Max's horse—he was called Arrow—had been sold in London at Tattersall's. As soon as she finished these notes, she planned to pen a letter to Lucien asking if he could possibly find the animal.

She was so involved in her task and in thinking that she didn't hear the viscount until he cleared his throat. Pausing her pen, she looked up to see him standing not far from her table. He was dressed as usual in his outdated coat and waistcoat and his simply knotted cravat. If she hadn't known he didn't have a valet, she might have guessed it. Perhaps she could persuade him to at least buy new garments. There had to be a tailor in the village. She should have asked when she'd gone to hire Teresa to help Mrs. Kempton. Ah well, she'd be making another visit the following day to hopefully hire maids and grooms. Mrs. Bundle was ecstatic at the prospect of having help, even if she didn't quite believe it. She'd also advised Ada not to say anything to Mrs. Debley until she had a kitchen maid already employed. Then the cook couldn't refuse. Or so Mrs. Bundle thought.

Ada found the cook's loyalty to the viscount endearing, if a little frustrating. She realized she'd been woolgathering once again while Warfield was staring at her. "Good evening, my lord. What a surprise to see you here at this hour. Can I be of help?"

His gaze flicked to the open ledger before her. "You're still working?"

"Just finishing up. Give me one moment." She wrote another two lines, then set her pen down. She'd draft the letter to Lucien later. "All done," she said, turning in her chair to face him. She saw he had a book in his hand. "Is that another ledger for me?"

"Er, no. It's a book. For me to read. I thought I might join you in your relaxation time this evening. That is what you called it?"

"Oh!" Ada shot out of her chair in shock and awe. He'd come to read with her? Had something happened last night to change his opinion of her? The kissing perhaps? Her gaze strayed to his very tantalizing mouth, which a grave mistake because she could practically feel his lips on hers and the resulting pleasure that stirred in other, more private areas. "Yes, time to relax." She wasn't sure she could do that around him after last night. Did he even remember the kiss?

She was fairly certain he'd been asleep. It was possible, if not likely, that even if he did recall it, he thought it was a dream.

"Will you mind if I read my romance novel?" she asked, wondering if she ought not tease him. Probably not, but it was too late now.

One of his golden brows arched, and she saw the rake he'd once been. "No. I will be reading about sheep."

"Splendid." She was encouraged by his choice of subject matter. Perhaps he meant to truly take a more active role at Stonehill. "Shall we sit together?" She was already moving toward the settee in the center of the library before realizing that was a rather forward invitation for a secretary who wasn't really a secretary to make. But was it, when that secretary who wasn't really a secretary had been in your bed the night before?

She really needed to stop thinking about that.

Her eye moved to a chair, and she wondered if she ought to sit there instead. Except she'd suggested they sit together and if she sat in a chair now, she'd look silly. Or stupid.

Ada dropped onto the settee and held her breath. He sat down at the other end. They weren't really sitting *together*, but they were on the same piece of furniture. She realized he could be sitting across the room, and it wouldn't matter. She was still intensely aware of his presence and of her growing desire for him.

No, she would not take that path again. She would not repeat the mistakes she'd made with Jonathan.

"I had a very productive day," she said, pretending he wanted to know. "Archie is an excellent guide."

"I'm glad to hear it."

"Tomorrow, I'll be visiting the village again to hire two kitchen maids, a housemaid in addition to Teresa, who is currently helping Mrs. Kempton and will hopefully come here after, another footman, and a pair of grooms. Mrs.

Bundle was thrilled that you decided to expand the household."

"She mentioned that when she brought my dinner. I can see it's made her happy. I should have done it sooner."

Ada didn't want him to wallow. He was on the cusp of making true progress; she was certain of it. "It only matters that you're doing it now."

He grunted in response.

She wanted to ask why he hadn't joined her for dinner again. She'd hoped he might, especially since he'd had breakfast with her. But she didn't want to put pressure on him.

He opened his book, and she took the signal that he was ready to read, not talk. Ada found her place and began to read. Unfortunately, she wasn't very successful at retaining anything on the page.

Casting him a sideways glance and seeing that he *was* actually reading, she tried again. He was so distracting! Not just because she was now attracted to him. He was interesting. She wanted to ask him a million things. And unlike when she'd first arrived, he now occasionally answered her.

Was he remotely intrigued by her? Let alone attracted to her? She had no way of knowing, especially since their kiss was probably unknown to him. Should she tell him and see how he responded? No, she wasn't going to poke that bear.

Turning so that she was angled slightly toward him, she cast surreptitious glances in his direction. His attention didn't waver from the book, and he turned pages at regular intervals. Ada cast her head back and looked up at the domed ceiling. Though it was dark, she could make out the flowers in the stained glass.

She simply couldn't contain herself. "I've been meaning to ask about the flowers in the ceiling. And the rooms with the flower names. Someone must have loved flowers."

His gaze lifted from the book and fixed on her. She felt a

rush of anticipation, which was ludicrous. He was only looking at her!

"My great-grandmother loved flowers," he said, thankfully appeasing her interminable curiosity. "And books. She had this library built, and she named all the bedchambers after flowers."

"What's yours called?"

"Except mine. My great-grandfather refused to let her name the viscount's suite."

"What about your room when you were younger? Did it have a flower name?"

"In her time, it was the Lily Room, but my father wouldn't let anyone call it that. Or my brother's chamber, which was the Peony Room. Indeed, the only rooms that really have flower names anymore are yours—the Primrose Room—and the one that used to belong to my great-grandmother. That adjoins my chamber and is called the Rose Room. Those were her favorite flowers."

"Is there a rose garden? I'm afraid I couldn't tell." Because the gardens were in such bad shape.

"There is." He grimaced. "Not that you can see it. I suppose I should hire a gardener to fix that."

"I'd be happy to make inquiries while I'm in the village tomorrow." She considered inviting him to accompany her, but she was almost certain he'd decline. Besides, she'd already courted rejection by inviting him to sit with her.

"You should do that." He returned his attention to his book, and she was sorry the conversation was over so quickly. But then he surprised her yet again by looking toward her once more, an expression of bemusement etched into his handsome features. "What have you done to me?"

"Nothing on purpose." That wasn't precisely true. She was trying to bring forth his better nature—for those around him as much as for him.

"I can almost believe that," he said softly and with a shocking dash of humor.

"I probably shouldn't say this, but in meeting the tenants around the estate, I've heard a number of things about you that stretch credulity."

His brow quirked again, and damn if her breath didn't catch. "Such as what?"

"That you were a rake. I struggle to see it."

He exhaled, sounding weary. "That was a *very* long time ago."

"You don't deny it?"

"I barely remember it, to be honest."

She doubted that, but he didn't seem keen to discuss it, which was vastly disappointing. When his gaze dipped to his book once more, she didn't interrupt again. She tried to focus on hers and even managed to read a few pages before he was the one to speak.

"How is your work coming overall? Will you be done in your allotted fortnight?"

"I should be, yes. I've five more days." She still had several tenants to visit and had allotted two days at the end to write her report and finalize the ledgers to ensure they were current. Goodness, that wasn't much time. Perhaps she should abandon her novel and return to work. Except sitting with him, even several feet away, was exceedingly pleasant.

"Good."

His simple, emotionless response gave her the truth—he wanted to make sure she was still leaving as scheduled. He wanted her to know that even though she'd made progress, he didn't want her to stay. Not that staying was an option. She needed to return to the Phoenix Club, to her real job. "I won't stay past my welcome," she assured him. "Furthermore, I'd be happy to share my progress. You're welcome to review any of the ledgers as well as my notes." She'd been careful not to document anything about him specifically. That information was stored entirely in her mind.

"I'll consider that, thank you. Now, I think I must retire. Sheep, it happens, are rather sleep inducing." He stood and inclined his head toward her, then departed the library.

Ada drooped back against the corner of the settee. She hadn't realized how tense her body had been in his presence. She hadn't felt like that on other occasions.

It's because you want him.

Damn and blast, she didn't want to want him. She was a grown woman who'd learned from her mistakes.

At least she bloody well hoped so.

CHAPTER 8

$\mathcal{A}$fter taking breakfast in his study the following morning, Max made his way into the library knowing Miss Treadway was out with Archie. He also hadn't dined with her last night.

Because he was avoiding her.

Yet he was unable to ignore her invitation to review her work. So here he was, about to sit at her table and go through her ledgers.

Her table. *Her* ledgers. How quickly he'd adapted to her presence.

He spent the next hour reading through her notes, part of them, anyway—she'd written an astonishing amount. It was an excellent overview of Stonehill and the tenants. He would need to read all of it. And try not to feel defeated.

Hell, she really could be his steward. She was more than qualified. She was at least more qualified than him, which probably wasn't saying much.

If she was his steward, she'd live here. He wasn't sure he could tolerate that. Not because he found her annoying—

which he still did—but because she'd tempt him in ways he didn't want to be tempted.

He hadn't been with a woman in years. Not since Spain. He swallowed past the tightness in his throat. It was natural that after kissing her the other night that he wanted her. Especially since he'd kissed her thinking she was Lucia.

Until he realized he wasn't dreaming, that he was awake. That it was Miss Treadway in his bed. Somehow, he'd mustered the fortitude to pull away. And it had haunted him since.

Last night had been a torture he'd forgotten—longing for a woman and not being able to have her. She'd sat on the other end of the settee, not terribly far, but she might as well have been in India.

The entire time he'd been consumed with thoughts of her —her lips on his, her body writhing beneath him, the touch of her hand on his neck as her tongue tangled with his. Hell, he was growing hard thinking of her now.

Had she given the kiss a second thought? Or did she think he'd been in the throes of his nightmare, unaware of what he'd done? She hadn't mentioned it, but then neither had he. He was too ashamed for taking advantage.

And so he'd pretended to read the book about sheep instead of engaging her. She'd tried and he'd remained aloof. Hell yes, he'd been a rake in his youth, but to admit that would be to open a part of himself that was long buried. That carefree lad was gone, killed in Spain, never to return.

Oh, but what a time he'd had those years in London, swanning about with Lucien and Dougal MacNair. Occasionally, his brother Alec would come along. Max smiled, thinking of the good times they'd shared. Until his father had put a stop to their fun.

Max indulged a moment of emotion—he missed his brother. Learning Alec had died when he returned from

Spain had been a crushing blow. He simply hadn't known how he was going to manage. So he didn't.

You aren't really alone.

No, he supposed he wasn't. Apparently, he had a half sister. He now recalled the young woman who'd come here looking for a job several months earlier—just before Yuletide. She hadn't revealed her identity, not her real one. If she had, would he have employed her?

He didn't like the answer.

Thankfully, Lucien had been here that day, and Miss Treadway said he'd helped her—Prudence. Lucien had done that again when he'd come here recently pleading for her dowry. Twice, Lucien had rescued Max's half sister when he wouldn't. Because he'd been too mired in his despair.

He really was the horrible beast everyone thought. But he knew that already. Hadn't he aspired to be that awful? It was the best way to ensure everyone left him alone.

Now it seemed he might be ready to…not be alone.

Miss Treadway was right about his half sister, as she was turning out to be about so many things. Their father's adultery wasn't her fault. Max was angry with his father, whom he'd admired and whose legacy he couldn't possibly live up to. Especially after what Max had done in Spain.

Max took a breath to soothe his suddenly thundering heart.

You were thinking about your half sister.

Yes, her. Prudence. Perhaps he should give her the dowry.

He sat back in the chair. Damn. Just look at all the change Miss Treadway had wrought in not even ten days in his household. She was a veritable storm, leaving devastation in her path.

Was she really, though?

In truth, he felt better today than he had in years. He probably owed that to her. He should thank her, but he doubted he would. He wanted to kiss her again so that she would know it was him and not some fevered dream. But he wouldn't do that either.

She would leave in a few days, and he'd let her go. He just hoped the light wouldn't go with her.

∾

"I'm still not convinced this is a good idea."

Ada looked over at Mrs. Tallent as they walked from the stables to the house. "I understand you're nervous, but I truly believe this is an easy and excellent answer to what the estate needs."

Mrs. Tallent narrowed one eye at Ada. "His lordship is supportive of this?"

"Er, yes." Ada hadn't found the time to speak with him about Mrs. Tallent specifically, but she was running out of time. "I believe he's ready to hire a steward."

"But is he ready to hire *me*?"

"He needs someone as soon as possible, and you are more than capable."

"I am also a woman," she said wryly. "I don't know a single man who would employ a woman as a steward."

Ada could understand that view. She'd been shocked when Evie had wanted to bring her back to London so she could work as a bookkeeper at a private club. But Evie had been confident that the owner—Lucien—would hire her. What Ada hadn't realized was that Lucien saw Evie as a partner in the business. He was the owner, and she was the manager, overseeing the daily operations with Ada's help. It was a unique and surprising relationship. Would Warfield be open to a similar arrangement with a woman?

She hoped so, or this meeting could go very badly.

They entered the house, and Ada took Mrs. Tallent to

Warfield's study, only to find it empty. Puzzled, she went into the library, but he wasn't there either. Perhaps she should have organized this in advance. But why would she bother when he was always here?

Looking out the windows to the messy garden, she gaped. There he was, elbow-deep in overgrown greenery.

"This way," Ada said, taking Mrs. Tallent into the drawing room next to the library, which had doors leading outside. "He's in the garden, apparently."

As they stepped into the sunlight, Mrs. Tallent gasped. "My goodness. The garden is…in need of attention."

"There haven't been gardeners for at least a year."

"I'd say longer than that," Mrs. Tallent observed with a cluck of her tongue.

They walked past some overgrown beds to where Warfield was working—in the rose garden. Ada nearly smiled. Had their conversation about flowers the other night prompted him to action? Whatever the reason, Ada was shocked. And thrilled. This was surely a good sign for positive change.

As they reached the rose garden, he stood straight and adjusted his hat. Brown gloves encased his hands, and he was working without a cravat. Ada's gaze was drawn to the exposed flesh at his throat. She was catapulted back to a few nights ago when he'd sprawled on top of her kissing her senselessly as she clutched at him. Heat spiked through her, and it wasn't from the early afternoon sun.

"My lord, I've brought Mrs. Tallent. I'm sure you've met at some point. Her son, Archie, works in the stables, and her daughter, Molly, helps in the kitchen."

He looked at Ada in mild amusement. "I know who Mrs. Tallent is as well as her children."

Of course he did. "Well, yes. I'll get right to the point,

then. I'd mentioned to you that I may have found the perfect candidate for the steward position."

Warfield darted a glance toward Mrs. Tallent, but spoke to Ada. "Her?"

Oh dear, that wasn't the reaction she'd been hoping for. She slid a look toward Mrs. Tallent. As expected, she appeared perturbed. Her lips pursed, and her eyes narrowed. Perhaps this had been a bad idea—not Mrs. Tallent being the steward, but the way in which Ada had gone about it.

Stiffening her spine, she refused to let this go badly.

"Mrs. Tallent keeps excellent records of her farm, and I must say hers is the most efficient *and* most profitable on the estate. She would be an excellent steward. Furthermore, you could then lease her farm, and this would allow her children to attend school, which she would like them to do."

Warfield seemed to assess Mrs. Tallent. "I see."

Ada held her breath. He wasn't saying no. Nor did he seem annoyed by this beyond his initial poor reaction.

"You'd rather not be a farmer?" he asked Mrs. Tallent.

"My husband was the farmer. I'm just doing what I must to provide for my children. I'm not sure Archie wants to be a farmer either. He's very good with the horses—Og will tell you. But he's also very good at mathematics. Honestly, he'd probably make an excellent steward someday."

Ada heard the motherly pride in Mrs. Tallent's voice and felt a surge of envy. She would likely never be a mother— she'd have to marry to do that, and she just didn't see that happening.

You don't have to marry to be a mother, and you know that.

It was as if an icy hand reached across Ada's shoulder. She twitched, hoping to banish the chill.

"I'll consider it," Warfield said, then turned back to pulling giant weeds from the garden.

"I'm still considering it too, my lord," Mrs. Tallent said,

making Ada tense. "I'd want to know that this would be a long-term engagement. My children need stability, and if I give up the farm, I need to know I can care for them."

"Of course you do," Ada said, looking toward the viscount. "His lordship knows that and would ensure you were content in your new position for years to come." She gave him an expectant stare.

He grunted as he tossed a tall weed from the bed. "Nothing in life is guaranteed. Work hard and do your best. That's all we can do."

"We can also be kind and pleasant in our work," Mrs. Tallent said plainly. The expectation was clear—at least to Ada. She wanted to be sure the viscount wouldn't be his usual beastly self.

"The viscount is committed to change at Stonehill." Ada looked from one to the other, noting that each seemed guarded. "He's hiring retainers and providing aid to tenants. Indeed, one of the first things you'll do as steward is arrange repairs on several farms. His lordship wholly supports that endeavor and will provide you whatever you need —cheerfully."

Perhaps she exaggerated. Given the looks both Warfield and Mrs. Tallent directed at her, they knew it too.

"Aspiration is a lovely thing," Mrs. Tallent said evenly.

"I'll consider this." Warfield's tone was gruff, but his expression beneath the brim of his hat conveyed honesty. He *would* consider it. Ada felt a surge of relief with a dollop of glee. He was making such progress!

Mrs. Tallent curtsied. "It was a pleasure to see you today, my lord."

She turned, and Ada walked with her back toward the house. "You can go around that way to reach the stables." Ada gestured to the right, knowing Archie was waiting for her.

"I will, thank you." Mrs. Tallent paused. "His lordship did seem different. You must be a magician."

Ada laughed. "Hardly. I'm just persistently optimistic. It's gotten me this far."

"You are a delightful person, Miss Treadway. I hope I'll see you again."

"I hope so too." Ada thought they might cross paths once more before she left. But, goodness, that was in only a few days. Today was Friday, and the coach from London would arrive Monday. She'd be leaving first thing Tuesday.

Ada watched Mrs. Tallent for a moment before turning back to the garden. She had to know what had prompted Warfield's gardening.

He was still ruthlessly pulling weeds from the dirt in the rose garden. He did not look up as she approached.

"That went very well," she said.

"You should have told me." He still didn't look at her, and his jaw clenched as he worked.

"I did tell you I had someone in mind."

He paused, throwing another weed from the bed and spearing her with a dark glare. "But not that it was Mrs. Tallent or that you planned to ambush me with her today."

Ada flinched. She'd hoped he'd moved past such fits of pique. But in this, he had a right to be at least...annoyed. "I should have done, my apologies. I'm just running out of time to get everything done."

"Then perhaps you should arrange to stay longer," he grumbled, plucking at another weed.

What a change this was. Would she stay? It was a moot question because she couldn't. "I need to get back to London. This was a temporary assignment. I have responsibilities I can't ignore."

His shoulders twitched, and when he threw the next

weed, it landed at her feet, sending dirt onto the bottom of her skirt. "I didn't mean to do that," he said.

She understood his reaction, quietly saying, "I didn't mean to imply that you were ignoring your responsibilities."

"But I was, wasn't I?" He stood still, breathing heavily, and put his hands on his hips. "I'm afraid these roses have gone wild."

"They may need a trim," Ada suggested. "I'm no expert. I'll hire a gardener as soon as possible. Or Mrs. Tallent will. If you decide to hire her."

He only grunted in response.

Ada moved to the corner of the bed and grasped a stem to pull a rose toward her so she could smell it. Her finger pressed into a thorn. She gasped, pulling her hand back.

"What is it?" Warfield moved quickly to her as blood beaded on her finger.

With her thumb, Ada smeared the blood to better see the wound. Just a small puncture. "I found a thorn."

"That's a rather accurate metaphor for your visit, isn't it?" Warfield said, sounding angry. "You grabbed that rose without care, and look what you've done."

Ada stared at him, uncertain why he was so furious.

"You've done nothing but upend my life since you arrived. I didn't ask for this. I didn't want it."

The pain in Ada's finger dulled as she suffered his ire. It was as if all the progress they'd made together had evaporated when she'd pierced her finger. She didn't understand. "I'll be fine," she said softly. "It was an accident—I wasn't careless." She felt defensive. When Clara had died, her mother had called her careless, and her siblings had echoed that sentiment for months until Ada had finally left.

"I didn't mean—" His jaw clenched, and he looked away, his hands fisting briefly at his sides. He shook his shoulders out. "My apologies." He stalked to the house without another word, leaving her to stare after him, wondering why things had taken a turn.

He's wounded both inside and out.

Prudence's words came back to Ada. She'd seen it herself. Whatever had happened to him in Spain had left an indelible mark. Ada had no idea if he could truly recover. Perhaps he would just have good days and bad. For the rest of his life. Her heart ached for him, but what more could she do? She'd be leaving soon.

Then she'd likely never see him again. It was time to distance herself. Perhaps he realized that too. His behavior a few minutes earlier would certainly make it easier for her to leave. And easier for her to avoid another situation like Jonathan.

She *had* learned from her mistakes!

Buoyed by this, Ada returned to the house in search of Mrs. Bundle. She found the housekeeper cleaning the front sitting room near the entry hall.

"I'm sorry to disturb you, Mrs. Bundle, but I wanted to share the good news that your two new housemaids will be starting on Monday. Teresa Chapman, who is currently helping Mrs. Kempton, and Mary Wendell."

Mrs. Bundle wiped her hands on her apron as she stood from cleaning beneath a chair. "I'm familiar with them both, and they'll be excellent additions. I can't tell you how thrilled I am to have help."

"They are also thrilled," Ada noted with a smile. "I think they find moving here to be a grand adventure."

"And you'll still be here to welcome them," Mrs. Bundle said. "I'm so glad you'll be able to see the fruits of your labor —at least a glimpse of it, anyway. I'm astounded by all you've accomplished."

Ada merely nodded in response.

"I must confess I'm concerned about when you leave. What if his lordship reverts to his old self?"

That was perhaps already happening. Ada hoped not. A thought struck her—was his mood today because she was leaving soon? Was he going to miss her? A happy jolt shot through her, but she tamped it down. What a ludicrous idea. She *annoyed* him.

But only for three more days. Then she'd be on her way, and he could be free of her forever.

CHAPTER 9

*H*is face was on fire. And his shoulder. The pain didn't stop or even slow him. He sliced and thrust, wreaking as much havoc as possible amidst the screams. Until they stopped.

Sweat dripped from his brow, down his back. He looked around, but there was no one left to kill. The heat and savagery faded. Now, he stood on a hilltop, the breeze an irritation instead of a balm to his burned flesh. Again, the pain was inconsequential—outside. Inside, searing agony threatened to tear him in two as he looked down at the fresh mound of dirt, the slender wooden cross marking her final resting place.

This wasn't a memory. Because he'd never seen where she was buried. He'd never seen her again after finding her bruised and broken body.

"Shhh, you're safe."

The soft words broke through his torment. He brushed his hand across his brow and met an arm.

Max's eyes flew open.

Miss Treadway was above him, perched on the bed, one

hand on his head and another on his bare, heaving chest. He blinked, and she came more into focus, her blue-gray eyes gazing at him with such concern. And perhaps something else.

Her lips were parted, inviting his kiss. He almost pulled her down.

Instead, he pushed himself into a sitting position, glad he wasn't nude, not that the small clothes were enough to cover his hardening cock. "Do you station yourself outside my door every night?"

"Er, not exactly." She'd withdrawn her hands from him when he sat up, and he regretted the loss of her touch. "I've been taking nightly strolls."

"And you just happened to hear me having a nightmare."

"Tonight, I did. Do you have them every night?"

"No."

She gave him a faint smile, but it didn't carry her usual brightness. "Well, I'm sorry you have them at all. If you ever want to talk about them…"

"It's about the war." He said the words before he could censor himself. "Something bad happened. I can't tell you what." His eyes met hers, and he knew in that moment that he could happily and easily drown in their depths—in the care and understanding he saw in them.

She nodded, her gaze dipping to the bed. "Did you lose someone?" she whispered.

"I did." Lucia's face rose in his mind. He worked so hard to keep her away, to maintain his defenses. Seeing her, remembering her, invited the pain and the grief. But for some reason, he felt safe at the moment, protected somehow. Lucia's dark curls blew about her sun-drenched cheeks as she laughed up at him. Max caressed her cheek before he kissed her. Jolting back to the present, he said, "I was going to marry her, but then…" His voice was low and raspy. He was surprised the words made it out. He hadn't ever told anyone that.

Miss Treadway took his hand between hers. She didn't say anything, just stroked his flesh and breathed with him.

"You aren't going to pester me about this?" he asked in surprise.

When her head jerked up and hurt flashed in her eyes, he felt immediately guilty.

She exhaled. "It's a valid question. I pester you about everything else. But no, I just want you to know that I'm here for you."

"For the next few days."

"Yes."

Then she'd be gone. The urge to take her in his arms, to kiss her and caress her, to show her how much he appreciated her kindness was almost overwhelming. He nearly asked her about the kiss they'd shared the other night, but he couldn't find the courage.

"Are you really considering hiring Mrs. Tallent as the steward?" she asked. "Is it all right that she's a woman?"

He was grateful for the complete change of topic. Had she realized how close he was coming to making an inappropriate advance?

"My initial surprise was because I already had someone in mind—also a woman."

Her hand stilled, and she blinked at him. "You did?"

"Someone very capable who has already demonstrated a better grasp of Stonehill in a very short time than I have done in years."

She clasped his hand tightly. "You mean me."

He nodded in response.

"But I annoy you."

He shrugged. "Less than you did at first."

"I'm flattered." She seemed to struggle to say more. "I would consider it if I didn't already have a job that I love."

"I understand." Even if it was disappointing. She might annoy him, but he liked her. What's more, he craved her—or more accurately, the way she made him feel: less afraid, strong, capable. But he was going to have to manage without her. "I'll hire Mrs. Tallent."

Miss Treadway's face lit. "Truly? I'm so happy! She will be too. I know this will be excellent for everyone."

"I'm sure you know this, but there's a house for the steward on the estate. It's likely bigger than where she is now."

"I did know there was a house, but I wasn't sure if you wanted her to live there." She looked a bit sheepish.

"You were hesitant about something?" he asked in disbelief.

"I rather botched this by not telling you about Mrs. Tallent in advance. I wasn't going to press matters by asking if she could move to the steward's house."

"She can't very well stay in the farm if I'm to lease it." He frowned. "I'll need to find someone to farm that this summer if she becomes the steward."

"Yes, unless she does both for a while."

Max shook his head. "I'm not going to expect her to do that. Now that I'm hiring grooms, perhaps Archie can take on more of the farming responsibilities. And yes, I know she wants him to attend school. I've already decided to write him a recommendation."

"You have?" She took her hand from his and threw her arms around his neck, hugging him fiercely. "Thank you."

He felt her breath against his neck. She wore a dressing gown and probably a thin night rail beneath it. He could feel the heat of her as well as the lush contours of her body. Her breasts pressed into his chest, and his cock lengthened once more.

She smelled of apples and spice. He closed his eyes and inhaled deeply, wondering if she'd bathed earlier. He wanted to press his nose to her flesh, to lick her neck, to immerse himself in her completely.

What was happening to him?

He'd never imagined he'd feel this way about anyone ever again. That he would dream of Lucia in one moment and want Miss Treadway—Ada, her name was Ada—so ferociously in the next was galling. He was a beast.

Gently, he disentangled himself from her, pushing back against the headboard. She withdrew, her cheeks pink. "My apologies," she murmured. "I got carried away."

"It's fine," he said stiffly—as stiff as his cock. God, she'd probably felt that and didn't know what to think.

She plucked at a thread on her dressing gown. "I should go."

"You could stay." He hadn't meant to say it, just think it. "For a few minutes."

"Would it help you go back to sleep?" She was asking another question, he thought. She wanted to know if sleep was his objective. It had to be. She would be leaving him in a few days, and he wasn't sure he was in any shape to engage in sexual relations with anyone.

"It might. It's also inappropriate. You should forget I asked."

She shook her head, then waved him over so she could lie down beside him. He noted she did not get under the covers with him, which was for the best.

He scooted down into the bed and brought the other pillow closer so that he could transfer to that one and not crowd her. How desperately he wanted to press against her, to fall asleep in the comfort of her warmth and scent.

She rolled to her side and faced him. "Good night," she whispered.

He turned to face her as well, and the inches separating them might as well have been a canyon. "Good night."

He closed his eyes and tried to sleep.

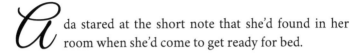

*a*da stared at the short note that she'd found in her room when she'd come to get ready for bed.

If you want to stay again—to sleep—you are more than welcome.

She'd slept in his lordship's bed the night before until just before dawn when she'd awakened and stolen from his room before anyone realized she was there. And who would do that? No one, but that would change when the household grew in a few days.

By then, she'd be gone.

So what harm would there be in sleeping with him again? They were just sleeping, after all. He'd made it clear that he didn't want her. With the exception of his unmistakable erection.

Those could happen with a stiff breeze!

Except there wasn't a breeze. He was alone with you in his bed. Of course he wants you.

No, he does not! We were in a bed, and his body just reacted. It doesn't mean he wants me.

You're being purposely obtuse.

Isn't that for the best?

Ada refolded the note and set it on the desk. "Oh, good heavens, who argues with themselves?"

Before she could think better of it, she strode from her room and went directly to his. Unlike the past few nights, she hadn't meandered, using the excuse of "walking to get tired" to explain her ramblings. The truth was that she'd wanted to be there for him if he had another nightmare.

That he'd told her even a little of what tortured him made her feel incredibly special. He had loved someone. Enough to marry her. She understood that the "something" that had happened was that she'd died. She could also guess that her death was traumatic, but whether that was due to only his grief or some additional tragedy, such as his wounds, she had no idea. Whatever had occurred had affected him deeply, and he was only now beginning to emerge from the darkness.

She *hoped* he was emerging.

When she reached his door, she wasn't sure what to do. She hadn't knocked on her previous visits because he'd been in the throes of distress. Plus, he'd been asleep.

Tonight, she should knock. It was far earlier than the other nights, and he would still be awake. She brought her hand up and rapped firmly. Nervously, she pulled her long braid over her shoulder so that it fell over her left breast. Then she fidgeted with the end.

A moment later, the door opened. He stood, gripping the wood, his gaze moving over her in what looked like appreciation.

Heat rose in her cheeks and flooded other parts of her body. Perhaps this had been a foolish idea. She was rubbish at resisting temptation. She dropped her hands to her sides.

"You came," he said, opening the door wider.

"Against my better judgment, probably. It's a good thing you have such a thin household. If there was a chance I'd be seen, I would not have come." She moved into the chamber.

He closed the door once she was inside. "If there was a chance you'd be seen, I would not have asked."

His voice rustled over the back of her exposed neck like silk. "I was a bit nervous to ask you to come again tonight, but my motives were rather selfish." He moved around to stand in front of her. "Last night was the best sleep I can remember."

Joy radiated through her, and she had to stop herself from hugging him again as she'd done the night before. "I'm so glad."

They stared at each other, and the moment bloomed into an awkward silence. At last, he pivoted and lifted his hand toward the bed. "Shall we?"

Feeling nervous again, Ada nodded. Last night, she'd kept her dressing gown on and slept on top of the bedclothes. Was she to join him beneath them tonight?

"Er, how do you want to do this?" she asked, too timid to meet his gaze.

"However you like. If you want to sleep in the bed with me, as opposed to on top of it, I have no problem with that. I want you to be comfortable. You are doing me a great favor."

She lifted her eyes to his. "I want to do it." Shaking away her reservations, she unfastened her dressing gown and slid it from her shoulders. Then she draped it over a chair and made her way to the bed. She pulled back the coverlet and slid between the bedclothes. Pulling the covers up to her chin, she laid her head on the pillow. "Is this all right?"

"It's fine."

Had his voice gone husky?

Ada made herself yawn, hoping it would help her feel tired. At the moment, she was rife with anticipation and that simply wouldn't do. "I've so much to do before I leave Tuesday." Perhaps conversation would distract them.

He threw off his dressing gown, and she noticed he was wearing a nightshirt, unlike the other nights she'd come to his room. Disappointment curled through her, for which she quickly and silently admonished herself.

"I was hoping to take you to see the remains of the castle

stones tomorrow. If you have time," he said, situating himself in the bed. With each shift of his body, she was more aware of their proximity. In a bed.

It wasn't as if they hadn't done this before! Just last night, in fact. Tonight was somehow different. They intended to sleep together.

Sleep!

What he said finally permeated her overtaxed brain. She turned her head on the pillow to look at him. "I'd *love* to see the castle stones." She'd stay up all night tomorrow to finish her work if necessary.

He lay on his side facing her, his hand propping his head. "Excellent. I'll have Mrs. Debley pack a picnic."

"That sounds delightful." Decadent, really. Picnics near castle ruins were for other people of a higher station than Ada. Oh, she'd taken her charges on picnics, but that was completely different. "When I was a governess, I would arrange picnics for the children. But honestly, they were for me. I enjoyed the change of scenery. However, I never seemed to remember that they ran amok, and it was far more work than eating inside."

"How long were you a governess?"

"Four years."

"Did you enjoy it?"

"Mostly."

His brow arched in that thoroughly alluring fashion that never failed to make her heart flip. "I'm surprised by your short answers. I expected you to tell me all about the household, the children, and probably ten other things."

Ada laughed. She absolutely would have done that, but she didn't like discussing that period of her life. "In the end, I don't think it was the right kind of work for me."

"I wouldn't think so. You should be organizing battalions, not a few children."

His high opinion filled her with pride. Ten years ago, she never would have imagined where she was today. In a viscount's bed.

But it isn't like that!

You'd like it to be.

She ignored the debate raging in her head. "While I was toiling as a governess at nineteen, I daresay you were devouring London at the same age."

"Devouring? That's an awfully colorful word."

"What were you doing then? Attending balls and routs or other, more salacious things?" She waggled her brows at him.

His lip quirked into a half smile, and Ada nearly gasped at his beauty, even with the scar marring his face. It was probably good that he never smiled fully. No woman in a fifty-mile radius would accomplish anything.

"I mostly made a nuisance of myself along with Lucien and Dougal MacNair."

"I know Dougal," Ada said, thinking of the charming second son of the Earl of Stirling who frequented the Phoenix Club. He was still a close friend of Lucien's.

"Dougal knows bloody everyone—like Lucien. They're birds of a feather. I suppose we all were since we were second sons. We felt it was our duty to make merry and, ah, commit debauchery. Our favorite haunt was the Siren's Call."

"That sounds like a bawdy house."

"We'd hoped it was, and it certainly seemed to be with plenty of beautiful women to look at. But that's all we were allowed to do—look. It's a gaming hell run by women. They drew men in with their seductive appearance and behavior. In return, they offered excellent food and drink and some of the finest gaming in London."

"That's bloody brilliant. I'm surprised I haven't heard of them."

"You aren't their audience," he said with a smirk.

She turned her body toward him, astounded at what he was sharing and wanting to know everything he was willing to reveal. "No, I suppose not. That was your favorite place to go?"

"We certainly didn't like balls or"—he shuddered—"Almack's."

"I can see why not. Committing debauchery there would be frowned upon. So did you?" she asked enthusiastically, wanting every detail.

Now he actually laughed. It was short, but so sweet, she wanted to weep with joy. "I have never been to Almack's, nor do I ever want to go. I'm fairly certain they wouldn't want me." His voice had trailed off, and she thought she glimpsed the darkness creeping back.

"The Phoenix Club is a wonderful counterpoint to Almack's. We have weekly assemblies, and while you do have to be a member or sponsored for attendance by a member, our punch won't make your face pucker. Furthermore, the membership isn't stuffy or self-important. Indeed, we boast many people who would not be invited to White's or Brooks's or other private clubs—and not just women. Though the inclusion of my sex is what truly sets us apart."

"You sound quite proud of the club."

Her chest swelled. "I am. Lucien and Evie have done a wonderful job. I'm privileged to be a part of it."

"Are you trying to convince me to join?"

"I wasn't intentionally, but you should."

He took his head from his hand and moved to his back, his attention directed straight up, toward the bed hangings. "Assemblies don't interest me."

"Whisky does. And perhaps gaming? It sounds as though you enjoyed it in your youth."

"I enjoyed a great many things then that I wouldn't now. I'm a much different person."

She worried she'd pushed too far, that he was withdrawing. "We all change with time," she said carefully. "And that's probably a good thing. I'm a much different person too. Hopefully I've learned from my mistakes."

His head turned sharply toward her. "You can't think what happened to your sister was your mistake?"

"I will always feel some guilt about it. I definitely learned from it." And from what happened after. "There are...other mistakes, however." Now she wanted to withdraw. She held her breath, hoping he wouldn't ask.

Exhaling, he turned his head back against the pillow and faced the ceiling once more. "Guilt and regret are impossible to avoid in life, I suppose."

"Yes. It's how we manage them that matters." She stared at the side of his face—the right side—wishing it was his left so she could move closer and touch his scar. Then she would put her hand on the other side of his face and turn him toward her so she could press her lips to his.

The kiss from the other night burned in her mind, and the memory aroused a fierce hunger in her body. But she was alone in her desire. He didn't even know they'd kissed.

"Good night, my lord." She turned her back to him.

"My name is Maximillian. But you may call me Max. If you'd like."

Her insides clenched, and she fought to breathe. "I would like. I am Ada. Good night, Max."

"Good night, Ada." He moved, but she didn't see how. She only knew he hadn't come closer. "Thank you for staying tonight."

She bit the inside of her cheek lest she say more, things that were best left unsaid. With just two days left, they ought not become friends. And they must definitely not become lovers.

CHAPTER 10

The cart was packed with their picnic when Max drove Ada from the stable yard. Last night had been the longest stretch of uninterrupted sleep he'd had since before he'd left for Spain. How could he let Ada go now?

Because you must.

There was no reason for her to stay. Was he to pay her to be his sleeping companion? She wouldn't leave her position as bookkeeper to the Phoenix Club, nor would he ask her to. He probably shouldn't even be out with her today, for she was a temptation he wasn't sure he could resist. She was so lovely, with a smile warming her pretty, heart-shaped face and her blue-gray eyes glittering, even though the sky was overcast and the sun was nowhere to be found.

He looked over at her to his right, hating that she could see his scar so well. He'd already angled his hat to create more of a shadow. "We will be driving by the lake on our way to see the ruins. Will that bother you?"

"Not at all," she said sunnily. "I have no problem *looking* at water. I've just no desire to be in or on it." Her shoulders twitched with a gentle shudder.

"I'm sorry that was ruined for you. I do enjoy sailing. And rowing."

"Do you? Perhaps I'd try it if you promised to take me." Was she flirting with him? He didn't want her to do that. He wasn't sure he recalled how. Furthermore, he wasn't sure he could. Flirtation required a lightness of heart and a sense of whimsy. He no longer possessed either.

When he didn't respond, she asked, "Is that how horses are for you? Ruined, that is. I understand you used to love to ride."

He hadn't thought of it that way, but he supposed so. "I did. Since returning home, I prefer not to, however. Perhaps that will change someday. Do you think there is any chance for you and the water?"

"I suppose I should remain optimistic. I am about most everything else," she added with a light laugh. "I hadn't thought of it that way. Now, I really must consider getting into a boat again. I'm afraid my nature demands it."

God, she was fearless. His desire for her increased tenfold. How he wished he could be like her.

As he drove toward the south end of the estate, she told him about the tenants she'd met when they drove past various farms. Then he started up the hill, the track curving around it as they ascended.

"This is an excellent place for a castle," she said as they neared the top. "You can see for miles."

"On a clear day, yes. Today isn't too bad." At least the clouds weren't thick. They were, however, darkening a bit. He would keep an eye on them.

"Do you think it might rain?" she asked.

"I doubt it, but one must always be prepared, even in summer. There's a small folly near the castle ruins, and it has enough cover if we need to escape a downpour." He stopped the cart and set the brake.

"You didn't mention a folly. I find them strange."

"Strange how?" He climbed down and came around to help her out.

She put her hand in his, and while he'd touched her before—even kissed her—today, the connection was electric. Her gaze snapped to his, and he knew she felt it too.

Damn.

Attraction was easier to ignore and dissuade when it was thought to be one-sided.

"Perhaps strange isn't the right word," she said, drawing him back to what they'd been discussing. "They seem indulgent. What are they even for?"

"To enjoy. For instance, they make excellent picnic scenery."

She grinned. "I thought hermits lived in them."

He couldn't help but crack a smile. More and more, she battered his defenses and made him question why he still had any. "Sometimes. But not here. As far as I know." He looked at her in mock apprehension. "You don't suppose there's a hermit?"

"We'll have to investigate." She turned from the cart and looked about. "Ah, is that it there?" She pointed to the other side of the wide rise, where the folly was nestled amongst some shrubs near a small stand of trees.

"Yes. Shall we go there straightaway, or would you rather picnic amongst the castle stones?"

"That is a very difficult decision. Can I enjoy myself if I'm concerned there may be a hermit lurking nearby?"

"Hermits can be quite harmless." This was the most absurd conversation he'd had in years, perchance ever, and he never wanted it to end.

"You've extensive experience with them?" Her eyes

widened. "Oh! This is what you didn't want to tell me about your wild youth. *You* were a hermit. It certainly aligns with your present demeanor."

He stared at her. "How do you do this?"

The little spot between her brows pleated in that manner he found so endearing. "What?"

"Be effortlessly charming and witty. Do you never have a bad day?"

"I've had plenty of bad days. And I hate them. Which is why I do my best not to have them. And if I do, I endeavor to turn them into good days. Some might say an impending rainstorm is bad, but I shall look at it as an excellent way to study the ridiculous folly in depth, hopefully with the assistance of the resident hermit."

He feared the days would grow bad again once she left. He should make her stay.

Looking up at the darkening clouds, he went to fetch the picnic basket and blanket from the cart. "Should we even have the picnic?"

"We probably have time, if we're fast."

"Any other female I've known would have asked to return to the house, except..." He'd almost said Lucia's name. He couldn't believe he'd mentioned her so casually.

"Except whom?" she asked quietly, then seemed to immediately regret it, given the way her face fell. "You don't have to tell me." She turned and walked hurriedly toward the random collection of stones that still remained from the ancient castle.

He followed her, dropping the blanket and basket near a larger stone before approaching her from the side.

"You're right," she said. "This wasn't a very big castle."

"These stones only mark the keep. The walls went out to the edge of the rise. I can show you some of those too. In fact, over there is the biggest collection—enough to make a wall."

She stared in that direction, but he reached out and snagged her elbow, drawing her to turn her head toward him in surprise. "Her name was Lucia. The woman I'd planned to marry. She would have been happy to picnic in the rain."

"She sounds like someone I would have liked to know," Ada said softly.

He let go of her, and she continued toward the wall. After a moment, she looked back over her shoulder. "Aren't you coming?"

In that moment, he wondered if he might follow her anywhere so long as she continued to lead him from the abyss.

Max caught up with her, and they spent some time investigating the wall. She imagined how tall it might have been and whether the gate was nearby.

He shook his head. "I think it was probably where the track is now—how we came up. That's the easiest side to scale."

"That makes sense. Do you know what would be a worthwhile folly? Rebuilding this castle."

That made him laugh, and the joyful reaction in her gaze made him want to never stop. "I have to think you know how much that would cost."

"Not really, but I've seen your ledgers and you can probably afford it. I was wrong to think the estate wasn't profitable, but then you didn't have enough retainers and weren't supporting the tenants as you should have been." She grimaced. "I shouldn't have said any of that, not today."

"But you're right about all of it. I'm glad you came here and pointed out my...oversight." What a pathetically inadequate word to describe his mismanagement and willful ignorance. "It needed to be done. I'm only sorry it took me so long to listen to someone."

"I'm only shocked you listened to *me*!" She laughed and skipped around in a circle. Her foot caught a piece of loose dirt, and she slipped.

Max dove to catch her before she tumbled down the hill. He clasped her waist and pulled her toward him. She crashed against his chest with enough force to send him backward to the ground.

He grunted but held her close. "Are you all right?"

"I'm fine. The question is, are you?"

"I've suffered far worse."

Her gaze, dark with alarm a second ago, softened. Then it fixed on the left side of his face. "I know." Her whisper was a preliminary caress just before she stroked her fingertips along the ripples of his scar. "This had to have hurt terribly."

"That entire day was the most painful of my life." He stared up into her captivating face.

And got a raindrop in his eye. "Here comes the rain." He rolled with her to their sides, then jumped to his feet, helping her as he stood. "You go to the folly. I'll get the basket and blanket."

"What about the horse?"

"She'll be fine." It began to rain in earnest, not a downpour, but gentle drops, and Max ran to fetch the picnic. By the time he joined her in the folly, he was damp.

"At least it's not raining hard," she said.

"No, and I doubt it will last long. We should eat and be on our way before it decides to pour." He spread the blanket over the stones, and she set the basket on top of it.

As she arranged plates of food, he removed his hat and shook the water from it at the side of the folly. His face tingled where she'd touched him. How did he not horrify her?

Because she was a singular woman.

He sat down with her on the blanket and ate from his plate. There was ham, cheese, bread, and apples. She poured ale into a mug and handed it to him, her fingers grazing his. He could almost imagine this was four years ago when he'd first met Lucia.

No, he didn't want to compare them. For as much as they both stirred something within him, they were completely different.

Distant thunder shook the sky, and Ada startled. She looked out at the heavens. "I always believed thunder was the sound of giants dancing. That's what I used to tell my charges when there was a storm and they were afraid."

Of course she did. "And did they believe you?"

"Certainly. I also told them the rain was from the giants' exertion."

Max nearly spit out the ale he'd just drank. "That's a great deal of energetic dancing."

"I believe that's what Rebecca said. She was the eldest." Ada's eyes sparkled with mirth as she popped a piece of ham into her mouth. Then her gaze dropped to his plate. "You ate nearly everything."

So he had. He shifted uncomfortably, but he didn't know if that was because he'd eaten more than usual or because she'd noticed. "It wasn't a large plate."

"I think it's wonderful." She finished eating and began packing everything into the basket. He helped, and they both grabbed the bottle of ale at the same time, their hands colliding.

The electricity was still there, perhaps emboldened by the currents in the air. Whatever the reason, neither of them pulled away.

"I know I kissed you the other night," he said, his voice low and hoarse.

Her eyes rounded. "I thought you were asleep."

"If I could sleep through that, I would have even more problems than I thought."

Her brow creased. "Please don't be witty too."

He held her hand, taking it from the bottle. "I doubt anyone would accuse me of that."

"Really, you have to stop." She took a shaky breath, and he could feel the tremors racing through her. "I'm already far too tempted, and, well, I don't want to encourage anything."

She was tempted…

His primitive man brain somehow managed to parse the second half of what she'd said. But he was unable to formulate a coherent response, and he'd already grunted enough in her presence.

"It's best for both of us if we part as friends," she added, slowly taking her hand from his. "I can see your heart was broken. Mine was too." She looked away, and he realized the rain had stopped. "I like you. Far more than I expected to. In truth, I'd planned to avenge Prudence, not that I'd any idea how I might accomplish that." A faint smile teased her lips. "In any case, I was prepared to dislike you. I meant to do my job and be on my way." Her gaze locked with his. "But this has been so much more. I feel like I helped you, at least with the estate, and I hope you don't mind."

"Not at all. I'm surprisingly glad you came. And you *have* helped, with more than just the estate." She'd awakened him from his misery.

"I'm so glad. You *will* find a path through this." She gave him an encouraging smile, but it didn't soothe the sting of her dismissal of their mutual attraction.

He *would* find his way. He'd just do it alone.

That was why he had defenses and why he needed to keep them in place. He'd suffered so much pain. It was impossible to manage. If he didn't care and didn't feel, he could stumble through each day without anguish.

But that also meant he went without joy and a multitude of other emotions. He began to wonder if it was truly worth the effort.

"We should get back," he said. The magic of the afternoon had passed. "I know you still have a great deal of work to do, and you've only tomorrow left to complete it."

"I hope you'll have dinner with me," she said tentatively.

"It might be best if we don't." He stood and helped her to her feet. Then he packed up the rest of the basket while she picked up and folded the blanket. "You're right that this is a temptation we should avoid. Besides, I need to learn to get on without you here."

He ought to have offered her his arm, but he didn't want her to touch him again. He didn't trust his most basic impulses. It was torture not to kiss her.

Without looking back, he carried the basket to the cart and set it inside. He lingered there while she made her way to join him. She set the blanket on the basket and went to climb into the cart. Again, he should have helped her and again he didn't, like the dolt he was.

She might have helped him step back into the light. He just wasn't sure he could stay.

~

*A*da stared up at the bed hangings. Was Max really going to let her leave without saying goodbye? Without even seeing her? She hadn't clapped eyes on him since they'd returned to the house yesterday following their picnic.

During which he'd admitted to knowing they'd kissed, and it seemed likely he was going to kiss her again. Until she'd put a stop to it. She feared she would regret that for the rest of her days.

More than you'd regret having sex with him? Because you know that very well could have come next.

I'll never know, shall I?

These arguments with herself were becoming quite tedious. She looked forward to returning to London tomorrow and prayed for a quieter mind.

Except she suspected her thoughts would be occupied with the beast of Stonehill for some time. She nearly giggled at the title. Now he definitely sounded like some sort of gothic romantic hero.

Her humor faded quickly. There was no romance here. She wondered if there was truly even friendship since he hadn't bothered to come to dinner last night or tonight. He hadn't even popped into the library.

Perhaps she'd hurt him yesterday. Did he feel rejected? She'd hate it if she caused him pain. This was about her and not repeating past mistakes. It had nothing to do with him at all, beyond the fact that she found him too damn tempting. If she could live without consequences, she would have greedily taken him in her arms yesterday.

Even with consequences, she'd considered it.

But aside from repeating mistakes, she was far too romantically minded. She fell in love easily—or at least with the idea of being in love. One would think she'd be safe from any sort of romantic inclination where the viscount was involved, but he'd shown himself to be a man of great depth. He realized he needed to change, and he was trying to do so. That took an enormous amount of courage, particularly given what he'd been through.

How she wished she knew the specifics, if only because she thought it would likely help him to unburden himself. He had, at least somewhat, and she was grateful she could be a support to him.

Turning to her side, she closed her eyes. She needed to sleep. Morning would come far too soon.

A sound made her eyes jolt open. Was that a knock? Rolling back over, she slipped from the bed and padded to the door on bare feet.

Without waiting for a second knock—if there'd even been a first—she opened the door. Framed beyond the threshold stood the primary object of her thoughts.

The edge of Max's mouth lifted in a near smile. "I can't sleep."

"Me neither." She opened the door wider in silent invitation.

He stepped inside, and she closed the door behind him. "I probably shouldn't have come."

"I'm glad you did. Now I can berate you for ignoring me since yesterday."

"I wasn't ignoring you," he said a bit wearily. "There have been plenty of days during your stay that I haven't seen you."

She crossed her arms over her chest and gave him a perturbed stare. "I misspoke. You were *avoiding* me. Which is what you were doing on the days we didn't see each other. Don't bother denying it."

"You're really angry with me." He sounded surprised. "I didn't think you got angry."

She unfolded her arms with a weighty exhalation. "I'm not angry. I was disappointed. I thought I might not see you again."

"And that upset you?"

Was he being purposely obtuse?

He lifted his hands. "I thought you wanted distance. You said you were tempted yesterday, and I—"

"Oh, be quiet." She grabbed the front of his dressing gown

and stepped toward him. Then she stood on her toes and kissed him.

He kissed her back, but tentatively. She pulled back and looked into his eyes.

His brow furrowed. "I'm confused."

"I wanted to keep you at arm's length because I'm leaving." *And because I shouldn't take you to my bed.* "I've since realized it's precisely because I'm leaving that I don't want you to stay away."

"Ah. I think I understand. Should I stay, then?"

"Do you know how to prevent a baby?"

"Ah, yes. To try, anyway."

"If you'll do that, then yes, stay."

He wanted to be clear. "Not just to sleep?"

She shook her head.

He wrapped his hand around the end of her braid, which hung down her back. "You're certain?"

She nodded, and he tugged the ribbon from her hair before pulling the braid loose. He lowered his head and kissed her, but there was no hesitation this time. There was heat and desire, his tongue licking into her as she clutched at his shoulders.

Her body sang with want. This was what she'd craved, what she'd been longing for without entirely realizing or at least acknowledging it. She connected to something within him, something that made her feel valued and appreciated.

Or was she only romanticizing things because that was what she wanted to feel?

Stop thinking.

She twined her arms around his neck, and he lifted her in his arms. She went to curl her legs around his waist, but had to pull up her night rail first. Linking her feet behind him, she held him tightly, her sex pressed against his, though his dressing gown separated them.

He groaned, and it was a much different sound from his irritated grunts and growls. This was low and hungry, and it made her want to provoke him to do it over and over again.

One of his hands moved down to her backside, cradling her against him. Sparks of desire shot through her. She dug her fingers into his neck, deepening their kiss to a frenzied exploration. She wanted to know all of him. *Now.*

He walked with her to the bed, at least she assumed that was where they were going. She honestly couldn't pay attention. He might have walked her across the house, and she wouldn't have realized. It was all she could do to hold on to him as her body quivered with need.

Then he set her on the bed and tore his mouth from hers so he could whip her night rail over her head. His gaze dipped to her chest, and he cupped her breast with one hand. "I don't think I can go slow."

She arched into him, eager for his touch. "Then don't. You can go slow later." Lifting her hands to his chest, she unfastened his dressing gown and pushed it from his shoulders.

He was entirely nude beneath it, the light from the embers of the fire casting shadows over his taut flesh. He was too thin, but still muscular and, of course, covered in those scars she'd seen the other night.

Ada wanted to kiss and caress each one, as if she could make him whole again. Could anything make him whole again?

She lifted her gaze to his and found him watching her.

"I'm not the most attractive of men anymore."

"You are beautiful," she whispered, gingerly putting her fingertips to the burn scar on his left shoulder. "When I think of the pain you suffered, I want to hurt someone. I want to make sure you never feel that again. I'm so sorry if I hurt you yesterday."

He clasped the back of her neck. "You didn't. I appreciate

your honesty—always. Which is why I don't want you to lie to me. Ever. You can't think I'm beautiful."

"You're magnificent, actually." She kissed the thin scar on his chest, moving her lips softly over his flesh.

His fingers twined in her hair and his other hand gently caressed her breast. Then he tugged her head back and kissed her again with a savage intensity that set her entire body aflame. She didn't think she'd ever been this aroused. Desperate, really.

He pinched her nipple, pulling it so sensation exploded through her, arcing straight to her sex. She moaned into his mouth, wanting more. She pulled him closer, and he leaned over her, pushing her back onto the mattress.

His mouth left hers, and he seared a path down her throat and into the valley of her breasts, his lips and tongue scalding her flesh. She gripped his head, guiding him to her breast, needing to feel his mouth on her. He obliged, holding her as he closed over her nipple. He sucked, then grazed his teeth over the tip, making her cry out as a desperate hunger pulsed between her legs.

"Max," she breathed, her fingers digging into his scalp as he devoured her breast. Sensations overwhelmed her, and she wrapped her legs around him.

He turned her on the bed and moved over her. His hand skimmed up her inner thigh, and she spread herself for him, holding her breath until he touched her where she most wanted him to.

His fingers gently stroked her sex, spreading her folds on his way to pressing her clitoris. She moaned again, his mouth still tormenting her breast. It was too much and yet not enough.

Ada lifted her hips, seeking more of him. Then he slid his finger into her, and she cast her head back as pleasure built. She wanted him—all of him—inside her. "Now, Max, please."

He lifted his head and met her gaze, holding it as he slid his cock into her. She hadn't even had time to touch him, to explore him, but she would. She didn't need to sleep tonight.

She was so close and moved closer still when he thrust fully into her. She wrapped her legs around him once more and drew his head down to kiss him. He began to move, his hand still between them as he stroked her clitoris. It was all she needed to break apart. She came hard, her muscles clenching as ecstasy washed over her.

It was never-ending, for as he continued to drive into her, she rose even higher, her body cresting on new waves of rapture. At last, her orgasm faded, but the pleasure remained. She wanted more of him and wasn't sure she'd ever get enough.

She clutched at his back, moving her hand down to the curve of his backside, reveling in the delicious firmness of his muscles. He slowed his movements, thrusting harder and deeper, claiming her with relentless purpose. He would take everything, and she would eagerly give it.

His mouth was still on hers, his breath rasping into her. Their bodies slicked together as they moved. She dug her heels into him, and he groaned just before snagging her lower lip with his teeth.

He kissed along her jaw to her ear, whispering, "Come again. Please."

She was already on her way, her body climbing to the precipice from which she would tumble into a rapturous abyss. His hips snapped against hers, and he picked up speed again. Over and over, he drove into her until she fell a second time. She cried out as he thrust twice more. Then he pulled away from her with an anguished moan.

Ada turned with him, her hand finding his cock as she stroked him through his release. He collapsed to his back, and when he was finished, she snuggled next to him.

"You've done that before." He was still breathing fast, and she couldn't tell if that bothered him.

"I told you I did."

"I meant that last part. After I left you, and you...helped."

"Er, yes. I had a lover, and we did that." Until they'd gotten lazy. "Does that trouble you?" Her breath held as she waited for his response.

He turned toward her and gathered her close. "Not at all. You are perfectly wonderful just as you are. Was he the man who broke your heart?"

Ada now knew what it felt like to be on the other side of intrusive curiosity. "Yes, but it wasn't his fault." Not entirely, anyway.

"I'd thrash him if I could." He gazed at her intently, and she knew he meant what he said. "Did you mean what you said about later?"

"That we could go slower then?" Grateful that he didn't ask her more about the past, she kissed him, then hovered her lips over his. "Yes."

He swept her hair back from her face and kissed her deeply, pressing her back into the mattress. When he finally lifted his head, she was breathless.

Ada caressed his cheek, her thumb sweeping over his scar. "I'm glad you came to see me. I regretted what I said yesterday."

"It's probably for the best, or you wouldn't have finished your work. Now you are unencumbered."

She narrowed her eyes playfully. "I can focus entirely on you for the remainder of the night."

"You should also sleep."

Pulling his head back down to hers, she murmured, "We can sleep when we're dead."

There was no way she was wasting a moment of their last night together.

CHAPTER 11

*A*da had only been gone half a day, and it was as if there was no light at all. Though she'd often sat working quietly next door in the library, the house seemed eerily silent. He didn't like it, which made no sense. This was how it had been before her unwanted visit, and he'd enjoyed the silence. He'd hated that she'd come to Stonehill.

Until he didn't.

He frowned at his desk and the neat stack of ledgers she'd left. He'd grown used to her energy and persistence, the very things he'd found so annoying at the start. Now he was annoyed that she was gone. There was, apparently, no pleasing him.

Except he'd been plenty pleased last night. Or pleasured, anyhow.

He'd never expected she'd invite him to her bed. He'd planned to say goodbye, to tell her he hoped she would visit again sometime. Instead, they'd spent the night learning each other's bodies until he'd crept back to his room just before dawn. Then he'd slept like the dead, completely missing her departure.

She likely thought him a beast. Wasn't he? She may have prompted him to change somewhat, but he was still the same monster who'd returned from Spain.

Mrs. Bundle pushed open his door, which had been ajar. "Mrs. Tallent is here. Do you want to receive her here or elsewhere?"

He'd completely forgotten he was meeting with his new steward today. Ada had left a note about it on his desk, which he'd found earlier. "Here is fine."

"You sound aggravated," Mrs. Bundle said, her eyes narrowing. "Do not drive Mrs. Tallent away."

He glowered at her. "Don't pester me."

"Here I hoped your gentler nature would remain," she murmured as she left.

Max sat up straighter behind his desk. What on earth was he going to discuss with the woman?

A few moments later, Mrs. Tallent entered. She'd removed her hat so he could fully see her dark hair pinned neatly atop her head. Her green eyes assessed him, and her hands were clasped before her. She appeared nervous.

"Good afternoon, my lord."

"Please sit."

She perched on a chair near his desk—the small one Ada sat in on the few occasions she'd come to his study.

They stared at each other, both expectant, and Max wondered if she knew what they were supposed to discuss. "These are the ledgers Miss Treadway organized and brought up to date." He indicated the stack on the corner of the desk.

Mrs. Tallent edged forward on the chair. "Excellent. Should I just take them?"

"I suppose."

Silence stole over them again, and this time, she broke it. "Do I need to find a tenant for my farm?"

"Isn't that what a steward does?"

"I believe so."

He clasped his hands atop the desk. "Perhaps you should visit with Sir George's steward for guidance." Sir George was Max's neighbor to the north.

She pursed her lips. "I will do that. And what of my family's living arrangements?"

"What of them?" Had she asked for this meeting to barrage him with questions he didn't know the answers to?

"It is my understanding that once a new tenant arrives for our farm, I and my children will move to the steward's house."

"Oh, yes. Of course."

"May I look at it?" she asked politely. "I should like to ascertain its condition and whether there are furnishings."

"Talk to Mrs. Bundle about that." He wasn't sure if Mrs. Bundle could help her, but in the absence of a steward and a butler, she was the ranking retainer in his employ, so she seemed the likeliest to provide assistance.

"It seems I have bothered you, my lord," she said tightly, rising to her feet. "I thought you wanted to meet with me today."

"No, I didn't ask to meet with you. Miss Treadway left a note." A disappointingly short and impersonal missive in which she'd said he had a meeting with his new steward this afternoon.

"I see. She also sent me a note. It seems she neglected to tell either of us why we were meeting."

"She should have stayed to help with this transition," he said darkly, angry that she was gone, that she'd left him with what he now saw as a mess. How he hadn't seen it before, he didn't know.

"I'll learn quickly, my lord," Mrs. Tallent said with confidence. Max only grunted in response. "Do you wish me to check in with you regularly?"

"I suppose you should." Max knew enough from his youth that his father met with the steward at least weekly, if not more often. Indeed, the steward had typically been present at their dinner table. He tried to imagine dining with Mrs. Tallent and perhaps her children and immediately chucked the idea.

"Are you entirely certain this arrangement is acceptable?" she asked.

No. "It will be fine. You need time to learn and become acclimated. I shall be patient."

"How magnanimous of you." She gave him what he suspected was a fake smile. "You also need time to learn and become acclimated. I am also patient. I'll visit Sir George's estate and I'll secure a new tenant. In the meantime, I'll acquaint myself with these ledgers." She picked up the stack and departed before he could say another word.

Or help her. He should have carried the bloody books. He also could have been more pleasant. At least he hadn't been outright rude, like he'd been before Ada had visited.

A moment later, Mrs. Bundle came back to the study. "What did you do?" she demanded.

"Nothing."

The housekeeper put her hands on her hips. "Mrs. Tallent said she hoped this arrangement would work, but did not appear or sound optimistic. I'll ask again, what did you do?"

"I didn't *do* anything. Ada—Miss Treadway—apparently set this meeting and didn't inform either of us what we were to discuss. If you want to be irritated with someone, it should be her."

Mrs. Bundle relaxed slightly and dropped her hands to her sides. "I see. You're angry with Miss Treadway and allowed Mrs. Tallent to feel the brunt of that. Shame on you, my lord. Here I thought you'd made good progress."

He didn't want to be chastised by his housekeeper today. He was in too foul a mood. "You berating me is going to ensure I make *no* progress. Mrs. Tallent will be fine. I need you to help her with the steward's house. Give her the key."

"I've just done that, and I'll go inspect it myself first thing tomorrow. It will be some time before she moves in, I expect."

"Thank you." Max rubbed his hand across his brow.

Mrs. Bundle lingered. "Are you upset because Miss Treadway is gone? I can understand why you would be."

Max said nothing. If he admitted his emotions, he'd have to deal with them. Wouldn't he?

"It's nearly the end of the London Season, isn't it?" Mrs. Bundle asked. "Perhaps you should go. It's been some time since you visited." Having planted that seed in his brain, she slipped from his study.

Normally, he would find his housekeeper's meddling annoying, but in this case, he didn't hate her idea. Not the going-to-London part, but the reason for doing so— following Ada.

Which he absolutely should not do. What would he do once he found her?

He had no idea.

Anyway, following Ada seemed a rather weak reason to travel to London. He didn't have lodgings there, and if it became known that he was in town, he'd be expected at Westminster. Plus, people would approach him and thank him for his military service. He flinched.

There was another reason he ought to go to London, he realized. His half sister. Not only should he give Prudence her dowry, he should at least meet her. As Ada had pointed out, he wasn't really alone. Furthermore, if Prudence was a close friend of Ada's, it seemed likely that Max would perchance find her interesting.

Fine, he'd go to London. But he wouldn't commit to enjoying it.

~

*A*da had barely deposited her traveling case in her bedchamber before there was a knock on the door of her private apartment located on the second floor of the ladies' side of the Phoenix Club. Moving into the main room, she hastened to the door, certain of who it would be.

"Evie," she said warmly.

Evangeline Renshaw was one of the most strikingly attractive people Ada had ever met. She was classically beautiful, with sculpted cheekbones, a dazzling smile when she chose to give it, and the most remarkable round blue eyes that turned up at the outer corners. She was also graced with astonishing russet hair that always looked as though she stood in the sunlight or beneath a glittering chandelier. Evie just…sparkled.

She was also incredibly clever, with a no-nonsense head for business that inspired Ada in all she did. When she'd first met Evie, who was somehow only slightly older than Ada, two years ago in Cornwall, Ada had been entranced. She'd wanted nothing more than to be just like her. In time, she'd realized that was silly, that she needed to learn to be Ada. She hoped she was doing that.

They embraced, and when Evie stepped back, she said, "You look like you're still in one piece. Was Warfield as awful as expected?"

"I would say more awful, actually." Ada recalled the first few days and his efforts to get her to leave. "But I managed to wear him down. He hired a steward before I left."

Evie gaped at her. "Astonishing. I shouldn't have doubted it, however. You are remarkably skilled at bringing out the best in people."

Had she done that? Ada wasn't sure she'd seen Max's best. She'd certainly seen his better, in any case. She only hoped he continued to improve. She truly believed he was ill, in a manner of speaking, from whatever had happened in Spain and was finally on the path to recovery. "He's been through a difficult time." She couldn't deny wanting to defend and protect him.

"You got on well with him, then?" Evie asked.

"Eventually." During the journey back to London, Ada had considered whether she would tell Evie or Prudence what had happened. She feared telling Evie would invite reproach. Evie had rescued Ada at one of her lowest points, after she'd left her employment as a governess and feared her life as a respectable woman was over.

In the end, since there was no chance Ada and Max would repeat their night of passion, Ada had determined it was best to just pretend it had been a lovely dream. That was precisely how she'd remember and treasure it.

"I know Lucien is eager to speak with you if you're not too tired," Evie said.

"Not at all. He's in his office?"

Evie chuckled. "I told him you would be full of energy even after the long ride in a coach. He really ought to know better by now, but men will always discount us, even those who know us best."

Ada wasn't sure she agreed with that, but didn't say so. Evie was the most independent-minded woman Ada had ever known. She often found men, particularly their opinions and interference, to be a nuisance. If ever there was a woman who would never marry, it was Evie. Her identity as a widow was a complete fabrication—a secret known only to Ada and Lucien and perhaps a few others.

"Do you want to walk with me?" Ada asked.

"I'd planned to go over, since it's Tuesday." The men's side would be bustling with activity as women joined them this one night of the week.

They went down to the first floor and took the shortcut through the gallery that overlooked the ballroom. Lucien's office was situated at the back of the first floor. His door was open, and Ada moved inside.

Evie followed her in. "Ada's back," she said, perhaps unnecessarily.

Lucien jumped up from behind his desk, his features eager. "Welcome home, Ada. I can hardly wait to hear all about your adventure."

"I'll leave you to it." Evie closed the door behind her as she departed.

Tall, with dark eyes and darker hair, Lucien was nearly as attractive as Evie and equally driven. They'd once been lovers, Evie had confided to Ada, but they were now just the best of friends.

"Your letters were not nearly descriptive enough." Lucien gestured to a pair of chairs near the hearth. He waited for Ada to sit before he took the other chair, sitting far forward in his enthusiasm. "Tell me everything."

She wouldn't come even close to doing so, but he didn't need to know that. "I believe I conveyed the important parts —that he was disagreeable and that I was making progress."

He smacked the arm of his chair with his palm. "I can't believe you got him to agree to hire a steward!"

"He actually hired one before I left." She nearly laughed as Lucien stared at her in unabashed shock. "I recommended Mrs. Tallent, a farmer on the estate, and he agreed."

Lucien's expression sobered. "Is Mrs. Tallent qualified?"

Evie's words came back to Ada, and she resisted the urge to roll her eyes. "*I believe so, yes. She's an excellent book-keeper—the best on the estate—and she's managed to not only maintain her husband's farm since his death last year, she's increased profit and productivity.*" Women could and probably should run the world, Ada thought.

"She certainly sounds good at farming," he said evenly. "However, Max doesn't know a thing about running the estate. He needs someone with experience. I was able to come up with a list of candidates." He stood and went to his desk.

Ada clasped her hands in her lap and stiffened her spine. "Too late. Mrs. Tallent has already started in her position." At least Ada hoped so since she and Max were supposed to have met that afternoon. She wondered how that had gone and wished she'd had more time to help them. Perhaps she should have stayed another week.

To spend more time in his arms?

She ignored the overzealous part of her brain.

"Could we at least send someone to guide them?" Lucien asked, his brow furrowing and his jaw tightening.

"You entrusted this mission to me. I don't know that his lordship would appreciate another meddling figure. It took me some time to win him over." And she still wouldn't consider the war won, just the battle she'd been sent to fight. Whether Max would continue on the path to being more amenable was anyone's guess. He had so many things to work through—the sleeping and nightmares, the eating, the not riding. Ada felt a pang of guilt at leaving him with regard to the sleeping in particular.

"You truly won him over?" Lucien asked.

"I think so." She wasn't about to say more than that. "I will write to him and ask how things are progressing with Mrs. Tallent—the new steward. If he indicates he needs help, we can offer to send someone." Or Ada could learn what needed to be done and return herself…temporarily, of course.

Lucien came back to the chair, his expression still weighted with disbelief. "I can hardly countenance him responding to you, let alone indicating he needs help. What did you do to him while you were there?"

"I was merely my usual cheerful self. I think I wore him down. Lest you think it was easy, I assure you it was not. He was most reluctant."

"That's the Max—er, Warfield—I know." Lucien gave his head a shake. "Sometimes I forget he's the viscount. I've always known him as Max, and we never expected him to inherit. His brother was quite healthy."

"You haven't said how he died. I know their father was ill."

"It was a terrible tragedy. Alec was thrown from his horse. He hit his head and seems to have died immediately, which is a comfort, I suppose."

Ada thought of Max's refusal to ride. Was that why he'd sold nearly all the horses at Stonehill? Or was it just whatever had happened in Spain? Likely, it was both. Her heart ached for him, especially since riding had seemed to have been something he'd enjoyed in his youth.

Since she'd written to Lucien about Max's horse, she decided it was worth discussing. They both cared about him. "I wonder if that is part of the reason he no longer rides."

"I hadn't considered that." Lucien looked to the side, frowning. "I've tried to be a good friend, but I've done a rather poor job." His gaze met hers again. "I did find his horse. I know the gentleman who bought him, and I believe he'll sell him to me. Do you suppose Max wants him back?"

"I have no idea. But I do think he should ride again." The same way she should get in a boat again. Just the thought of that made her quake with fear and unease.

"I can still scarcely believe he doesn't ride at all. He is one of the finest horsemen I've ever known. I think I'll pay him a visit in a few weeks. Perhaps I'll bring Arrow as a peace offering."

"Does peace need to be made?"

Lucien leaned back in his chair, slumping slightly. "I'm not sure, but I don't think Max has appreciated my meddling. He definitely wasn't thrilled about you coming to Stonehill."

"Yet you sent me anyway," Ada said wryly.

"I knew it would benefit him. Or it would be a colossal failure. You were my last hope." He smiled, and it carried relief. "I'm so glad you found success. I hope he appreciates it. And you."

"I think he came to."

Lucien stood. "I'll buy the horse."

"I hope he accepts the gift." As much as Ada thought she might have come to know Max, she acknowledged there was far more of him that was a mystery to her. She truly had no inkling how he might react to receiving his former horse. She rose.

"Are you coming into the club for a bit, or are you tired from your trip?"

"I think I must step into the members' den and the library, at least," she said, taking his arm as he offered it.

They left his office and made their way toward the front. "Drinks first, and you know the best is in the library."

"Of course I do." She slid him an amused glance. "Who ensures we have those beverages?"

Lucien laughed heartily. "This club would fold without you. While I'm glad you agreed to do this errand for me, you were sorely missed."

She felt a moment's alarm. "I worked hard to make sure everything was taken care of. Did things not run smoothly?"

He put his hand over hers. "Things were just fine. I only meant to convey that you are highly valued."

"Thank you. I appreciate hearing that."

The moment they stepped into the library, a blonde figure rushed toward them. "You're back!"

Prudence St. James, the Viscountess Glastonbury, smiled broadly and only just kept herself from embracing Ada.

Ada put her arms around her. She was far less concerned about showing her feelings than Prudence was. "I'm so glad to see you."

They parted, and Prudence cocked her head. "I wasn't sure you'd be here tonight, but I'm so glad you are." She linked her arm through Ada's.

Lucien waved them off. "Go. I'll bring you a glass of port, Ada. Unless you'd prefer something else?"

Ada thought about the whisky she'd drunk with Max and how she'd tried to persuade him to join the Phoenix Club to broaden his palate. "Irish whiskey, if you don't mind."

"Indeed?" Lucien looked to Prudence. "Anything for you?"

"Not at the moment, thank you." Prudence set her expectant gaze on Ada. "Tell me everything, starting with how horrid Warfield was."

"Just as nasty as you described. However, and I hope you won't hate hearing this, he did become less…terrible over the course of the fortnight. I was rather persistent with my cheer and charm."

Prudence laughed. "How I would have liked to see that. I'm so glad you wore him down. Is that what happened?"

"Somewhat. He liked to tell me as often as possible that I annoyed him. He was generally unhelpful. But then he realized I was going to do what I was going to do whether he provided assistance or not." Ada sobered somewhat. "Ultimately, he saw that he was not doing his best for those around him, and I persuaded him to make some changes."

Prudence's expression was much the same Lucien's had been—total disbelief. "Such as?"

"He hired a steward and more retainers. His poor housekeeper has help now."

"I'm astonished he agreed to that, but glad for Mrs. Bundle. I liked her. She apologized profusely for Warfield's behavior." Prudence looked away, her lips pursing. "Did you, ah, discuss me with him?"

"Yes. I took him to task for his treatment of you. He thinks he's alone in this world, but I reminded him that he is not."

"Did that seem to make a difference?" Prudence sounded as if she hoped so.

"Pru, are you hoping you might forge a sibling relationship with him?" Ada would do whatever she could to facilitate that if Prudence wanted it.

"I doubt that's possible. His disdain of me was quite strong."

"I think it was largely bluster," Ada said softly, thinking of the vulnerabilities he'd shown her. "It is my fervent hope that he is changing, that the wounds he suffered at war are finally beginning to heal. With that, anything is possible."

Prudence gave a dry laugh. "You are the most optimistic person I know."

Lucien returned with Ada's whiskey. "Did I hear you praising Ada's eternal optimism?"

"Praising is perhaps not the best word. Marveling at it is a better description."

"It is a wonder to behold," Lucien agreed. "That's how I knew she was the right person to send to Stonehill. Did she tell you that he hired a steward and that she's a woman farmer from his estate?"

"How did that come about?" Prudence asked.

"Her husband died last year, and Warfield allowed her to

continue on." *Because that was easier for him than overseeing a change.* She left that last part out. Again, she felt defensive and protective of him. She wished they could all see the man she'd come to know.

"The whole thing is beyond astonishing. My hat's off to you, Ada." Lucien lifted his glass in a toast and took a drink before leaving them.

"Where is your husband?" Ada asked, scanning the library before seeing the Viscount Glastonbury standing in the corner, speaking with Dougal MacNair.

"Never too far away," Prudence murmured, a smile lifting her lips. She was so clearly in love, and Ada couldn't have been more thrilled. No one she knew deserved to be happy more than Prudence.

Perhaps that wasn't exactly true any longer. She desperately wanted Max to find happiness. He'd suffered so much.

"I still can't believe you're the one happily married," Ada said with a light laugh.

"Me neither. You are far more likely to fall in love."

"You know I've already done that."

"Just as I know that it didn't work out," Prudence said. "My hope for you is that it happens again, but that it's forever."

Ada wasn't sure she wanted that. She'd loved Jonathan very much. Leaving him had been incredibly difficult, but then she'd had no choice. She'd created her own miserable and awful situation because she'd been foolish and overly romantic. Honestly, she should turn her back on romance and perhaps even optimism entirely. That wasn't her nature, however. So she would continue to be romantically minded —for others.

And yet, she couldn't deny that she felt...*something* for Max. She'd come to care deeply for him, but that didn't mean it was love. Honestly, she didn't want to think about what she felt.

"As it happens, I'm too busy at present for any of that," Ada said breezily, glad she'd decided not to tell anyone what had happened between her and Max. What would be the point when it was a singular event?

Lucien had gone to speak with MacNair and Glastonbury. Ada recalled what Max had told her about his escapades with Lucien and MacNair. She wished Max would come to London and see his friends. It would only help his healing.

Perhaps she ought to write to him about that. She could ask about his former horse and Mrs. Tallent, and suggest he come to town. Would he write back? She regretted not seeing him that morning before she'd left. But what was she to do, ask Mrs. Bundle to wake him?

No, it was best that they'd parted as they did. Her last memories of him were of her body entwined with his, their lips joined, and shared joy.

"Why are you smiling like that?" Prudence asked. "I can see you're thinking about something, as you so often are."

"Woolgathering, you mean. Nothing in particular. I'm just glad to be home. Now, tell me all about your newly married life." Ada escorted her to a settee and put Max from her mind.

For about an hour, anyway.

CHAPTER 12

*M*ax shifted anxiously in the hack on the way to the Phoenix Club. It was Friday and there would be an assembly, so he'd changed his clothes at the hotel. He hated that he felt harried, but he'd only arrived in London a short while ago.

He was still irritated that he hadn't been able to leave Stonehill the day before. The new grooms had started that morning, which meant Og could drive him to London. Except Og had been exceptionally disagreeable regarding the new grooms and leaving them in charge of the animals on their first day. Max had nearly directed one of the new lads to drive him instead.

But Og had insisted he would drive the coach, provided they left today. Max had acquiesced, if only because he understood what it felt like to battle one's own mind. Og was mired in his ways and in having independence, and Max was asking him to do two things that would cause him stress: welcome new retainers and drive him farther than the village.

The hack stopped in front of the Phoenix Club. Max

stepped out and immediately considered climbing right back in. He rarely went out in public and hadn't in some time. Was he ready for the stares and murmurs his appearance would provoke? His scarred visage was bad enough, but they would also speculate about him and his notable absence.

He pivoted, but the hack was already pulling away. Exhaling with resignation, Max faced the club once more and noted there were two entrances. Because, as Ada had explained, there were two sides of the club. Which one should he use?

The gentlemen's side, he supposed. But which one was that?

Max loitered for a moment, hoping for some sort of divine indication. Except he didn't believe in divinity. Not after what he'd seen and done.

Scowling, he was about to march toward the door on the right side of the building when he saw a trio of ladies walk up the short steps. They were quickly admitted inside.

Not that door, then.

Veering left, Max made his way up the steps. The door opened, and a green-liveried footman held it while Max moved inside.

Immediately, he was greeted by another fellow in dark green livery, but this one had gold on his collar. He seemed to be someone of import.

"Good evening," he said to Max, his voice even with an edge of curiosity. "Forgive me, but I don't recognize you. Are you a member?"

"Not officially."

The man's eyes flickered with surprise and dismay. "Then I'm afraid I can't admit you."

"I'm the Viscount Warfield."

"Ah, yes, however, I don't recognize that name from the membership roll."

Max tamped down his annoyance. "Fetch Lord Lucien."

"I'm afraid his lordship is exceedingly busy. There is an assembly this evening."

"I am aware of that as I've come to join the bloody assembly," Max growled. "If you don't fetch Lord Lucien this instant, I guarantee he will not be pleased."

The man, who was perhaps a few years younger than Max's thirty years, blanched. Still, he hesitated until Max growled again. Max may also have turned his scarred face toward the bloke and bared a few teeth. The man took himself off at last.

Occasionally, being a beast had its advantages.

While Max waited, he studied the large entry hall. Hung above the staircase, a massive painting of a bacchanalia was the focal point. The more he studied it, the more he seemed to recognize some of the figures portrayed within it. There was Pan, of course, and Dionysius. But in the lower right, it seemed Lucien and Dougal laughed with another pair of gentlemen. Another figure caught Max's eye—just up the same side of the painting, a man arrived at the feast on horseback. Max recognized both man and beast—it was him astride Arrow.

He was completely unprepared for the sweep of emotion that stunted his breath.

"Good God, Warfield?" Lucien's voice broke into Max's haze of befuddlement.

Blinking, Max turned his head and focused on Lucien. "What the bloody hell is that?" He jerked his head toward the painting.

"I had it commissioned. Isn't it marvelous?"

"You've no right to put me in a damned painting. Especially like that." Seeing himself on Arrow... Max still couldn't breathe properly.

"I like it," Lucien said coolly. "It's a wonderful reminder of my old friend." He moved closer, lowering his voice. "Let's not begin this way. I'm so very pleased to see you. What on earth brings you all the way to London and to my club of all places?"

Max grunted. He definitely should have climbed back into the hack. He wasn't sure this aggravation was worth seeing Ada or meeting his half sister.

"I came to give Prudence her dowry."

Lucien gaped at him. "Come to my office for a moment." He led Max up the stairs. As they ascended, they passed a few gentlemen. Max didn't know any of them, and to a man, they registered Max's face and quickly averted their gazes.

At the landing, Lucien went to the right, and Max followed. Once they were inside, Lucien closed the door. "Brandy?"

"I understand you have Irish whiskey."

Lucien stared at him. "You are full of surprises," he murmured. "Yes, but it's in the library."

"Take me there," Max said, recalling it was the place Ada had said he might like best.

With a nod, Lucien led him from the office back past the staircase to the front of the club, where a long rectangular room overlooked Ryder Street. Though the room was large, it was inviting with dark wood bookshelves and several seating areas. A sideboard with a varied collection of liquor atop it stood between the windows.

"How did you know about the Irish whiskey?" Lucien asked as he went to pour the alcohol. "It's primarily for Wexford, and he likes to hoard it."

"Miss Treadway told me about it. She thought I might enjoy it." Max took the glass and inhaled the scent of the whiskey. There was sweetness with a bit of fruit and vanilla. Honestly, it reminded him of Miss Treadway in a subtle way, not that she smelled like whiskey.

Lucien poured himself a glass of brandy. "I am utterly baffled by whatever happened during Miss Treadway's visit."

"She didn't tell you?"

"Should she have?"

"She drafted a report, which you've surely read. She also likes to talk."

"That she does," Lucien said with a chuckle. "Her written report was quite extensive, and I read every word. We also spoke, and she mentioned your resistance to change, but that you eventually came round. I'm still in awe as to how she did it."

"Can we not belabor this?" Max asked wearily. He realized he was tired from the journey and annoyed by a number of things, namely that asinine painting. "I came tonight hoping I might meet Prudence. Is she here?"

"In fact, she is, along with her husband. I will warn you that Glastonbury may be angry with you."

"That's to be expected."

"I continue to be astonished by the fact that you are well aware of your surliness and yet you do nothing to change it. Except apparently you did with Miss Treadway."

"She said that?"

"Not entirely, no. I just assumed you'd mellowed since you'd agreed to hire a steward. And a woman to boot!"

"Assume nothing," Max said tersely. He took a drink of the whiskey at last, finding it spicy yet smooth. He could see why it was Ada's preference.

"What prompted you to give Prudence her dowry?" Lucien asked skeptically.

"Miss Treadway was a rather strong proponent on that front."

"So, she wore you down about this where I could not. Amazing." Lucien shook his head, and while Max recognized that his change of heart and mind on these issues was astounding, he didn't appreciate how bloody flabbergasted Lucien continued to be.

Max glowered at him. "You're still carrying on."

"My apologies. I don't wish to drive you away. I am delighted you've come to your senses when it comes to my cousin. You will like her immensely. She's a lovely woman with a great deal of sense and wit."

In response, Max drank more whiskey.

Lucien took a quick sip of brandy. "Your Phoenix Club membership is official. I apologize for the head footman. His job is to ensure nonmembers don't gain entry, and you are an unfamiliar face. Furthermore, you didn't officially accept the invitation I sent over a year ago."

"I will remain an unfamiliar face as this is likely the one and only time I will visit. Don't be surprised—or harass me—if I allow my membership to lapse."

Lucien's expression dimmed. "Does that mean you won't be in London long?"

"A few days, I suppose. I should like to spend a little time with my half sister." Unless he met her tonight and found her completely irritating. He was also considering meeting with her mother—his father's lover, Lady Peterborough, who was Lucien's aunt. Max thought back to the handful of times he'd met her in his youth, never realizing her link to his family. That ignorance ate at him. He'd been friendly to this woman who had heartlessly stolen another man from his loving wife.

"I'm so glad to hear it. We'll organize a family dinner—"

Max lifted his hand and cocked his head with a grimace. "If you don't mind, I'd rather not attend a large event. I'm certain we can get along on our own."

Lucien couldn't seem to stop from meddling. Max could see why he'd hired Ada and found her so valuable. They shared that annoying trait. Except Max had come to accept her meddling and even appreciate it. Could he do the same with Lucien? Perhaps it was time. He was just trying to be a good friend. And perhaps he was trying to make up for what he'd done—saving Max when he hadn't wanted to be saved. Not that Lucien would ever regret doing that. Max believed he would defend his actions, both what he'd done in the moment and what he'd done afterward to ensure Max was seen as a hero, with his dying breath.

"Of course. I just thought it might be nice to get together as a family." Lucien looked him in the eye. "We are family now, Max."

That hadn't occurred to him, and Max didn't know how he felt about it. He'd gotten rather accustomed to being alone, to accepting that and perhaps even using it as an excuse to remain apart from everyone. What an uncomfortable thought.

"Just because I want to meet my half sister and give her the dowry she deserves doesn't mean I want to join a family." He drank more whiskey.

Lucien appeared briefly disappointed, but nodded to cover that up. "Understood. I don't know where you're lodging, but if you'd prefer maximum privacy, I invite you to stay here. We've excellent rooms on the second floor just above me, and the kitchen is quite good, if I may say so."

Max had gone to the Stephen's Hotel on Bond Street. It was the only place he thought he might be remotely comfortable since it was where military men lodged. But the lure of a place where he could be relatively alone was too attractive to ignore. "How many gentlemen lodge here?"

"At the moment, none."

Perfect. "Can someone fetch my things from the Stephen's Hotel? I'll also need to notify my coachman. His name is Francis Ogden, and he's situated in the mews nearby."

"I'll have someone take care of everything." In this case,

Lucien's managing was bloody helpful. Max would try to remember—and appreciate—that. "But first, I'll take you downstairs to meet Prudence."

Max twitched. The idea of going into the assembly and seeing so many people all at once was a bit distressing. He nearly asked for Lucien to bring her upstairs, but didn't want to seem a coward.

Except he was. Or wanted to be, anyway. But since he'd come all this way, he'd brave the stares and the murmurs. "Let's go." He finished his whiskey and set his empty glass on the sideboard.

Lucien tossed back the rest of his brandy, and when they started toward the door, Dougal MacNair blocked their path. Broad shouldered with ink-black curly hair, Dougal possessed the ability to look both imposing and approachable at the same time. The latter was due to his brilliant smile, which was not currently on display.

"Max?" Dougal shook his head. Then came the smile, or at least a hint of it. "I mean, Warfield. I apologize for the many times I will likely forget." His features creased with genuine joy, and Max was hard-pressed not to feel a rush of sentiment. "It's been too long, my friend." His Scottish brogue was thick with emotion.

Then Dougal embraced him, and Max froze. He'd barely touched anyone the past few years. Only Ada had gotten this close.

Giving Max's back a thump, Dougal stepped back. "It's so good to see you." He looked to Lucien. "Did you know he was coming and not tell me?"

Lucien shook his head. "He surprised me as well."

Dougal looked from Lucien to Max. "Would it be boorish of me to suggest we abandon the assembly and go directly to the Siren's Call?"

Laughing, Lucien said, "No, but I can't leave my own

damn club in the middle of an assembly. I haven't thought of the Siren's Call in years. Tomorrow night?"

"I think we must," Dougal said, grinning. He gave Max a pointed look. "Don't try to refuse. I won't allow it."

"I haven't been out in years."

Lucien's gaze was earnest and sympathetic. "If you're uncomfortable, we'll leave."

Max was torn. Facing people—exposing himself—made him anxious. But he'd come all the way to London, so perhaps it was time he tried.

"We'll force you if we must," Lucien said with humor, but Max recalled the numerous visits he'd paid to Stonehill over the past few years and how he'd tried to force Max to do any number of things. The last time he'd done that, they'd come to blows.

"You won't force me to do anything," he told Lucien with a considerable chill. "I'll go."

Dougal clapped his hands together. "Brilliant!"

"We were on our way downstairs," Lucien said. "Care to join us?"

"In a while," Dougal said. "I just came from there, and after dancing with Miss Jones-Fry, I find myself in need of a large glass of whisky."

"Are your feet all right?" Lucien asked with a faint grimace.

"They will be." He grinned toward Max once more, then gave his arm a quick, firm clasp before going to the sideboard.

Max continued from the library. Lucien caught up with him, and they made their way downstairs.

"This way." Lucien led Max through a wide arched doorway cloaked with dark green draperies. They stepped into the large, sparkling ballroom. Along with the windows across the far wall, mirrors reflected the flames of hundreds of candles in the chandeliers overhead. Dancers glided across the parquet floor, and nondancers were gathered at the opposite end—the ladies' side. The musicians were situated above them in the mezzanine. It was a marvelous scene, and in that moment, Max was rather proud of Lucien's accomplishment. He'd always worked to bring people together, both for good and...not so good purposes.

"They'll likely be on the other side," Lucien said. "Unless they're dancing, but I don't see them. Come." He walked along the edge of the ballroom.

Max trailed him, trying to keep his attention focused on Lucien's back so he wouldn't see people looking at him. Or more accurately, he wouldn't see their reactions.

He did an excellent job until they were nearly to their destination. Then his gaze strayed to a group of four ladies huddled together, their attention fixed on him. They stood to Max's left, so of course they could see his scarred face. Two of them wore matching expressions of revulsion while the third looked away. The fourth studied him intently as if she wanted to remember every ripple in his flesh so she could draw it later.

Somewhat repeating what he'd done earlier with the footman, Max sneered before he snapped his teeth together, lips bared, as if he would take a bite from them. All four recoiled, and he nearly smiled.

"Here we are," Lucien said, stopping. He turned, his expression darkening. "You're ready? I confess I feel a trifle wary surprising her like this."

"I'm not going to be rude, if that's what you're worried about."

"Well, I wasn't actually, but you make a good point. Though, you seem to be on your best behavior tonight. Or at least better behavior."

"I'm trying."

A brief smile flitted across Lucien's mouth. "I can see that, and I can't tell you how happy it makes me. Truly."

"None of this is for you." Max realized he sounded cruel, but it was the truth. He wasn't sure if he and Lucien could ever return to the friendship they'd shared before the incident in Spain. If Max thought deeply about it—and when did he ever do that—he might realize he hated knowing Lucien had seen him at his very worst, that it was easier to keep his distance from the one person who had witnessed the worst day of Max's life.

More than that, Lucien had interfered where he shouldn't have. Never mind the fact that he'd saved Max's life. Max hadn't wanted to be saved, and he certainly hadn't wanted to be recognized as a hero after what he'd done. "If you please, introduce me to my half sister."

"Very well." Lucien frowned slightly before turning once more and leading Max to an alcove with chairs. Two ladies were seated, and Max recognized the brunette as Lucien's younger sister, Lady Cassandra. She was Lady Wexford now.

She, in turn, recognized Max, the color draining from her face before she reached for the other woman's hand. She had to be Prudence. Pale skinned with blonde hair and light moss green eyes, she possessed an almost ethereal beauty. He now recognized her too—as the woman who'd come to his house seeking employment. And whom he'd tossed out with considerable vitriol.

She'd caught him on a particularly bad day.

Max bowed without waiting for anyone to introduce him. "Good evening, Lady Glastonbury. I am Lord Warfield. Maximillian, I mean. Or Max," he added quietly, wondering why he suddenly felt nervous.

Perhaps it was the cool, furious way in which she regarded him. She'd not forgiven his horrid behavior, and he didn't blame her.

"You've a great deal of nerve." This came from a gentleman to Max's left. Also blond with an athletic build, he stepped close to Max, his hands fisting. His gaze trained on Max, he gritted his teeth. "Lucien, I apologize for the scene I'm about to cause, but I think I must hit Warfield in defense of my wife."

"Don't." Prudence had stood and now moved between her husband and Max, her back to Max. "Ben, you aren't going to make a scene. Furthermore, it wouldn't be fair. You're a pugilist, and Warfield looks as if he couldn't last ten seconds in the ring."

Max's pride stung, but she was probably right. He'd never gained back all the weight he'd lost after being so severely wounded, and he certainly didn't get enough exercise. He suddenly wanted that to change too.

Prudence pivoted, her eyes glittering as she looked up at Max. "Besides, if anyone is going to hit him, I think it should be me."

"On that we agree," Max said. "If you'd like to go outside, I will suffer whatever you wish to do to me."

"What the devil is going on here?"

Everyone turned. Max knew that voice. His heart leapt.

Ada stood with one hand on her hip. "No one is hitting anyone."

~

*A*da could scarcely believe her eyes. Max was here. In London. At the *Phoenix Club*. She immediately assumed something was wrong even as giddy emotion swirled inside her.

She also realized they were seconds away from creating more of a scene than they already were. Summoning a bright smile, she turned her body toward the door leading outside.

"Shall we adjourn to the garden? It's a lovely summer evening."

Before she could make eye contact with Max, he'd pivoted and started toward the door. Curiosity burned within her, but she'd have to tamp it down until later. Assuming there would be a later with Max. She had to know why he'd come.

Lucien and his sister Cassandra followed Max, and Glastonbury offered Prudence his arm. Ada hastened to move close to Prudence as they walked outside.

"Don't judge him too harshly," Ada whispered.

Prudence slid her a wide-eyed stare. "That's precisely what he deserves."

Ada couldn't argue, and yet she had to. "He's been through a great deal. That doesn't excuse his behavior, but it explains it, I think."

Prudence's eyes narrowed. "What do you know about what he's been through?"

"Not much," Ada admitted as they stepped into the garden. "And I won't betray his confidence. Trust me when I say I know enough to understand why he's been such a colossal mess these past few years. I should think that his coming here is a step forward. Can you give him a chance?"

"I will try, but I can't promise Bennet won't trounce him."

"I won't promise that either," Glastonbury said, indicating he'd at least heard what Prudence was saying.

Ada stepped forward and pivoted to give the viscount a haughty stare. "I would beg you to remember the compassion and understanding that others have shown you."

Glastonbury exhaled. "Yes."

"I will try, Ada," Prudence said. "So long as Warfield tries too."

Nodding, Ada motioned for everyone to move to an area near a torch where they could conduct their discussion. They formed a circle, and Ada positioned herself between Max and Prudence.

"I'll reiterate that there will be no hitting," Ada announced. "Now, who would like to speak first?"

No one said anything. Cassandra, who could always be counted on to talk, finally spoke. "Lord Warfield has come to town to speak to his half sister, apparently." Her voice carried disdain, indicating she was clearly in support of her cousin, Prudence. Ada would have been too, but she'd come to know and understand Max. She was thrilled that he'd come to see Prudence.

Max's expression was impassive and perhaps bordering on irritated, which worried Ada. "I came to give Prudence her dowry."

Ada brushed the back of her hand against Max's. It was the best she could do when what she really wanted was to take his hand and kiss it and convey how happy she was that he'd decided to do this.

"That's wonderful," Ada said, barely containing her joy.

Max looked down at her, his brow slightly creasing. She had no idea what he was thinking.

Cassandra, who stood between Glastonbury and Lucien, smiled at Prudence. "Better late than not at all, I suppose."

Max flicked a glance toward Prudence, but fixed his gaze across the garden. "I want to apologize for not giving it to you before. I was, er, shocked to learn you existed."

Ada could feel his tension. She inched closer to him, hoping her nearness would soothe him. Or at least let him know he had an ally.

"Is three thousand pounds adequate?" Max asked.

It was an astonishing sum, but Ada knew he could afford it. She brushed her hand against his again, hoping he understood how proud she was of him. She'd tell him so as soon as she had the chance.

Prudence exchanged a look of surprise with her husband before she addressed Max. "That's most generous, thank you. I know you don't have to give me anything. By law, I have no claim whatsoever."

"You aren't responsible for the circumstances of your birth," Max said quietly, which was almost exactly what Ada had said. "Nor are you to blame for my father's perfidy." The anger and hurt in his voice were unmistakable.

Prudence's features softened. "Thank you. No one was more distressed to learn of my real parents than me. My mother—the woman who reared me—told me before she died, and I sometimes wish I didn't know."

Max nodded slowly. "I can understand that. I wish I didn't know that my father had been unfaithful. It rather changes what we thought we knew to be true, doesn't it? The very way we view the world."

"Precisely," Prudence said softly.

Ada's heart swelled. She hoped she was seeing the beginning of a wonderful sibling relationship—they could both benefit from it. Or perhaps Ada was just projecting her own desires on them. Having lost her family, she realized she was always looking for a replacement, even if it wasn't in her best interest.

Prudence gave him a look that was both tentative and sympathetic. "I'm sorry for all you've been through."

Ada felt Max tense—his arm twitched, sliding gently against hers. She wanted to clasp him, to let him know she cared.

Glastonbury cleared his throat. "Thank you for the dowry, Warfield. It is deeply appreciated. I hope this won't be the last time you and Prudence talk or spend time together." He slid his arm around Prudence's waist and drew her close.

"I'm grateful that you appear to care for my sister," Max

said rather flatly, making Ada wonder what was going on in his mind. "Just promise you'll never be unfaithful."

Glastonbury's blue gaze turned to flint. "I would *never*. Pru has my entire heart."

A lovely smile lit Prudence's face, and Ada felt a surge of envy. What she wouldn't give to share a lasting love like that. Alas, she doubted that would ever happen. Ada certainly didn't expect it to, nor was she certain she'd have the courage to pursue it. It seemed that fate kept telling her she should be alone.

Ada slid a covert glance at Max. Brow furrowed and jaw tight, he appeared unsettled. She didn't want to ask and draw attention to any discomfort he might be feeling. Disappointment snagged at her mind—she thought this encounter had gone rather well.

"I should get back inside," Cassandra said. "No doubt Ruark is wondering where I've gone to."

Max inclined his head toward Prudence and Glastonbury. "I'll arrange for the dowry payment."

Prudence looked him solemnly in the eye. "Thank you. Truly."

Nodding, Max clasped his hands behind his back. Prudence and Glastonbury turned and walked toward the club. Cassandra and Lucien followed.

Ada stayed back, waiting until they were out of earshot before facing Max. The same thrill she'd experienced upon seeing him wound through her again. She was so glad he was here. "I'm so pleased to see you. Now tell me what's wrong."

"Why do you think something's wrong?"

"Because I know you, and there's a telltale set to your jaw."

He shook his head at her, exhaling. "You are far too clever for your own good. Certainly for mine. I was hoping I might have a few minutes to speak with Prudence alone. I should have realized that was too much to expect."

"Tonight, perhaps, yes. But I feel confident she'd like to speak with you too. Will you allow me to arrange a meeting?"

"You'd do that?" He nearly smiled. "Of course you would. Is 'meddlesome' your middle name?"

"No, actually it's Constance. That was my mother's name."

"That's an even better fit—you never waver. In anything."

Ada laughed. "I want to be flattered, but coming from you, I'm not sure that's the way you mean it."

"It is a compliment. But only for you."

A ridiculous flutter passed from her heart to the pit of her stomach. This emotion swirling inside her—this *besottedness*—was most persistent. "Thank you. Once I set up your meeting with Prudence, where shall I send notice?"

He blinked at her.

"Your lodgings here in London," she prodded.

"Oh, yes. I'm staying here, actually."

"At the Phoenix Club?" Her voice climbed on the last word, and she hoped he didn't notice.

"Lucien invited me since I was staying at a hotel."

Dear sweet temptation! That meant he'd be on the second floor of the club on the men's side—a short walk through a hidden doorway from her own apartment. Ada wasn't going to tell him that. She knew what would happen next. Or at least later, after the assembly.

Assuming he still wanted her the way she wanted him. Perhaps he didn't. There was always the chance that their one night together had been plenty for him. Yes, that would be for the best.

Still, Ada wasn't taking that chance. Knowing he was so close was bad enough. *Telling* him would be even worse.

Ada glanced toward the club. "I suppose I should go back inside."

"Does your job require it?"

Did that mean he wanted her to stay? "Not really."

"It's good to see you."

Ada's entire body flushed with heat along with that incessant emotion. "I'm glad to see you too. How did things go with Mrs. Tallent?"

He frowned. "Not well. I forgot about the meeting. You could have done more to prepare me than leave an impersonal note on my desk. Neither of us knew what we were supposed to discuss."

"Oh dear, that is entirely my fault. I'm afraid I was rushed. I slept later than I should have for some reason." Her cheeks flushed, and she avoided his gaze. "In hindsight, I think I should have delayed my departure."

"Mrs. Tallent and Mrs. Bundle would have appreciated that. I'm afraid I wasn't my best self." He blew out a breath. "I was my old self."

That he thought of himself in terms of old and, hopefully, new made her want to turn circles of joy. "I hope they weren't too upset. This is a transition for everyone."

"They're fine. I think. Og is the one who got worked up. I wanted to leave yesterday, but the new grooms started, and Og was adamant that we couldn't leave his precious stable with brand-new retainers."

Ada laughed at the edge of sarcasm in Max's speech. "Was he horribly put out?"

"You should have seen him stamping about and growling. I believe he was also hissing."

"Like a snake?" Ada giggled.

"That's what Archie said—he was there to help."

"Poor Og." She realized that Og must have driven him to town. "Where is Og now? Should I fear for London?"

Max quirked a brief smile. "Perhaps. I doubt he'll cause any trouble, but then it's been a while since he was here."

"How long has it been for you?" she asked quietly.

"More than a year." He sent a furtive glance toward the club. "I admit to feeling uncomfortable." Taking a deep breath, he shook out his shoulders. "I'll manage. I won't be here long."

Ada cloaked her disappointment. "Well, let me see how quickly I can arrange your meeting with Prudence." She wondered if she could postpone it—just a bit—in order to keep him here longer.

That would be rather self-serving. Ada was many things, but selfish wasn't one of them.

"I'll escort you back inside." Max offered her his arm.

She knew the moment she touched him, her body would react with heat and hunger. She wasn't wrong. As soon as her fingertips grazed his sleeve, she had to tell herself not to grab him shamelessly.

Attraction was a fascinating thing. It took no thought and seemed to be some sort of natural connection between certain people, or sometimes only for one person, Ada supposed. Attraction after being intimate with someone was an entirely different animal. There was a knowledge and awareness that made every look, every touch, every moment in that person's company something greater and more arousing than before.

Ada was still very attracted to Max, but it was worse— now she knew exactly what she was missing. She sighed softly as they walked together back into the club.

More's the pity since she'd never experience it again.

CHAPTER 13

*W*hat in the bloody hell was Max doing crammed into a London hack with Dougal and Lucien as if they were twenty years old? Although, they were rather more subdued now as compared to then, and far more sober.

Max was aware that his clothing was slightly out of fashion and his hair too long. He didn't think he would care, but now that they were out, he wished he'd taken the trouble to visit the tailor and the barber. Or perhaps hire a valet.

Good God, he was becoming the man he'd been trying not to become. The old Max. No, the Viscount Warfield.

He didn't deserve to be that man. He was such an imposter filling his brother's shoes.

Would Ada help him hire a valet while he was in London? She was the only person he trusted to do that.

Ada had sent him a note earlier that Prudence had agreed to meet with him tomorrow. Which was good because then Max could leave Monday.

Only, he wasn't sure he wanted to. This was the first time he'd been in London in years that he wasn't a *complete* disaster. He'd actually made it through last night's assembly without feeling awful. He suspected that was because of Ada. She'd hovered around him until he'd retreated to his new chamber on the second floor. It was easier to ignore those around him when he had Ada to focus on.

Leaving Monday meant he wouldn't have time to meet with Lady Peterborough, which he was still considering. He was stupidly curious about aspects of her relationship with his father. How had it happened? Had he loved her? Did she regret it? Perhaps most importantly, had his father?

He realized he might not like her answers. Indeed, he expected not to. Why torture himself, then? Because he had to know, and he bloody well couldn't ask his father.

"You're pensive this evening," Dougal said, looking at Max, as if it wasn't obvious who he was talking about. Max wasn't sure Lucien could ever look pensive.

"Pensive or disgruntled?" Lucien asked with a laugh.

"I'm not in the mood for teasing," Max growled. "Ever."

Lucien's eyes narrowed. "If you're going to be sour, why are we doing this? I'd be perfectly happy back at the Phoenix Club."

Dougal snorted. "We know. Getting you to come out tonight was more difficult than persuading Max." Apparently, Lucien rarely left his club in the evenings.

Max wanted the make the most of this night. Who knew when they would ever do it again? "I'll endeavor to be more...pleasant." He realized—without the unhelpful stares of doubt from his friends—that pleasant was a lofty aspiration. "Er, how about just less sulky?"

Dougal laughed, and Lucien smiled.

They approached the intersection of Piccadilly and the Haymarket. The Siren's Call was just beyond it on Coventry Street.

The hack dropped them on the other side of the intersection.

"Ready, lads?" Lucien asked with a hearty grin, just as he used to do in their youth. Max felt an odd but welcome buoyancy, as if he could let go of his cares for a while. He hadn't done that in ages.

"Do you remember the first time we came here?" Max asked.

Dougal laughed. "When we thought it was a brothel? How randy we were, and so sure of ourselves." He rolled his eyes. "I forget who told us to come, leading us to believe we would be able to dip our quills in the well, and had a good laugh at our expense."

"It was Oliver Kent," Lucien said. "He still crows about it."

Max hadn't thought of Kent in years. A powerful and well-regarded member of Parliament, Kent could easily be their father, but possessed the sense of humor of a lad at school. He'd never been married and managed to be liked and respected by nearly everyone. He was particularly known for guiding young bucks on their path to debauchery. But he did it with such good humor and efficiency that no one faulted him for it. Probably because he was the first to help someone in need—quietly, of course. Indeed, he'd visited Max after he'd returned from Spain and still wrote from time to time. Max had never responded.

"Does Kent still frequent this place?" Max asked, wondering if he was going to have to answer for his rude behavior.

"No idea," Lucien responded. "I haven't been here in years."

"Me neither," Dougal added as they neared the club.

"You know I haven't," Max said rather unnecessarily.

Dougal moved between them and put his arms around

their shoulders. "I'm glad we're here now. Into the breach!" He led them to the door, where a footman admitted them.

Memories assaulted Max as he stepped inside the large main room of the club. Round tables covered with purple linen sat at intervals, many of which were occupied by gentlemen. Provocatively dressed women glided about, some offering drinks while others simply stopped to chat with patrons.

A large arched doorway with purple drapes led to the gaming room. Shouts and laughter carried into the main room, tempting Max. He'd won—and lost—a great deal of money here.

"Gambling tonight?" Dougal asked as if he could read Max's mind. But then he likely recalled how much Max had enjoyed the tables. They all had.

"I'm a bit long in the tooth for that," Max responded wryly.

As they made their way into the main room, heads turned, and the murmurs started along with the looks—gazes focused on Max's face briefly until they turned away in alarm or disgust. He gritted his teeth and clenched his fists, determined to stay.

He could suffer this. He'd endured far worse.

"Och!" A woman with bright red hair stopped in front of them. She put her hands on her ample hips and looked from Lucien to Dougal and then to Max, where her attention arrested on his face. "Hunt?" she asked, her eyes agog. "What the devil happened to ye?" Her Scottish brogue, thicker than Dougal's, was as pronounced as it had been a decade earlier.

"The war, Becky," Max said evenly. "I was in Spain."

"I forgot about that." She leaned close, standing on her toes so his cheek was at her eye level. "Looks like ye were burned. Imagine that hurt like hell. I'd say it makes ye ugly, but in truth, it gives ye a dashing, mayhap dangerous, air."

She stood back and narrowed an assessing eye at him. "I like it."

Max didn't know whether to be offended or complimented. He preferred the latter, so that was what he decided to be. "Thank you."

Dougal leaned toward her and spoke in a low, gravelly voice. "He's dangerously dashing. Spread the word."

Becky snorted. "Hunt never had trouble turnin' heads, and he won't now. Nothin's changed—we still aren't offering services," she added with a touch of sternness.

"He's the Viscount Warfield now," Lucien said with mock authority.

Her eyes widened, and she sank into a deep, overwrought curtsey. "Your lordship. I am honored to be in your presence." When she rose, she surveyed the three of them. "Ye lot want a table? Ale?"

"That would be most welcome," Dougal said, rubbing his hands together.

She showed them to an empty table near the middle of the room. Max nearly protested in favor of something on the periphery, but there wasn't much available. Besides, he didn't want to be difficult. He tugged his hat a little lower on the left side.

Becky went to fetch their ale.

"You aren't going to cover your scars doing that," Lucien said.

Max glowered in his direction. "Mind yourself."

"What was the name of the actual brothel we went to after we discovered we weren't getting shagged here?" Dougal mused.

Lucien drummed his fingertips on the table briefly. "I don't recall."

"Madame Helene's." Max remembered it quite well.

"Holy shit, I'd forgotten that!" Lucien slapped the table. "I wonder if she's still in business."

"Thinking of going there later?" Dougal asked slyly.

Before Lucien could answer, Becky returned with the ale. She stayed to chat for a few more minutes before moving on to another table.

Dougal lifted his mug. "To old friends and new memories."

"Hear, hear." Lucien raised his ale.

Max said nothing, but held his mug out before taking a long drink. Being here was like a dream. He could almost forget the pain of the past few years, imagine he was the carefree young man who thought he was invincible.

So why not do that for one night? Couldn't he pretend he hadn't gone to Spain? Hadn't suffered tremendous loss and committed terrible acts?

"Ho, there, look what the wind blew in!" A jolly voice carried over them, prompting Max to look up at the new arrival.

Oliver Kent stood behind an empty chair at their table, his dark blue eyes piercing as he looked at each of them in turn, ending with Max. "Warfield, haven't seen you in London in some time. A year at least."

Max stiffened, wondering if he would mention the unanswered letters he'd written. "Evening, Kent."

Kent greeted Lucien and Dougal, who invited him to sit. The older man set his glass of port on the table and took the empty chair in front of him. "It's a coincidence to see you here tonight, Warfield. I was just talking about you earlier."

"Oh?" The back of Max's neck prickled. He expected people to talk about him, whether he was in London or not, but that didn't mean he wanted to hear about it.

After taking a sip of port, Kent set his glass back on the table, keeping his hand around the stem of the glass. "There's talk you're to be elevated to earl. Well deserved, wouldn't you say, gentlemen?" He lifted his glass again and took another drink.

Max gripped his mug as if he had to hold on to it to keep from drowning.

"Excellent news!" Dougal said, grinning toward Max. "I can't think of a man more deserving after what you did in Spain."

"It wasn't just me," Max muttered. "If they're handing out peerages or elevating peerages, Lucien should get one too." He sent a glower across the table at Lucien.

"Honestly, it seems egregious to award either of us for committing the atrocities of war," Lucien said quietly. He took a long drink and kept hold of his mug after setting it down, as if he might need to swallow the remainder of the contents at a moment's notice.

Max realized he was doing the same.

While he agreed wholeheartedly with what Lucien was saying, the only reason they were lauded was because of Lucien. Without his interference, Max would probably have died. And he'd been ready to do so. Without Lucia and knowing how she'd died, he hadn't wanted to continue on. More importantly, he'd wanted to punish those who'd brutalized her.

"You're too modest," Kent said with a wave of his hand. "We love to celebrate war heroes, and that's what you both are, whether you like it or not."

Max didn't like it at all. He finished his ale and abruptly stood. His hopes for the evening had been completely dashed. There was no putting the past out of his mind now. Not tonight.

"Evening, Kent." Max looked to Lucien and Dougal. "I'm fatigued. No need to cut your evening short. Enjoy yourselves." With a nod, he started toward the door.

He didn't make it out before Dougal was beside him. "What's wrong?" he whispered.

"After my time as a hermit these past years, I find this... difficult." That wasn't it exactly, but it was close enough. He thought of Ada and her conjecture that he actually *was* the hermit living in his folly at Stonehill. While he didn't live in the folly, he absolutely was the Hermit of Stonehill. Perhaps he could convince whoever had suggested his title change that he should be Hermit of Warfield instead of earl. That he could live with.

Max walked out into the warm night intent on finding a hack to take him back to the Phoenix Club.

"Max, wait!" Lucien called after him. He hurried past Max and moved to block his path. "Don't let Kent's gossip ruin our evening."

"This was a mistake. I can't pretend I'm a green lad without a care in the world."

Lucien's jaw clenched. "No one's asking you to do that."

Dougal had stopped beside Max. He pivoted so that he faced both Max and Lucien. "Ignore Kent. We can always go back to the Phoenix Club and enjoy ourselves there."

"Capital idea," Lucien said.

"Did you know about the title?" Max asked, his voice low and raw.

Lucien's response came fast and terse. "I'd heard."

"And failed to mention it, to warn me."

"It's just talk as far as I know."

Max hoped that was all it was.

Dougal looked to Max. "Why does this bother you so much? It's just a bloody title, which you already possess. So what if it's an earldom instead of a viscountcy?"

"I don't want it. Or the celebration or the notoriety. I don't want to *remember* why I received it." The scars on Max's face burned as if he'd just been scalded. He hadn't experienced that in some time. He pinned Lucien with a bitter stare. "Just as I didn't want your help. You had no right to interfere."

"You'd be dead if I hadn't."

"I'm supposed to thank you for that?"

Lucien threw his hands up, his voice spiking with anger. "It would be nice."

Max lunged forward, his hand already making a fist.

Dougal grabbed his arm and hauled him backward as he positioned himself between Max and Lucien. "People are staring," he whispered urgently.

"People always stare," Max shot back, his lip curling. He felt Dougal release him.

Lucien held his gaze. "I won't apologize for saving you, nor will I regret it. I will always be here for you, whether you want me to be or not. If you want me to try to stop the elevation, I will. I'll speak to my father and anyone else who will listen." He edged forward, his features creasing with sympathy. "Your life wasn't over when Lucia died, and it's not over now."

"You know what I did." Max barely heard the words he murmured. "Try living with that."

"I do, because I helped you," Lucien said simply, and Max couldn't tell if he carried the same weight of remorse and self-loathing. He certainly didn't seem to with his successful club and his ever-increasing popularity. He sailed through life with a wide, self-assured smile and a surfeit of magnetic charm, while Max could barely eat or sleep.

Max stared at him, feeling as desolate as he ever had. "How are you not fucking broken?"

Lucien swallowed, his frame stiffening. "How do you know I'm not?" He turned and stalked off toward the Haymarket.

"Well, hell. Who am I supposed to go with?" Dougal asked. "You're both bloody messes."

"Go after Lucien. He will always be better company than me."

Dougal clasped his shoulder. "I don't want that to be true, Max. I've missed you. I don't want us to lose this chance—I believe you should be here. Not just in London, but with us. With friends."

"I'm not leaving yet." Neither was Max promising anything. He hadn't come here to renew friendships or forgive past mistakes, including the ones he'd made, which were far worse than anything Lucien had done.

"I'll go talk to Lucien," Dougal said, taking his hand from Max's shoulder. "Are you going back to the Phoenix Club?"

Max nodded. "To sleep." If he could. "I'm meeting with my half sister tomorrow. I have to think of what to say."

"Just be yourself." Dougal smiled. "Mostly."

"Good night, Dougal."

"Night, Max."

Dougal hurried toward the Haymarket, and Max crossed over to Piccadilly, where he caught a hack to the Phoenix Club. By the time he stepped out of the vehicle on Ryder Street, he was annoyed with himself.

Perhaps he shouldn't have left. Before Kent had interrupted them, Max had glimpsed a night where he could have let go of everything that kept him bound up and tethered to the past. He briefly considered going back and trying to find Dougal and Lucien, but the hack had pulled away.

Frowning, Max started toward the door to the club, but stopped. Was Ada here this evening? If so, she'd be on the ladies' side, of course. Or perhaps in her office, wherever that was located. He suddenly wanted to find out.

In his youth, he might have garbed himself as a woman and stolen into the ladies' side. Since he couldn't fathom where to come up with a costume of women's clothing, he'd have to settle for just stealing into their sanctuary. There had to be a servants' entrance.

He pivoted and walked around to the side of the club. There it was. Stairs led down to the kitchen level below the ladies' half.

Anticipation curled through him in a way it hadn't for quite some time. This was incredibly unusual for him—or at least for who he'd become.

Max crept down the stairs and slipped inside. This area was quiet as he made his way along a corridor. Sounds of the kitchen came from his left, and he noted a staircase on his right. Where would Ada be? He couldn't very well stroll up the stairs and find her.

Hell.

A woman dressed in smart livery came toward him, her brow furrowed. Max had never seen such a costume for a woman. It was a feminine version of something a footman might wear. It occurred to him that the ladies' side might not have footmen but instead employed footwomen. Extraordinary and brilliant.

"You shouldn't be down here," she said.

"My apologies," Max said smoothly, angling himself so that she could see his best side—or more importantly, not see his scarred side as well. "I am looking for Miss Treadway. I'm lodging on the other side of the club, and I require her assistance with something. I don't suppose you could deliver a message to her?"

"Certainly." The footwoman appeared skeptical.

"I assure you, Miss Treadway knows me and will be eager to help. Can she meet me in her office?"

"I'll ask her, but if she refuses, you'll need to return to the other side. This is highly inappropriate."

"I do beg your pardon." He flashed her a smile that used to draw the ladies to him like magnets.

Her features softened, and he felt a heady rush of victory.

"Where is Miss Treadway's office?" he asked.

"Second floor, front." She nodded toward the stairs that were now just behind him. "Take those straight up."

"Thank you." He turned and dashed up the stairs, moving faster and with more intent than he had in a very long time. With excitement, even.

What did he plan to do once Ada came upstairs? He had no idea and that unknown only added to his anticipation.

CHAPTER 14

*S*aturday evenings during the Season at the Phoenix Club always felt subdued after the potent excitement and bustle of the assembly the night before. Ada enjoyed the quiet, however. It was unlikely she'd be called upon.

This was the night she typically went to the ladies' library to find the book she would read over the next week. She'd just replaced her last book on the shelf—the one she'd started before going to Stonehill and inadvertently left here. It was another romance, and she couldn't help but think that Max would find fault with it.

Instead of scowling or otherwise reacting with disdain, she smiled. Even when he'd been insufferably aggravating, she'd enjoyed their banter.

She wondered where he was tonight. Was he in the library on the other side? Sipping Irish whiskey, perhaps? Or was he already abed where nightmares awaited?

Now, she frowned. She hated to think of him struggling. And she wasn't around to help him.

Except she *was* around…

"Miss Treadway?"

Blinking her reverie away, Ada turned from the bookshelf to see one of the footwomen standing with her hands clasped. "I've a message from a gentleman. I forgot to ask his name." Pink crested her cheeks.

"That's all right, Joanna. Is there a problem?"

"He said he needed your help and would meet you in your office. He's waiting there now."

"You let him into this side of the club?" Ada couldn't imagine how Joanna had come to encounter him in the first place, unless she'd needed to fetch something from the men's side.

"He was already here—downstairs. I told him he shouldn't be there. He said he's staying on the men's side."

What was Max up to?

"Thank you, Joanna. I'll take care of this." Ada stalked from the library and went to the backstairs. If he was in her office, he'd discover that she also lived there.

She went into the apartment, but found the main room, which included her desk, a table, and a seating area, empty. "Max?"

He appeared in the doorway to her bedchamber, then leaned his long, lithe figure against the frame. "You live here."

"Yes."

"You failed to mention that last night." He perused her lazily and thoroughly, making her feel as if she wasn't wearing any clothing. "I have to ask why."

"Isn't it obvious?" She licked her lips, too aware of how attractive he was and how much she wanted him. There was something different about him tonight. Dressed in dark blue with a light blue waistcoat, he made her mouth water with desire.

"I'm not sure it is." He pushed away from the doorframe and moved toward her. "Perhaps you'd enlighten me?"

Ada's heart began to pound a steady, hungry rhythm. "I thought it best for both of us if you didn't realize we were sleeping under the same roof."

"You didn't want me asking you to sleep with me again."

"I didn't want to have to tell you no." More accurately, she didn't think she could have. "You make resistance difficult."

He smiled slowly, seductively, and Ada couldn't breathe. "I'd apologize, but I feel no remorse about that."

"You're not being at all fair," she croaked, her body quivering with need. He'd stopped a foot away from her, and she took the respite to grab hold of what little sanity she currently possessed. "What is wrong with you tonight?"

His brow pleated. "Something is wrong?"

"Not *wrong*. Different. You are behaving in a wholly unusual manner. You're *flirting*."

"You don't like it?"

"You are making resistance nearly impossible."

His gaze dipped over her again, setting her entire body aflame with want. "I like impossible."

Ada was moments away from abandoning all restraint and sense. She fought to keep them talking. "Did something happen tonight?"

"I went out with Dougal and Lucien. We went to the Siren's Call. Do you remember me telling you about that?"

"I do, the not-brothel. How was that?"

"It didn't go well, and I came back here. I realized I wasn't in the right frame of mind to enjoy myself. The damned past keeps rising up. I've since decided it might be best if I could pretend the last five years hadn't happened. Just for tonight."

She saw a brief battle in his eyes, as if he were reconsidering his decision, or perhaps his ability to forget. She stepped toward him, finding it imperative that he win this battle, that he spend a night in which he would not be burdened by all that weighed upon him. "How can I help? I was told you needed my assistance."

He just stared at her, and she wasn't sure he was winning the fight within him.

"What would you be doing if it were five or ten years ago?" she asked. "We could return to the Siren's Call. Or go someplace else."

He shook his head. "Five or ten years ago, I'd be right here shagging *you*."

Oh God. She nearly threw herself into his arms.

A knock on the door interrupted them completely, momentarily disorienting Ada. She ought to have been thankful. Instead, she wanted to murder whoever stood outside.

"Ada, are you in there?"

Bollocks, it was Evie. Ada gestured toward her desk and urgently whispered, "Hide under there!"

Max scrambled to do her bidding. When he was stuffed underneath, Ada took a steadying breath and went to the door.

Opening it, she summoned a bright smile. "Evie."

"Is everything all right?" Evie stepped into the room, forcing Ada to move aside. "I heard there was a man up here and that he required your help." She looked about, her gaze lingering on the doorway to Ada's bedchamber. Ada should have sent him in there to hide under her bed instead.

"Ah, yes."

Evie turned to face her. "It was Warfield."

Ada spit out an explanation without forethought. "He just wanted a plate of food sent up. I told him I'd take care of it. He's gone back to his room now."

"Why didn't he just ask a footman for that on his own bloody side of the club?"

Shrugging, Ada said, "You know he can be difficult."

"Men," Evie muttered.

"Indeed," Ada agreed with a nod.

Evie cocked her head. "It's odd that he came in search of you. Is there something between you?" Again, she glanced toward the bedroom.

"We're friends. He's, ah, uncomfortable here in London, I think. I'm familiar." Ada would have believed that argument. She hoped Evie would.

"I'm glad you're his friend. It sounds as though he needs one." Evie started to turn toward the door. "Are you coming back down?"

"In a bit. I remembered there is something I need to take care of." Ada went to sit behind her desk, hoping that if she looked busy, Evie would leave.

"Always working," Evie murmured. "I'd tell you not to, but I know it makes you happy."

"Yes." Ada nearly jumped from the chair as Max's warm hand closed around her calf. She fought to remain still as he caressed her through the thin layer of her stocking.

"I'll see you later." Evie let herself out, closing the door behind her.

Ada looked down at Max crouched in the keyhole of her desk. "What on earth are you doing? Were you trying to announce your presence?"

He pushed her chair back with his other hand and came forward, but stayed on his knees. "I was not. I'm afraid, unlike you, that I couldn't resist. Shagging might be out, but when you said I wanted a plate of food, I came up with another idea, if you're amenable." He skimmed his hand up her leg, sliding from the back of her knee to the top of her thigh.

She could imagine what he had in mind, and what remained of her resistance fled. "Oh." That was all she could manage to say.

He used his free hand to lift her skirt, settling it atop her lap. "Does that mean I may continue?"

"Yes," she rasped.

"Splendid." He slid both hands under her gown and clasped the tops of her thighs. "Open your legs."

Ada didn't need to be told. She parted for him and slumped down slightly, moving her pelvis toward him.

He pushed her dress up to her waist, exposing her flesh to the air and his gaze. "So lovely," he murmured as he stroked her folds.

Pressing her head back against the chair, Ada sucked in a breath. He teased her, his fingertips gliding along her sex and rubbing her clitoris. She closed her eyes and focused only on his touch.

His tongue replaced his fingers, and she arched from the chair with a soft cry, desperate for more. He guided her legs to his shoulders and cupped her from behind. Then he buried himself between her thighs, his lips and tongue savagely devouring her.

Ada moaned and lost herself in him. This wasn't a new experience for her, and yet it was unlike anything she'd ever known. He couldn't seem to get enough of her, and she knew she'd never have enough of him. Pleasure soared inside her, and she clutched his head, her fingers digging into his scalp. She thrust up, moving against him without care or shame.

He held her backside, his hands massaging her while keeping her steady in the midst of her abandon. She felt wild, untamed, glorious. Suddenly, his thumb was against her clitoris once more, and sensation exploded within her. Muscles clenching, she cried out over and over again as ecstasy pummeled her body.

At some point, she fell to earth, her body becoming aware of the seat beneath her and the awkward set of her head as she slumped against the chair. His fingers continued to stroke her sex as the last of her orgasm faded, leaving her replete and quivering.

He stood, and she managed to push herself up to a sitting position. "That was lovely," he said, moving to the settee, where he sat down and crossed his legs.

She noted the stiff line of his erection and wanted to return the favor he'd just bestowed on her. "I'm grateful your evening went awry." Her voice was harsh and scratchy, likely because she'd been making all manner of inhuman noises. She hoped she hadn't been too loud or drawn attention. It was unlikely anyone was on this floor at this time of night, particularly when members were in the club. Although, Evie had just come up here... Ada shook that thought away.

"I am too," Max said. "You've an insufferable boor at the Siren's Call to thank for that."

"I'm glad you went, even if it didn't turn out the way you'd hoped."

"I'd say this evening has turned out much better than I imagined. I actually finished a meal for once."

Ada clapped her hand to her mouth and goggled at him. He was positively indecent, and she loved every moment of it. "Well, if that's what it takes..." She shrugged. "Are you sleeping any better?"

"No, but I suspect tonight will be different."

Ada knew she would sleep wonderfully and was glad he would too. Perhaps they ought to do this every night he would be in town. But she feared he wouldn't be staying long. "Are you leaving Monday after you see Prudence tomorrow?"

He stretched his arm along the back of the settee. "I was considering it."

Since he didn't sound as though he'd decided, she pressed her advantage, hoping she actually had one. "Will you stay one more day at least? Then we can go to Vauxhall Monday evening. It's so lovely this time of year." When he looked away, she added, "With its size and myriad walkways, it's easier to avoid people than, say, at a ball. You'd get to enjoy a social outing without having to deal with intrusion, or much of it anyway."

"That is somewhat alluring, I'll admit." His gaze met hers. "You'd like me to go?"

"Please?"

He took his arm from the settee and stood. Ada leapt from her chair and met him in the middle of the room. "As it happens, one of the reasons I came to London was to see you," he said softly. He kissed her, his lips moving over hers gently before his tongue slipped into her mouth.

Ada splayed her hands on his chest, feeling his heartbeat, and angled her head to kiss him more deeply. He tasted of heat and her, and desire sparked within her anew. If it had ever truly faded.

He pulled back and kissed her forehead. "Thank you for a memorable evening. Good night, Ada." He let himself out, and Ada stared at the door for a long time.

Yes, it had been a most memorable evening. Probably because she finally acknowledged that pesky emotion she'd been trying so desperately to ignore and avoid. That her feelings for Max were quite strong and ran very deep. She was tumbling hopelessly in love with him, whether she wanted to or not.

～

*H*yde Park bustled with children running about, birdsong filling the air, and the scent of summer flowers dashing by on the breeze. Strolling in the park was yet another thing Max hadn't done in some time. And he wouldn't have done it if he wasn't meeting Prudence.

Which wasn't to say he didn't appreciate the beautiful surroundings. Perhaps he was just too wrapped up in last night.

It had felt so wondrous to let his guilt and sadness go, if only for a little while. Why had he not done that sooner?

Because he'd been too far gone, too deep in his own despair. It had taken a persistent woman with an annoying penchant for making him feel things he hadn't felt in a long time. And for making him smile and laugh. For making him *want* to smile and laugh.

Watching her face last night when he'd flirted with her had given him more joy than he'd had in years. He hoped he'd be able to do it again.

Max stood near the Ring and watched for his half sister. After a few minutes—he'd been early—she came toward him, her blonde hair mostly hidden beneath her bonnet, her flower-printed skirt moving as she walked with purpose.

"Good afternoon," he said when she approached. He glanced about. "Are you alone?"

"Yes. Ada thought this meeting should just be the two of us. Should I have brought Bennet?"

"No, I only mean that you don't have a maid."

"Our household is still rather small," Prudence said. "I suppose we can afford to hire more people now, but I don't particularly need a maid. I wasn't raised like you." She spoke matter-of-factly, without disdain or judgment. "As a viscountess, I should probably have a companion, but I don't, and furthermore, I don't particularly care what anyone thinks of that, least of all you."

He liked her. "Would it surprise you to know I don't have a valet?"

"Yes, actually. Why not?"

"When I returned from Spain, I was ill for a long time. There was no need for a valet. I've considered hiring one recently—very recently. Since coming to London, actually. My hair could do with a trim. And I should probably have someone to oversee my wardrobe." He glanced down at his five-year-old costume.

"So will you hire one?"

"I don't know. I'm still hesitant. It seems unnecessary. I'm also not accustomed to having people that…close."

"I see," she murmured. "Shall we walk?"

He started along the path, and she fell in beside him. "It's interesting that you came to me in search of employment instead of telling me you were my half sister and demanding money."

She looked straight ahead. "I don't feel entitled to anything. I wouldn't have asked for the dowry either. In fact, that was Lady Peterborough's idea."

"Your mother."

"Yes. Although, it's still difficult to think of her that way. She may have birthed me, but she hasn't been my mother."

"I understand." Max suddenly decided he *did* want an audience with the countess. He went back to something Prudence said. "You really needed that dowry. Lucien tried to tell me so, but I didn't care." Grimacing, he wished he could go back and behave differently that day. "Honestly, if you or Glastonbury had come and asked, I might have given it to you. Which isn't to make excuses for myself."

"Good. I appreciate someone who takes accountability for their actions."

"Is three thousand pounds enough?" he asked.

"It is," she responded firmly. "I refuse to accept more. I have pride, and I value my independence. Or I did before I married Glastonbury. Now, as a wife, I suppose I'm entirely dependent." She shook her head. "That isn't fair. Bennet treats me as a partner."

"He sounds like a good husband. I'm glad for you."

Prudence paused on the path and turned toward him. "Why did you want to meet with me today?"

Max looked into her green eyes. "You resemble him—our father. It's very strange. I thought I was utterly alone after my brother died. There are no cousins or far-flung relatives."

"So if you don't wed and have children, the title will die."

"Yes."

"Then I suggest you marry," she said drily.

"The title means nothing to me."

Her brow creased, and she cocked her head. "But it bothered you to be alone?"

He opened his mouth, then closed it again, not quite certain how to respond. "I loved my father and brother very much. I also loved my mother." He swallowed and stopped himself from mentioning Lucia. Her death had been devastating, and losing his father and brother so soon after had broken him.

"Did you want to meet with me to see if you still felt alone?" She started walking again, and Max joined her. "I'm trying to understand. Like you, I was also alone after my parents died. I expected to be that way forever, especially after you refused to even hire me. I was very fortunate to run into Lucien that day. He completely changed my fortune."

Max thought of Ada and how Lucien had apparently helped her too. "He seems to be everyone's savior."

"It sounds as though that might aggravate you," Prudence said softly.

"He can't help himself when it comes to saving people." Max knew that firsthand, and now began to wonder why Lucien was like that.

"I would think that's a good thing," Prudence mused.

"To answer your question, I wanted to see you because you are the only family I have. I wish my father hadn't been unfaithful to my mother, and that I could speak to him now and ask him why."

Prudence cast him a sideways glance. "Perhaps you should talk to Lady Peterborough."

He was glad she suggested it. "I've been thinking the same thing. Do you think that's a good idea?"

She shrugged. "It couldn't hurt. I didn't particularly want to confront her, so I will understand if you don't. I find that sort of thing—confrontation and the potential for emotional outburst—uncomfortable."

Yes, Max liked her very much. He certainly felt a kinship with her. "Then why did you do it?"

"It's complicated, but I felt I had to. I was in a...bad situation."

"Can I help?"

She smiled at him. "You are giving me a dowry. That is all the help I need."

Max didn't particularly understand, but he wasn't going to probe further. Ada would have asked more questions until she discovered the heart of the matter.

"You're smiling," Prudence said. "You don't seem to do that very often."

Only when he was with Ada. Or thought of her, apparently.

"I haven't had much cause for happiness recently." Until he'd met Ada. Could he stop thinking of her for one moment?

"Because you're too busy being surly?" There was humor

in her voice, and he appreciated that. There was definitely something sisterly about her tone.

"My housekeeper would say so. I didn't think I was doing it on purpose, but I think I might have been." He exhaled. "Like you, I prefer to avoid emotional entanglements." Especially since... Well, since he'd hurt so deeply that he never wanted to feel anything again.

"I can't help but notice you seem to have had a change of heart since Ada visited you. I know her rather well and can imagine the influence she might have had on you. Did she perchance talk you into this?"

"She took me to task for my treatment of you, but I decided to come here after she left. She did, in fact, have an impact on me. She made me see what I'd been missing, namely the people around me, people who depend on me. That includes you."

She looked offended. "I do not depend on you."

"No, but you could. If you wanted to."

"Are you suggesting we behave like family?" She sounded as though she were stuck somewhere between disbelief and sarcasm. He couldn't blame her.

"I'm saying we *are* family, whether we want to be or not." He took a breath, his heart picking up speed. "And I think I might want to be."

"You surprise me, Warfield."

"I surprise myself." Since Ada had lifted him from the abyss, he found he didn't want to fall back in. Perhaps more anchors would prevent that from happening. "You should call me Max."

"Then you must call me Prudence. I've never had a sibling. You had your brother, so I hope you don't mind me relying on you to show me how to act."

"You may not want to do that," he said, shaking his head with a slight smile. "I'm not sure I remember how to be...

close to people." He couldn't quite believe what he was revealing to her. It hadn't been his intent, and yet he couldn't seem to stop himself. But he would—there was no way he would expose his past or the horrible things he'd done.

"Then we'll move slowly. How about we start as friends?" She sent him a tentative look.

"I'm so sorry for the way I treated you." He paused and offered her his arm.

She took it, curling her hand around his sleeve. "I'll be here for you. If you need me to be."

"Thank you." Somehow, he breathed more easily, as if a burden—at least a small one—had been lifted.

"How long will you be in London?"

"I'd thought to leave tomorrow, but Ada—Miss Treadway —convinced me to stay at least one more day. She's dragging me to Vauxhall tomorrow night. You should come." He glanced toward her, but she was looking straight ahead. "If you'd like."

"That would be lovely. I'll speak with Bennet. We'll be returning to Somerset in the next week or so. A night at Vauxhall would be nice."

"Then I'll look forward to seeing you." The words felt odd coming from his mouth, but he meant them. He hoped this indicated he was truly able to move on, to leave the past behind.

～

*S*he didn't want to be in love with him.

Ada turned to her side and scowled into the darkness. Worried Max might try to come to her apartment, she'd had dinner with Evie at her house in St. James's. Indeed, she'd lingered as long as she dared, and upon returning to the Phoenix Club had hurried up to her rooms without stopping.

But Max hadn't come. Much to her annoyance, she was disappointed as well as relieved. Last night had been so wonderful. She'd felt certain she'd have to turn him away tonight. Because she must, no matter how much her heart craved his companionship.

Frustration bubbled inside her. Not with anyone or anything but with herself. She ought to have known better after her experience with Jonathan.

Foolishly, she'd thought age had given her wisdom or at least the ability to behave differently. It had done neither, it seemed, for she threw the covers back and slipped from the bed. Donning her dressing gown and slippers, she took a candle and left her apartment, making her way quietly to the cabinet at the end of the corridor.

It wasn't really a cabinet. Once she was inside, she found the lever that released the false back which was actually a door leading to another, identical cabinet.

Now, which chamber was his? She'd seen every inch of this club and if she had to guess which room Lucien would have given Max, she would say it would be the largest, which was situated in the back corner overlooking the garden.

Creeping as silently as possible, she slowly traipsed to the far corner. Then she stood outside the door and frowned.

Why was she hesitating?

Because she shouldn't be here. He hadn't invited her. Neither had she invited him the previous night, but he'd been in her apartment anyway.

She'd ask him about his meeting with Prudence. Yes, that was an excellent reason for coming to see him well past midnight.

Before she could stop herself, she knocked. A moment later, the door opened, and Max pulled her inside.

"I knew it was you."

"That's a relief. I can't imagine who else you'd be expecting at this hour."

"I should think that would be obvious." His brow arched. "A courtesan."

She wanted to argue, but she knew that occasionally, certain gentlemen—friends of Lucien's—had assignations on this floor. She was not in favor of it since the Phoenix Club was not that kind of establishment.

Narrowing her eyes, she took in his dressing gown and the exposed flesh at his neck. "Did someone offer to arrange that for you?"

"No. Should they have?"

"I would hope not, but I don't have a say in all that goes on here." She set her candle down on a table situated against the wall. Pivoting toward him, she clasped her hands in front of her and flexed her arms briefly. Anxiously. "I came to, ah, ask you how your meeting with Prudence went."

"I was hoping I might see you. I wish the men's club wasn't only open to women on Tuesdays." He gestured to the seating area that dominated the small antechamber.

Ada avoided looking toward the door to the bedroom as she perched on the settee. "Perhaps you should stay another day so you can experience that. It's my favorite night of the week, actually."

He sat down beside her—closer than he had when they'd shared a settee in the library at Stonehill, but not close enough for her to touch him. It was both a blessing and a curse. "I had the same thought. That would also allow me to see Lady Peterborough. I plan to send her a note tomorrow requesting an interview."

"I'm surprised you want to see her."

"Prudence suggested it, but I'd already been considering doing so. I have questions." He frowned into the distance.

"Then you should see her. It sounds like you're having a most productive trip."

"I suppose I am. I like Prudence, but then I expected to since she is your close friend. I think we will get on well, actually."

Ada beamed at him. "I'm so happy. For both of you." She couldn't wait to talk to Prudence about it. Hopefully, she'd be able to see her tomorrow.

"Thank you." He looked at her with a solemn gravity that tempered her joy, but not in a bad way. She could see how much this meant to him. "You've moved me in ways I thought impossible."

Oh dear. He was being irresistible again. But then, she didn't think she could see him any other way. She was absolutely in love with him, and if she didn't run now, she would be caught in the web. If she wasn't already.

She jumped to her feet. "I'm glad to hear things are going so well." She forced a yawn, putting her hand in front of her mouth. "Now, I must get to bed. I've an early morning, and we have an exciting evening tomorrow." How was she going to manage that? Strolling the dim, romantic walks at Vauxhall with a man who made her heart practically burst from her chest? Not to mention the way he made her body thrum with desire. As it was doing at that precise moment.

He stood. "You're leaving?"

"I think I must," she whispered.

"Probably." He sounded resigned. "Would you stay if I promised we would just sleep?"

She wanted to. So badly. She also wanted to return the favor he'd shown her last night.

But no, she could exhibit restraint. She'd already determined that she'd learned from her past mistakes, and she would demonstrate that she wouldn't repeat them.

"I'll have to leave very early," she said.

His eyes lit with warmth. "Just like Stonehill."

Except that last night. "Let us sleep, then," she said firmly. "*Sleep.*"

A few minutes later, she climbed into his bed, making sure to keep at least a foot between them. Sleep, however, did not come easily.

CHAPTER 15

*E*xcitement bubbled inside Ada as Max's coach stopped outside the gate to Vauxhall. She perched on the forward-facing seat with Max while Evie and Lucien sat opposite. They'd meet Prudence and Bennet inside.

"I came by boat once," Evie said. "I should like to do that again. What say you?" She glanced around the coach.

"I'd like that," Lucien agreed.

Max slid a look toward Ada as his hand brushed against hers. All through the ride to Vauxhall, which wasn't short, they'd touched intermittently, but this was a silent communication that he understood why a boat ride would not be appealing.

Ada smiled sheepishly. "I'm not terribly fond of boats."

Evie shook her head, grimacing lightly. "I should think not. My apologies."

"In truth, I've been considering whether I ought to face that fear," Ada said. "Perhaps we should take a wherry ride down the Thames."

Evie's expression brightened. "I'd love to do that with you."

The door opened, and Og helped Ada from the coach. Seeing him here in town, dressed in old but tidy livery, had been shocking when he'd picked her up earlier.

"Thank you, Og," Ada said, giving him a warm smile. She wondered if his demeanor had improved since coming to town as it seemed Max's had.

Evie departed the coach next, then Lucien, and finally Max. Lucien gave Evie his arm, and Ada took Max's. Once they moved inside, Ada immediately saw Prudence and Bennet a short distance away, whom they'd planned to meet just off the Grand Walk.

The orchestra's music drifted from the grove, and the glass lanterns glowed in the trees. People of varying ages and status milled about.

Ada smiled. "The first time I came here two years ago, I thought it was so magical. I still do." She tipped her head up toward Max. "Do you remember your first visit?"

"Not particularly. I think I'd overimbibed that evening. That was a rather common occurrence when I was running around town with Lucien."

"Then we shall make a new memory for you tonight." Ada squeezed Max's arm as they approached Prudence and Bennet.

Ada had seen Prudence earlier in the day and heard her perspective about her interview with Max. She'd come away as positive as Max. Nothing pleased Ada's optimistic heart more.

After exchanging pleasantries with Prudence and Bennet, they all walked into the grove. The crowd was thicker there, and Ada became aware of the way people stared at Max's face before quickly looking away. The more she paid attention to this behavior, the more she noticed the people casting him furtive glances also whispered amongst themselves.

"Evening, Lord Lucien," an older gentleman greeted. The

man was in a group of three couples, just as they were. Ada didn't know any of them. "Warfield?" he asked, his gaze squinting toward Max and then riveting on his scar. "Almost didn't recognize you with that."

"Nonsense, it's clearly him," another of the gentlemen said with a touch of acid. "Don't insult a war hero."

"I meant no insult." The first man gave a slight nod. "My apologies."

"We should be thanking you," the second man said to Max. "I'm glad to see you here in town. It's an honor."

Ada couldn't help smiling. "That's very kind of you to say."

Max's arm stiffened. "We were just on our way to find refreshment." He barely inclined his head before steering them away.

There had been no mention of refreshment. "Is something wrong?" she asked, sensing he was agitated.

"No." His clipped answer said the opposite.

"Let's go for a walk. Alone," she said quietly. She turned her head toward Prudence. "We're going to the Grand South Walk. We'll meet you back here in a bit." She pulled Max away before anyone could ask questions.

When they were out of the grove, he spoke. "Thank you." He was still rigid with tension.

"Is that why you rarely leave Stonehill?" she asked, wanting to lash out at everyone who stared and whispered.

"Partly. Being around people is difficult to manage."

"I'd like to smack every one of them."

He tossed her a wry glance. "I believe you would if you had the chance."

"How about we discuss something pleasant, then. I saw Prudence today. She said she enjoyed your time together, that you were surprisingly charming."

He let out a sharp laugh. "Is she delusional?"

"Not at all. I don't doubt you were charming. You must accept that you are not always a boor."

"Hopefully I will avoid being one tomorrow when I meet Lady Peterborough. She's invited me to call on her at the Duke of Evesham's house."

"You've been there before, I assume? As a friend of Lucien's."

He nodded. "Not in many years. I suppose I shall have to suffer the duke's appreciation for my military service." His lip curled.

Ada recalled his reaction to the praise he'd received in the grove. "Why does that bother you?"

They'd just passed under the first arch, and he steered her down a side path where there were fewer lights. Before she could say more, he pulled her off the walk into the trees and kissed her, his hands pulling her roughly against him as he plundered her mouth. Desire flared, and she grasped his coat, holding him tightly.

Just as quickly as he'd kissed her, he stopped. "Forgive me. I don't know how much longer that will be possible. Kissing you, I mean."

"Because you're leaving London soon?" she asked so quietly that she hoped he heard her.

"Yes. I'm just not...comfortable here. Not in public, anyway. Being alone with you is quite nice."

Ada felt both giddy and somber. "I wish it wasn't so difficult for you to be here."

"It's better than it was on my last visit. Or perhaps I'm just in an improved frame of mind." He took her hand and curled it around his arm once more before leading her back along the path toward the outer edge of the gardens. "I appreciate you taking me away from the crowd. This is what I'd hoped tonight would be."

"The two of us strolling the darkest, most unpopulated walks?"

A smile teased his lips, and she again saw just how devastatingly handsome he could be. "Exactly so."

They walked in silence for a moment, and Ada simply enjoyed his presence. She'd said they'd create a memory for him, but this was for her too. She'd treasure their stolen moments together always.

"I thought I might do one more thing before leaving town," Max said, sparking her curiosity.

"I'm breathless with anticipation."

"Don't say that unless you want me to drag you from the path again."

Heat kindled inside her, and she merely nodded. She would promise nothing.

"I discussed the possibility of hiring a valet with Prudence." He glanced at her in resignation. "You've completely ruined me."

Prudence couldn't help laughing. "That you see a valet as the final piece of your downfall is completely comical."

"I'm still not entirely sure I want one, but I probably need one. He must be the right sort of person, however."

She understood what he wasn't saying. His valet would hear his nightmares. "It might be best, after we find this person, if you are completely honest about what they ought to expect."

"You said 'we.'"

"I did. However, I probably shouldn't assume you want my help."

"I do, in fact. It's only fitting since this is your fault."

She chuckled again. "I will accept the blame and your request for help. But it may take several days."

"Are you trying to manipulate me into staying? I'm not

sure I can withstand the temptation of sleeping with you every night and trying to keep from touching you."

"We did a rather poor job of that last night." Ada had awakened before dawn to find herself entwined with Max. In his defense, it had looked like she'd invaded his side of the bed and basically wrapped herself around him.

"*You* did. I was a model of restraint."

She loved when he joked with her. He'd come such a long way. "To answer your question, I am not trying to get you to stay, though that would be nice. I can conduct interviews and dispatch a few potential candidates to Stonehill. If you trust me to do that."

"I trust you implicitly," he said. "One candidate. You may send *one*. Only the man you think I should hire. If you aren't certain, he isn't right for the position."

Ada practically floated along the path. Having his trust meant more to her than anything. She wasn't sure he even trusted himself. "I can do that." She was determined to find a valet he could rely upon and feel comfortable with— someone he could trust as he did her.

Damn, could she be his valet? She stifled a giggle.

"What amuses you?" he asked.

"I just wondered if I could be your valet, but I'm in no more position to do that than I was to be your steward."

"Because of your commitment to the Phoenix Club." He sounded slightly disdainful.

"It's more than that. It's a commitment I made to myself, to find my own way and be happy with where I am and the choices I've made."

"Choosing to work for me wouldn't have made you happy?" Now he sounded upset.

Ada hesitated as she tried to think of how to answer that. She had an important role at a hugely successful club in

London. She met all sorts of people, and the potential to keep learning new things was considerable.

But the real truth was that working for him *wouldn't* make her happy. She'd already worked in a household and fallen in love with its master, much to her detriment. She had to expect it would be similar if not the same with Max. He wasn't offering to make her his viscountess. Goodness, she couldn't even imagine that.

In the end, she said, "I think we both know that my working for you would be an irresistible temptation that is best avoided. Now, let's go look at the cascade. It's only open a short time." She pulled him in the direction of the fake waterfall.

"You're so managing," he muttered.

"You like me that way."

"I do." His response was low and seductive. She ignored the pulse of lust it sent through her.

When they arrived at the waterfall, they met the rest of their party. While Ada was glad, she was also sorry her time alone with Max had come to an end. Until later. When she slept with him.

She really needed to put a stop to that.

They watched the cascade in motion—sheets of tin accompanied by the sound of roaring water. "This is water I can appreciate," she said with a laugh.

"Shall we visit the hermitage?" Evie suggested.

Ada slid Max a secretive smile. "Yes, let's. I have it on good authority that Warfield is inordinately fond of hermitages."

Max rolled his eyes. "She's exaggerating."

"I think we must hear this story," Lucien said with a laugh.

Max complied. "After seeing the folly at Stonehill, she asked if that's where I'd been hiding the past few years."

"That is not what I said!" Ada laughed. "Not exactly, anyway."

They strolled to the far corner where the relatively new hermitage stood. Once there, they could turn onto the Dark Walk, though Ada didn't see the excitement in that now that she and Max were no longer alone.

Suddenly, a boom sounded, followed by lights in the sky.

"The fireworks!" Prudence exclaimed, turning her head up.

Another boom and more lights.

Ada grinned into the heavens. "I love fireworks, don't you?" She looked to Max, but he was not gazing upward like the rest of them.

He stared straight ahead, his face pale in the faint illumination from the lanterns and the lights dazzling the sky. She watched his features as another loud crack filled the air. He flinched, and she thought he might run.

"Max," she whispered, moving close to him and taking his hand. "Are you all right?"

"We need to find cover." He looked about, his wild gaze landing on Lucien. "Lucien! Get the women down!"

Lucien came toward him quickly, his expression distressed. "It's all right, Max. It's just fireworks." He touched Max's arm, but Max threw him off.

"It's not all right! We need to get out of here!"

"Yes, we should." Lucien spoke calmly, then looked over to Glastonbury. "Give me a hand?"

Ada didn't see this going well. Instinct told her she had to be the one to help him. She moved between them and Max, putting her body in front of him so her back touched his chest. "Don't come closer." She turned to face Max, lifting her hand to his cheek. "Max, let's go. You can protect me."

Someone gently grabbed her elbow. She looked over her shoulder to see it was Lucien.

"Ada, he thinks we're in the war," he whispered.

She'd assumed as much. "He'll be fine. Just follow us."

Taking Max's hand, she quickly walked the way they'd come.

"No! We need to hide." Max pulled her into the trees and crouched down, tugging her with him.

"Yes, this is safer." She hated the fear in his gaze, the coiled tension in his body. She worried that at any moment, he might explode. If he did, she'd no idea what would happen.

They crouched like that while the fireworks blazed overhead. The rest of their party remained on the path, and though Ada couldn't see their faces, she could feel their concern.

Her thighs burned as they stayed low to the ground, but she didn't dare move or speak. At last, the fireworks stopped. Silence filled the air.

Ada watched Max's face—his features remained taut, but the terror in his eyes had lessened. "Is it safe now?" she asked.

"I'll check." He stood. "Stay here."

Rising, Ada rubbed her aching thighs through her gown. Max went out onto the path where Lucien met him. A moment later, he returned for her. "Lucien says it's clear now."

"Good." She smiled, unsure what to do once they were on the path. Go back to the club, she supposed. This was not how she'd envisioned tonight.

When they were back on the walk, Max blinked. He looked around, his gaze fixing on Ada and then the others until he finally settled on Lucien. Opening his mouth, he seemed about to speak, his brow creased in befuddlement. He snapped his lips closed and scowled.

Ada pressed herself against his side, thinking he might just have realized where he was. "Shall we go?"

Max wiped his hand over his eyes. "I'm sorry." The apology was a ragged whisper. "That hasn't happened in a long time. I thought I was past that, except for the nightmares."

He'd kept his voice low, so Ada didn't think the others had heard. Still, she didn't want to take the chance that they would. She motioned at Lucien to go ahead and did the same to Prudence, who nodded in response.

The other two couples started along the path back toward the front gate while Ada walked a bit behind them with Max, her hands curled around his right arm.

"I've embarrassed you," he said.

The self-loathing in his tone made her want to weep. "Not at all. I didn't realize the fireworks would upset you. I should have known."

"Why would you? They're pretty and entertaining. I'm an aberration."

"You are not!"

He withdrew from her. "I need a moment." He walked to the outer wall, covered by shrubbery, and put his back to her.

Ada longed to go to him, to comfort him, but she wouldn't intrude. She looked to her left to see the other two couples were now several yards ahead of them—already past the next walk where the cascade was located.

A trio of young man approached. They talked loudly and weaved as they walked. Ada could practically smell the gin from where she stood. She stepped back, nearly to the trees to give them a wide berth.

"What's this?" one of them said, moving close to her. "All by your lonesome, sweeting?" His gin-soaked breath filled the air, and Ada brought her hand up to her nose.

"I'm not," she said firmly.

"Not anymore, love," another of them said as they encircled her. "Give us a kiss now." He reached for her.

Before Ada could cry out, before she could call for Max, he was there.

And he brought the darkness with him.

CHAPTER 16

$\mathcal{M}$ax watched the men close in around Ada, and for a brief moment, he couldn't move. The air left his lungs in a rush. His feet were rooted in the ground.

No, he wasn't losing someone else.

He launched himself toward them, the warm air washing over him, reminding him of another summer night when violence had been necessary. Gripping the back of the coat of one of the men, he pulled him to the ground, then stepped on his chest as he moved toward the assailant who had his hands on Ada.

The world blurred around him, but Max focused on the ruffian who was trying to kiss her. Grabbing the man by the shoulder, Max whipped him back before putting his fist into the man's face.

The criminal staggered back, and Max kept after him, hitting him viciously over and over. Another of the men tugged at Max, but Max kicked back. From the corner of his eye, Max saw the third man run toward him. After hitting the man in front of him again, he turned. But he wasn't fast enough to stop the blade that pierced his shoulder.

Max barely felt the sting as he circled his hand around the man's wrist, squeezing until he dropped the weapon. With a low cry, Max hit him hard in the gut. Then again. And again. The ruffian doubled over, and Max sent an upper cut to his jaw, snapping the man's head back.

The other two men came at him, catching Max's arms and waist. Whirling about, Max fought brutally, his fists and feet flying. He hit the ground hard, one of the men landing on top of him. Max's hand grazed something in the dirt—the knife. Clasping the handle, he drove it into the man's side, then pushed him over to the ground.

Max didn't hesitate as he leapt up and went after one of the other men. He was vaguely aware of more people. The ruffians had help.

Growling and baring his teeth, Max sprang forward and slashed at one of the brigands. They were faceless animals, threats he needed to kill.

"Max, stop!"

But he was already in motion. And he needed to prevent these men from taking Ada from him. God, they hadn't, had they?

Max had missed the man, so he lifted the knife for another swipe. A man's hand collided sharply with the base of Max's wrist, sending the knife flying.

Then a body slammed into him, driving him to the ground once more.

"Max, you have to stop. You're safe. *Ada* is safe."

Max fought to breathe—landing on the ground had knocked the air from his lungs again. He blinked several times, and the blur around him came into focus. Lucien's face hovered above him, and to the right, Glastonbury.

Where was Ada?

Max pushed Lucien away, then rolled to his side and leapt up. He looked around wildly.

"Careful, Max. Just take it easy." Lucien touched his arm, and Max shook him off.

"Where is she?"

"Here," Ada said, coming into his line of sight. Her face was pale, her eyes wide.

Relief poured through him, but it was fleeting. He spun about. "Where are they?"

"Gone," Lucien answered. "We fought them off, and they carried their wounded comrade away."

The man Max had stabbed? "He's not dead?"

"Not yet."

"We need to go after them." Max turned, looking for where they'd gone.

Lucien grabbed him again, more forcefully this time, his fingers biting into Max's arm through his coat. "No, just stop."

With a low, furious cry, Max hit him in the jaw. Lucien stumbled back. "I don't want your fucking help."

"Warfield, he's not your enemy," said a man, who Max assumed was Glastonbury.

"He's not my friend either."

"You can't mean that." A woman's voice, but Max didn't think it was Ada.

He couldn't look away from Lucien. "You can't keep from meddling in everyone's lives, whether they want you to or not. You always think you know what's best, that you can fix everything."

"That's not how I think." Lucien set his jaw, his eyes narrowing as he brushed his hand across his reddened cheek where Max had hit him.

They'd done this before during one of the times Lucien had come to Stonehill. It infuriated Max that Lucien continued trying to help when it was clear he wasn't wanted. "What will it take to get you to leave me alone?"

"Nothing," Lucien said fiercely. "I will never abandon you."

Max shouted in rage just before he lunged forward, wrapping his arms around Lucien's waist and taking him down to the ground. They landed in the dirt, and Max rose over Lucien, hitting him in the jaw.

Lucien had started the previous fight, hitting Max after he'd said something particularly insulting. Mrs. Bundle's arrival had stopped them after a few blows. No one was preventing this tonight.

"Max, please don't!"

That was Ada.

Lucien's fists slammed into Max's gut, pummeling him before Lucien tried to shove and buck him off.

Someone pulled at Max's coat. Snarling, he turned his head, ready to strike at whoever would dare to interrupt him.

Ada jerked her hand back, her gaze terrified. "Max, *please.*"

Max dropped his hand. He would have hit her. *No, no, no.*

He was a beast.

When Lucien again pushed at him, Max rolled to his back and let his arms fall onto the dirt. He stared at the sky and waited for the blows to fall.

"Let me help you." Glastonbury offered his hand.

Max took it, and the other viscount pulled him up. Shame and revulsion swept through Max. He couldn't bring himself to look at Ada. Or anyone, really.

"I'll get a hack," he muttered before taking off toward the entrance. His shoulder screamed with pain. He'd forgotten he'd been stabbed.

Ada caught up to him. "We came in your coach. I'll go with you. Prudence and Glastonbury will take Evie and... Lucien." She'd hesitated to even say his name.

"Are you all right?" Max was torn between wanting to check every inch of her to ensure she was safe and not wanting to see the fear in her eyes. So he stared straight ahead.

"I'm fine."

"How can you be fine?"

"I'm better than you," she said wryly. She gripped his elbow, and he started. Glancing at her, he saw the color had returned to her cheeks. Good.

He bent his arm and held it for her to clasp. He could at least pretend to be a gentleman.

When they arrived at Max's coach, Og gaped at him. "What the hell happened?"

"A drunken ruffian got a little too close," Ada explained.

"You're all right?" Og apparently wasn't satisfied with Ada's answer.

"I'm fine."

Og's deep frown remained. Max reassured him that he was all right before helping Ada into the coach.

As they moved away from Vauxhall, seated together on the forward-facing seat, she turned toward him. "That was not at all what I envisioned for tonight."

He couldn't imagine it was. He'd been a fool to think he could enjoy normal activities, that he could mingle amongst regular people. He was scarcely better than the animals who had attacked her.

She twisted her lips, her gaze settling on his right shoulder. "We need to get your coat off so I can look at your injury."

He pulled the garment back, wincing as it cut into his shoulder.

"Careful," she said, helping him ease the coat down his arm.

Tugging it down his other arm, Max tossed the garment

onto the floor of the coach. Then he removed his hat and sailed it to the opposite seat.

Ada frowned at the wound. "Waistcoat too."

Together, they worked that garment free, and it joined the coat.

"I suppose that's one way to justify new clothing," she quipped softly. "Not that you needed justification." Bringing her knee up, she half knelt on the seat, pushing herself against the cushion to allow light from the lantern so she could better investigate the wound.

"How bad is it?"

"A nasty scratch, really, thanks to your clothing. The bleeding has stopped, so I don't think you'll need stitching. I'll bandage it up when we get to the club. I should see if the cook has any poultice or herbs to help it heal."

He watched as she studied him intently, her face full of concern and gentle, but firm, capability. He thought in that moment that he might love her. That if he could ever love anyone again, it would be her.

Emotion welled in his throat. "I'm so sorry that happened to you, Ada." His voice croaked.

She straightened her leg and sat back down beside him. "I'm all right. Truly. I've fought off randy ruffians before. After I left my family, I had to fend for myself for several years."

He stared at her, uncertain if she was trying to make light of the situation or if she actually thought she could have defended herself alone. "There were three of them. And one had a knife."

"In any case, this is a moot conversation since I didn't have to fend for myself. I had you." She stared at him, and he nearly flinched at the depth of caring in her eyes. "Were you still in the war? From the fireworks, I mean."

"Not exactly. I just saw that you were threatened, and I

moved without thinking. I did everything without thinking." Just as he'd done that summer night three years earlier.

And he'd nearly hurt Ada. He could never let that happen.

He looked out the window into the dark night as they made their way toward the bridge that would take them to the other side of the river and to St. James's. "You can't fix me," he said softly, agony tearing at his insides. "I'm irreparably broken."

She cupped his cheek, drawing his head back around to look at her. "I refuse to believe that. You were wounded —*are* wounded. It will take time to recover, but you *will* recover."

He looked into her eyes and basked in the fierce devotion she had for him. How had he ever managed to deserve that from her? "You've no idea what I've done. There's no coming back from it." His insides twisted. In some ways, this was worse than any of the pain he'd suffered before. Or it would be, if he told her.

"Tell me," she said evenly, her gaze holding his with a command he didn't dare refuse. "I promise I won't judge you. I could never think badly of you." She continued to caress his cheek, soothing him, but only superficially. The devastation he felt cut straight to his soul.

He couldn't look at her, at the inevitable horror that would fill her expression. So he closed his eyes and leaned his head back against the squab. He forced himself to breathe, to try to calm the incessant racing of his heart. It hadn't slowed since the fireworks.

"It was a summer evening like this, three years ago. Lucia —she was my betrothed, and we planned to marry in the autumn. She followed the army, cooking for us, washing, ensuring our camp was as much of a home as it could possibly be." Max smiled, her face brilliant in his mind. "She was bright and cheerful, hopelessly optimistic even in war."

He cracked one eye open to see Ada watching him intently. "Like you in many ways."

Ada answered with a soft smile. "She sounds lovely."

He closed his eye again. "I loved her so much. I envisioned a life for us in Spain after the war, but everything changed that day. She'd made supper for me before going to wash clothes in a nearby stream. This wasn't unusual or dangerous. She'd gone to that very spot many times before. While I was eating, one of the boys who helped at camp came to tell me she was in trouble, that I needed to go."

Max swallowed, the memory moving slowly in his mind, ensuring he recalled each detail. As if he could forget. "I got up, fear churning in my belly so that I nearly vomited. I put on my coat and grabbed my hat, then went to saddle Arrow."

His voice nearly broke as he recalled his beloved horse. Why had he sent him away? Because between what Arrow had seen in Spain and the loss of Alec from an accident on his own horse, Max hadn't wanted to see the animal again. He thought of Prudence and the way he'd treated her—she couldn't help who her parents were or how she'd been born any more than Arrow was responsible for the tragedy Max had experienced.

Ada had dropped her hand to his lap, taking his hands between hers. Her gentle stroking gave him ease and...courage.

"I found Lucia near the stream. They'd choked her to death—her beautiful throat was purple already, her ebony eyes staring sightless at the sky." The pain was both fresh and distant. Max hadn't allowed himself to remember her like that in some time. In his nightmares, she appeared thus, her gaze accusing him in death of allowing her to die. "They hadn't just killed her, you understand." He wasn't sure if she could hear him—his voice was barely audible, the words so difficult to utter. "Her skirt was torn, her legs splayed—"

She squeezed his hands. "I understand. I'm so sorry, Max. I can't imagine what that was like for you."

"Think of the very worst thing and then magnify it by a thousand and a thousand more. Infinity, perhaps." He squeezed his eyes more tightly shut and grimaced against the wave of torment.

"Rage doesn't begin to describe what I felt. I went in search of them, uncaring how many there were or what weapons they had. I found them not too far away, laughing and drinking, utterly careless as to what they'd done or that there could possibly be repercussions." The memory was clear as he'd crept upon their encampment. However, from the moment he rushed forward atop Arrow, everything jumbled together—sound, smell, pain, fury.

"I rode Arrow into their camp and cut them down one by one until they pulled me from the saddle. Then I flew at them with my sword and my gun. One of them threw hot water at me—they'd been preparing their meal. That's how I was burned." His scarred face and shoulder twitched in recollection. "They shot me and cut me too. I don't remember any of it, not specifically. I just remember knowing I was going to die and that I didn't care. It was an honorable death, a necessary death, avenging Lucia."

Max felt wetness on his fingers. He opened his eyes to see Ada wiping her cheek. She dashed the back of her hand over her eyes. "I'm sorry."

"Don't be," he said softly, hating that he was hurting her. "I should stop."

"No, I want to hear the rest. Obviously, you didn't die."

"No." He took a deep breath. "Lucien came. The boy had told him what happened and that I'd left camp to find Lucia." The remaining memory was so clouded. It was chaos, really. But he remembered Lucien and his cold fury. "Lucien killed the rest of them. There were eight in total, but he won't tell me how many I took and how many were his. He says it doesn't matter."

"I think I agree with him," she said quietly, her hands still stroking his—methodically and with great care.

"He shouldn't have come."

"It sounds as though you'd be dead if he hadn't."

"Precisely. I didn't want to live without her. What was the point?" He let out a haggard breath and shifted his weight on the seat. "I was severely wounded. It was several weeks before they sent me back to England. By then, my father had died, which I learned before departing. When I arrived home, I discovered my brother had died too."

"He was thrown from a horse."

Max shouldn't have been surprised that she knew that. She'd conducted a rather thorough investigation at Stonehill.

"Is that why you sold Arrow?" she asked.

"I wouldn't have brought him back to England with me. He is emblazoned on my mind with the horror of that day."

"You told me you didn't finish meals because you were interrupted once. It was the boy coming to tell you about Lucia."

"Yes." Oddly, he'd eaten everything on his plate the past two days. He hadn't said anything to Ada about that, however. Perhaps he was afraid the change wouldn't last.

The coach fell silent. Though Ada wasn't pulling away— on the contrary, she continued to hold and comfort him— Max feared he'd finally turned her against him.

He stared at the opposite side of the coach, "I am not a good person, Ada."

"I don't believe that. You survived the unimaginable."

Glancing toward her, he gritted his teeth. "You didn't see what I did to those men."

"I told you that I wouldn't judge you. Please stop asking

me to. I wasn't there. Answer me one question: are you sorry they're dead?"

She'd cut right to the heart of it. Max had asked himself that question a thousand times, along with whether he would do it again if given a second chance. "No, I'm not sorry."

She exhaled and gave his hands a gentle squeeze. "What I don't understand is why you're angry with Lucien or think that he isn't your friend. From my perspective, he is the most steadfast and loving of friends. When people like that come into your life and stand by you…" Her voice trailed off briefly. "You don't refuse them."

He suspected she was speaking from experience, as a young woman who'd been utterly alone. "Who is that person for you?"

"Evie. And Lucien, to a certain extent. But Evie is the reason I am not eking out a living God knows where with a child who depends on me."

A child? Max never imagined she could have pulled him so quickly and thoroughly from his tortured thoughts. "You have a child?"

She met his gaze. "No. And I will tell you that story later since we are revealing our darkest truths. However, before we arrive at the club, I need you to understand that what happened tonight is not proof that you're a bad person."

Of course she knew that was exactly what he was thinking. "When I saw those men touching you, menacing you, I wanted to kill them. I may have, if not for Lucien and Glastonbury intervening."

"I think you should remember that you were fighting in a war. I'm sure there are many other things you saw—and survived—that are terrible and that may even haunt you. The way you've suffered since then, especially after everything you endured, is, I think, to be expected. You weren't just wounded in your body—you were also wounded in your mind."

She'd managed to put into words what the last few years had been like for him. As he'd healed on the outside, everyone expected him to just return to normal. Those who knew him, anyway. Those who didn't startled in fear or revulsion when they saw his face, confirming what he knew to be true—that he was a beast, unfit for human companionship. His external scars had helped to keep the internal wounds from healing.

"My body could be fixed," he said woodenly. "Mostly," he amended, gesturing toward his face. "But how can anyone repair my mind, my soul?" He genuinely wanted to know.

He suspected he already did.

"I think with time and with people who care for you, it's possible to heal," she spoke confidently, captivating him with her certainty. "To overcome that which you think is impossible and not only survive but flourish."

"How are you so wise about this?"

"Because I had the same wounds, only they weren't in my body at all. I carried guilt and self-loathing, and it was magnified by my brother and sisters. I saw myself as a worthless person, and it wasn't until I became what I thought I should be—someone who deserved to be treated badly— that I realized I didn't want that. Furthermore, I *wasn't* that person, even if my family thought otherwise."

He stared at her in awe. "You have such courage and strength. I feel rather weak next to you."

She tightened her grip on his hands. "No! You aren't weak at all, and don't you dare think that. As I said, it takes time to overcome wounds, to heal. You've been doing that—slowly. If you can't see the progress you've made in the past few weeks, then I will entertain the notion that you are at least feeble-minded."

That she could provoke him to feel a flash of amusement in this moment was astonishing. "I wouldn't want you to think *that.*"

"Good, because I wouldn't anyway." She narrowed her eyes at him. "You are, however, wrongheaded about Lucien."

He heard what she was saying, and she wasn't wrong. He hadn't meant what he'd said earlier about Lucien not being his friend. "Because of Lucien, I am a celebrated war hero. The truth, however, is that I attacked a squadron without provocation and had no orders to do so. Lucien reported to our superiors that we happened upon them by accident and had to defend ourselves."

"So you're angry with Lucien for not only saving your life, but also for protecting you from court-martial?"

"You make me sound ridiculous." He looked away.

"That is not my intent. You've been living under the belief that you deserved to lose everything. But I am glad you did not, and I am especially grateful to Lucien for being such a good friend to you."

"I did something stupid and horrible, and I shouldn't be rewarded for it. They want to elevate my title to an earldom." He curled his lip.

"Would you rather tell them the truth and see what happens then?"

His gaze snapped to hers. "I wouldn't do that to Lucien. He would suffer the same consequences as me. More, probably, since he lied."

A smile curved her lips. "You still care about him, then. I'm pleased to hear it." She glanced toward the window. "We're here."

The coach creaked to a stop, and a moment later, the door opened. Ada swept up his garments, including his hat, and stepped down with Og's assistance.

Max climbed out and immediately met Og's still-concerned face. "Are you sure you're all right?"

Ada took Max's arm. "He will be after I tend to him inside."

Og looked slightly relieved. "Are we still returning to Stonehill day after tomorrow?"

After tonight, Max wasn't sure of anything. "I'll let you know. Night, Og." Max walked toward the club with Ada.

She hesitated. "I don't want to go in through the club. I know how much you dislike people staring at you, and your lack of clothing along with your bloodied shoulder will attract all manner of interest. Let's enter on the side, down through the kitchen where I can fetch medical supplies, then we'll go up to my room."

Without waiting for his response, she started toward the right of the building, where he'd stolen into the ladies' side the other night. He followed her down the stairs to the entrance, but before she could open the door, he pulled her away, pinning her back against the outer wall. She held his garments between them.

"I will never understand why what I did tonight didn't prompt you to run away from me as fast as possible. I nearly hurt *you* in my frenzy." The thought of that brought an agony he'd hoped never to experience again.

She lifted her hand to his cheek. "But you didn't, and I trust you never will. The fireworks triggered something for you and put you in a terrible place. Then those ruffians accosted me, and you reacted from that place. It was a perfect intersection of awfulness for someone with your...wounds."

"You think those two things happening together is why I reacted that way?"

"I think it makes sense, and I love for things to make sense."

He stared at her clever eyes and her pert nose, the strong

jut of her chin. She was the most sensible person he'd ever met. "Nothing has made sense for me in years," he whispered. "Not until you."

Lowering his head, he kissed her, his mouth covering hers. She slid her hand back to his nape, holding him as she leaned into his embrace.

She kissed him until he was breathless, pulling back and bringing her palm down his throat to tug gently at his cravat. "Let's go up to my room." She narrowed her eyes slightly. "To clean your wound."

"All right." He tried not to sound disappointed.

"And I'll tell you my story. We'll see what you think of me then."

CHAPTER 17

*A*da finished tying the bandage that covered Max's shoulder and angled around his torso under his other arm. He looked like he was wearing a sash.

"Does it still hurt?" she asked as she tidied up, taking the basin of bloody water to a table near the door.

Max sat on a chair in front of the hearth, his head angled as he tried to see her handiwork. "Not really. Thank you."

Ada went back to him and sat in the other chair. "I suppose you're waiting for me to tell you about the child." She hadn't intended to tell him about it, but after what he'd shared with her, she wanted to, especially if it meant he would let Lucien back in.

"Only if you want to," he said quietly. "Don't feel as though you must."

"But I do. Your rift, or whatever it is with Lucien, troubles me. Friendship sometimes means doing hard things. Such as telling someone they're being foolish when they absolutely are."

"Is that what Evie did for you?"

Ada nodded. "Do you remember the lover I mentioned?"

At his nod, she went on. "I was pregnant and despondent. I didn't want to bring a bastard into the world." Her insides clenched—that was only part of it, and she couldn't tell him the rest. He would be horrified by her behavior. This much was shameful enough. "As an unwed mother, my choices, which were already slim, would be practically nonexistent. I'd already had to leave my position as governess."

"He should have married you."

Jonathan had loved her, but he was married. She couldn't bring herself to tell Max, knowing how upset he was about his father's infidelity. Max would never look at her the same way again. "He couldn't, and there's no sense being upset with him. It was *my* foolish behavior."

"What did you do?"

"I took Evie's advice, and I decided not to have the baby. There are...ways to do that." She clasped her hands in her lap. "I don't regret it. Sometimes I think of the child I might have had, and I feel sad, but it was the right thing to do—for me and the child. What I do regret is putting myself in a situation where I had to make that choice. I should have known better."

He was quiet a long moment before asking, "Is that why you try so hard to resist what we feel for each other?"

He'd seen clear through her. "Yes. Our attraction is something I should avoid." She said it with a light laugh, but that came from unease. It was more than just the physical pull they felt toward each other. She had to protect her heart. She didn't want to talk about that, so she diverted the conversation. "What are you going to do about Lucien?"

Max leaned back, frowning. "I don't know. Perhaps I'm angry with him so that I'm not always angry at myself."

"You shouldn't be angry at either."

He took a labored breath. "I failed to protect Lucia."

Ada heard the pain in his voice and would have done anything to take it away. "Don't let guilt rule your life."

"I should listen to you—since you're an expert on such things. I am trying."

"I know. I do think forgiving Lucien and reestablishing your friendship would help. As hard as you think that might be."

He ran his hand through his blond hair, tousling it so that she longed to make it tidy. No, that was just an excuse to touch him. Her fingers practically itched with the need to do so. After everything he'd told her tonight, she wanted to hold him, to comfort him, to give him the solace he needed.

He wiped his hand over his mouth and sat straighter in the chair. "I'll try. Lucien will crow about that, I imagine."

"I don't think he will. He only wants you to get better. His concern for you has been at the crux of everything he's tried to do with and for you."

"When he came to ask for Prudence's dowry, he tried to persuade me that forging a relationship with her would be good for me." His jaw tightened. "He was right."

"I'm so glad you changed your mind about that."

His eyes met hers. "You were right too. About everything." He let his gaze dip to her breasts and then lower, heating her already aroused body, before finding her face once more. "It's a pity I can't show you how much I appreciate you."

"It's not even your turn," she said, sliding from the chair onto her knees. Moving forward, she gripped his thighs and positioned herself between his legs, which he widened to accommodate her. "It's my turn to appreciate you."

"Ada, I thought you were trying to resist me."

"There can be no harm in this, can there?" She glanced toward his thick erection straining beneath his clothing. Then she looked up at him, working hard to keep the love from her expression. It was difficult. "If I can't touch you after all you've shared with me tonight, I'll go mad. Will you let me?"

"Only if you let me do so in return." He caressed her cheek and cupped her chin. "That's not negotiable."

She nodded. "All right."

He leaned forward and captured her mouth in a sweet but savage kiss, his lips and tongue plundering hers as he held her. His other hand gripped her head so he could keep her captive as he deepened the kiss, forcing her head back.

Desire throbbed between her legs as she clutched his thighs, her fingers digging into his breeches. She moved her hands up, searching for the buttons. Finding them, she plucked them free, anticipation building with each one.

She pulled down the fall and slid her hand into the slit of his small clothes. His cock nestled there, thick and hard, his flesh warm and smooth against her. Tucking her fingers beneath him, she encircled him with her hand and moved from the base to the tip, where she pushed back the skin and skimmed her thumb across the top.

He moaned into her mouth before pulling away and falling back against the chair. He slouched down, giving her better access. It wasn't enough, however. She wanted him bare.

Reluctantly, but necessarily, she let him go to quickly remove his boots. He growled, sounding most aggrieved until he realized what she was doing. When she tugged at his clothing, he lifted his hips so she could more easily peel it from him.

As she exposed his flesh, she licked her lips, then tossed the garments away, including his stockings. Her gaze fell on the scar on his thigh. It was the worst one, really. Long and still reddish where the rest were pink.

"This must have been awful," she whispered, tracing her fingers along the ruined flesh.

"I barely felt it when it happened. Later, it was terrible. I think it was a bayonet. It apparently came quite close to severing an artery that would have caused me to lose all the blood in my body."

She snapped her head up. "I'm incredibly glad it didn't." She pressed her lips to the scar, then glided her tongue along the rigid flesh.

He moaned, and it was the most intoxicating sound she'd ever heard. Emboldened, she continued her path upward and then to his cock. It stood proud and eager for her touch. Blond curls cloaked him at the base. She cupped his balls, massaging them gently as she watched liquid bead on the tip.

Max thrust his hand into her hair, dislodging strands so they floated against her cheeks and temples. He gripped her head as she lowered her lips to him, kissing his shaft before curling her hand around the base. She licked him, moving up to the tip where she spread the liquid there with her thumb.

He held her tightly, his thighs tensing around her. She put her mouth over him and pressed her tongue against him. Then she began to move very slowly, using her hand and mouth in concert.

He growled and moaned, making all manner of erotic noises that aroused her even more. Her breasts tingled, and her sex throbbed. She wished she was bare too. But then the temptation to climb atop him and ride him to their mutual release would be impossible to avoid.

Suddenly, he dragged her from him, tugging her hair, but not painfully. His cock left her mouth, and she looked up at his lust-dazed expression. "What's wrong?"

"I can't enjoy this without you. Do you trust me?"

"Of course."

His eyes glittered with sensual promise. "Then I'm taking you to bed."

~

*M*ax hauled Ada to her feet as he stood, nude, and swept her into his arms. He carried her swiftly into her bedchamber and set her down next to the bed. "Too much clothing." He started to unfasten the front of her gown, which had a drop front.

She put her hands over his. "I'm not sure I can resist you if I'm naked too."

He smiled at her, kissing her softly. "You said you trusted me. I won't risk a child, and I don't mean that I'll leave your body. We're going to enjoy each other just as we were—but together. You haven't done that before?"

"No. Show me." Her eyes narrowed seductively.

He unfastened her gown and helped her out of it, then moved on to her petticoat. She turned so he could loosen her corset. That joined the other garments on the floor, leaving her in just a chemise, which she quickly drew over her head.

No, that wasn't accurate, for she was still wearing her boots, stockings, and garters. Max lifted her onto the bed, then crouched down to remove her boots, working quickly. When they were gone, he trailed his fingertips up her calf to the inside of her knee. He untied one garter and stripped it away with the stocking. Then he moved to her other leg and performed the exact same series of actions. When he was finished, her thighs were quivering.

He stood up between her legs and put his fingers on her sex, teasing her flesh. "You are so wet already."

"It's rather humiliating how much I want you." Her cheeks flushed.

"It's damned intoxicating." He bent his head and kissed her as he stroked his fingers into her.

She gripped his upper arms as she spread her legs wider and began to fall backward. He eased her down, never ceasing his thrusts into her wet channel. Breaking the kiss, he moved his lips down her throat into the valley between her breasts before sliding to the right and taking her nipple into his mouth.

He sucked hard, and she bucked up. He'd already been barreling toward his orgasm when she'd had her mouth on his cock, and if he wasn't careful, he was going to explode.

Pulling away from her, he worked to draw a deep breath. It was a trifle difficult due to the height of his excitement.

"I'm going to lie down, and you're going to get on top of me so that you can finish what you started. Understand?"

Her gaze was dark and heavy lidded. "I think so." She moved to give him room.

Anticipation screamed through him as he climbed onto the bed and positioned himself. He flattened his palms against the coverlet.

She flicked a glance toward his cock, her brow creasing so that those adorable pleats he loved formed between her brows. "And I'm to straddle you?"

"Put your mouth on my cock, Ada. Then let me put my mouth on your pussy. Now, please?" It wasn't a command, but if she didn't move quickly, he was going to frig himself out of desperation.

Her hair was still mostly held up by pins, but dark strands caressed her face and nape. She tucked errant curls behind her ears and lowered her head to his waist. She grasped his cock and put him in her mouth. Then she moved over him.

The scent of her arousal filled his senses as he clasped her thighs and positioned her. He started with his thumb, swirling over her clitoris. He'd forgotten the focus it took to give while receiving, but he was so eager to taste her again.

Holding her open with his thumbs, he licked inside her, thrusting his tongue in and out as he'd done with his fingers. She began to move against him, her hips rolling with a persistent rhythm that he responded to with his own body.

She sucked him deep, then lifted, her hand moving up his cock along with her mouth. His hips rose with her as pleasure coiled within him.

He increased the pressure of his tongue and moved one thumb up to her clitoris. She answered by taking him farther into her mouth and closing harder around him, her hand stroking him with ruthless, relentless vigor. The she cupped his balls, squeezing gently as she drew him to the back of her throat.

He cried out against her and gripped her backside, digging his fingers into her flesh as he rushed toward his orgasm. Working his thumb furiously over her clitoris, he speared his tongue into her and licked at her wet folds. Her muscles quivered, then clenched, and he sensed she was about to come.

Good, because he was lost.

Her muscles tensed as his hips jerked. Hell, he had no idea if she wanted him coming in her mouth, but it was too late.

Eyes closed, he fought to deliver her into ecstasy while riding his own. He'd no idea what he did next. There was only bliss and satisfaction and the desperate need to never let her go.

At some point, she left him, and he heard her deep, rapid breaths that matched his own. He worked to steady himself —his limbs were shaking. Damn, he didn't remember when he'd felt this *good*.

He felt the bed move and opened his eyes. She'd turned around and moved next to him.

"That was…astonishing," she said, pushing hair out of her face. More of it—much more—had come loose.

"I thought you might enjoy that."

"I think it's my new favorite thing." Her gaze fell on his

shoulder, and she gasped, her eyes rounding. "You're bleeding!"

He'd completely forgotten about his wound. "It doesn't hurt." Well, now that they were talking about it, it did.

She sat up and untied the bandage, which was close to her. Carefully, she lifted it from the wound. "It's just a trickle. Still, we should not have done that. I'll make a fresh bandage and re-dress it." She looked him in the eye. "Don't move."

"I don't think I could if I wanted to. You quite ruined me."

"Sorry."

He smiled. "In the best way." He pulled her head down and kissed her soundly but briefly. "Thank you."

She left the bed and went back into the main room. When she returned, she had a new bandage and a damp cloth, which she used to clean the wound again.

Max closed his eyes as she cared for him. He could get used to this.

To what exactly?

To her. With him. All the time.

He loved her, he realized. But he didn't want to. The pain that came with losing that love wasn't worth it. Ada had been right. He *was* wounded. What she couldn't realize was that, like the scars on his body, those wounds would always be there. He was not the man he was before, nor could he ever be. She deserved a whole man—someone who could be as brilliant and rapturous for her as she was for him.

That wasn't him.

She finished tying the new bandage around him. "There we are, all better. Now, no more exerting yourself."

He opened his eyes and looked up at her. She'd let her hair down and tied it over one shoulder with a ribbon. "You helped."

Her lips parted, and she gave him a scolding stare. "You're

teasing me." Then she laughed. "That is so delightful. You must do it again."

"Alas, I suppose I must dress myself and find my way to my chamber."

She shook her head firmly. "Nonsense. I said no exertion. That includes putting on clothes and leaving the bed. You're sleeping here, and I won't brook any argument."

"I would never argue with you." He couldn't stop the grin that split his lips.

She laughed. "You're rather good at this teasing thing."

After tidying up from rebandaging him, she helped him under the covers then rounded the bed to climb in herself. Turning toward him, she asked, "Do I need to put on a night rail, or will you behave yourself?"

He reached for her hand and brought it to his lips, kissing the knuckles. "Do you really think a night rail is sufficient barrier for either of us?"

She blew out a breath, making a silly sound with her lips. "You make a valid point. We shall both have to do our best. I don't want you opening that wound again, though. Do you understand?"

"Yes, mistress."

She smiled, then leaned over to kiss him before rolling to her side.

He stared at the back of her head and basked in the joy that always surrounded her. Somehow, she'd managed to not only bring it to him—she'd given it to him when he'd thought he could never feel it again. Whatever happened tomorrow or the day after that, he'd be forever grateful to her.

CHAPTER 18

*A*da helped Max back to his room early, but it was well past dawn. They'd overslept. She wasn't surprised, considering the excitement of the night before. She helped him get into his own bed and instructed him to go back to sleep to help his shoulder recover.

As she'd kissed him goodbye, she wondered if that would be the last time. Presumably, he'd leave tomorrow. Which meant they had tonight. But should they spend it together knowing they would part in the morning? It was getting more and more difficult.

For her, anyway. She'd no idea how he felt, and she didn't have the nerve to ask him.

What would he say? That he hated to be apart from her and wanted her to be his wife? There was no way he was ready to do that now—he was still healing. And when he was himself again, or as much himself as he could hope to be, there was no telling what he would do. He'd been clear about his intent to remain unwed and to allow his title to go extinct.

Last night had been full of revelations. She now fully

understood the weight of his burden and the depth of his guilt and despair. She also saw that he *was* healing, despite what had happened at Vauxhall.

It was difficult not to abandon her work in favor of checking on him. Had he already gone to Lady Peterborough's? Ada was eager to hear how that went. Hopefully, she'd see him tonight on the men's side of the club. After last night, there was no guarantee he would want to be in a group of people.

But it could be his last night in London. If he didn't come, she might consider pushing him into it. When he returned to Stonehill, he could go back to being a hermit.

The thought of that tore at her heartstrings.

It occurred to her in that moment that she ought to perhaps push herself. She'd been thinking of what Evie had said in the coach about taking a boat to Vauxhall. It was, mayhap, time to conquer her fear of the water.

She could take a small boat out onto the Serpentine. That would be easy enough. But the Serpentine was hardly the type of water that made her quake. Oh, she'd avoid it most certainly, but if she truly wanted to overcome her terror, she should take a wherry down the Thames.

The idea made her blood turn cold.

Perhaps she could ask Max to come with her. She knew he would. Even so, she couldn't depend on him—*shouldn't*. It would make his eventual departure that much more painful.

Evie or Prudence, or both of them, would go with her. They could make a day of it, perhaps traveling down to Hampton. Well, perhaps not *that* far.

Before she could relegate it to the back of her mind, Ada gathered her courage and stood from her desk. She made her way down one flight of stairs to Evie's office.

The door was open, so Ada stepped inside. Evie sat behind her desk writing, the late morning sun streaming from behind her. She looked up and smiled, but a touch of concern marred her normally smooth brow. "Good morning, Ada. I didn't want to bother you after last night's excitement. How is Warfield?"

Ada considered prevaricating, but Evie wasn't stupid. She at least knew that Ada had cared for his wound upon returning to the club. "His injury wasn't that bad."

Evie stood and moved around her desk, gesturing to the settee before taking a seat. "And his general demeanor? Is that improved?"

Sitting beside Evie, Ada again decided not to lie. "I think so. The fireworks seem to have put him in a place where he thought he was at war again. Then those men accosted me, and he reacted in a violent manner. He was quite shaken by it all."

"I could see that. He was also rather angry with Lucien." She frowned. "Lucien would not explain it to me. I don't suppose Warfield told you the truth of the matter?"

"That is between him and Lucien." It was the most diplomatic thing Ada could think to say. She absolutely wouldn't break Max's confidence. "I did advise him to speak with Lucien and to mend their breach, if he could."

"Will he?" Evie clucked her tongue. "I've never seen Lucien upset like that." That was saying something since Evie knew him perhaps better than anyone. She'd been his mistress for some time, and they were still close friends. Ada had asked her once if there was any hope for them in the future. Evie had responded there was not, that she had no romantic feelings for him, nor did he for her.

Ada shrugged. "I can't say for certain."

"You and Warfield seem rather close. Dare I hope there is something between you?"

"Why would you, of all people, hope for that?" Ada asked with a laugh. Evie was as against marriage as a person could be. As a former courtesan, she had no desire to be owned by a man ever again. She had no need of their money, and she argued that love could be had without the bondage that marriage required.

"Just because I don't wish to be a wife doesn't mean you shouldn't." Evie held up her hand before Ada could speak. "I know you prefer to remain unwed, to cling to your independence. But sometimes I think you're trying to emulate me."

Ada appreciated Evie's shrewdness, and she wasn't wrong. "I did once; however, I am quite content to be Ada Treadway, bookkeeper. For the first time, I feel needed and important, that my loss would be felt. I don't know that I can trade that for anything." Emotion tickled her throat, and she coughed gently.

"Hear, hear," Evie said softly. "I'm so very proud of you. I will be forever glad for the day we met in that tearoom in St. Germans."

"No more than I." It was there that Evie had detected Ada's sorrow. She'd just left her position as governess a few days before and was trying to determine how to make her way as an unwed mother without employment. Evie had taken charge, drying Ada's tears, and counseling her on how she could reclaim her life.

Buoyed by Evie's support and instant care for her welfare, Ada had decided not to have the baby. After a short time, Evie and Ada had traveled to western Cornwall. Those months had shown Ada what the life of an independent woman could be—and she wanted that.

Now she had it.

"I came to see if you might help me face my fear of the water."

A look of distress passed over Evie's features. She reached over and touched Ada's forearm. "Is this because of my insensitive comment last night?"

"Yes, but that's not a bad thing, truly. In helping Max—Lord Warfield—to heal, which requires him to overcome his own fears and challenges, I find I am somewhat of a hypocrite. So I'm going to get on a boat. I'd thought to take a wherry from the Horse Ferry perhaps down to Somerset House." She shuddered. "Will you come with me? I plan to invite Prudence too."

"Of course! Though, Prudence may not want to get on a wherry if she feels sick from the babe."

Prudence was expecting a child, which only a select group of people knew. Ada had talked Prudence through her shock and fear at learning she was pregnant—that was before she'd married Glastonbury. Fortunately, all had worked out well and they'd discovered a mutual love and devotion, but it hadn't been easy.

"That's certainly true, though I think she's felt well for the most part. I'd like to go tomorrow."

"So quickly?"

"I don't want to lose my nerve."

Evie grinned. "Then, let's do it. I'll arrange for someone to pick us up at Somerset House."

Joanna, one of the footwomen appeared in the doorway of the office. She wore a puzzled expression. "Pardon me for interrupting. There's a gentleman here to see Miss Treadway." She darted a glance toward Ada. "I told him that we don't receive gentlemen on this side of the club, but he was most insistent."

Ada's first thought was that it was Max, but it wouldn't be him. He knew the rules of the club and had demonstrated his ability to circumvent them. This sounded like someone who didn't know what the Phoenix Club was and had arrived here looking for Ada.

"We'll have to receive him on the men's side," Evie said

with authority, standing. "Instruct him to go to that door, and I'll have Sebastian show him up to Lucien's office."

Joanna nodded, then left.

Ada rose, wondering who it could be. "Before you ask, no, I don't know who it is. I'm as perplexed as Joanna."

"We shall find out soon enough." Evie preceded her over the threshold, and they made their way to the men's side, arriving quickly at Lucien's office.

Seated at his desk reading, Lucien looked up as they entered. "Good morning. Am I in trouble?"

"No, why would you think that?" Evie asked.

"Because you're both here, and last night was, ah, difficult."

"You aren't in trouble," Ada said, moving into the office to stand near the settee. "We aren't even here about that."

"How is Max?" he asked quietly.

"Better than you probably think," Ada responded. "I'm hopeful that you'll hear that from him, and that's all I'll say on the matter. We're here because a gentleman has come to see me. Evie thought I could use your office."

"Actually, I said 'we' would receive him," Evie clarified. "If you think I'm leaving you alone to meet some unknown man, even in the security of the club, you don't know me very well."

"Perhaps I should stay too," Lucien offered, rising from his chair.

Ada exhaled. "While I appreciate you both very much, I am a grown, independent woman."

Sebastian appeared in the doorway, his blue gaze sweeping the occupants of the office. "Mr. Jonathan Hemmings is here for Miss Treadway."

Thankfully, the settee was close, for Ada sank onto it, her jaw dropping just before she clapped her shaking hand to her mouth.

Evie sat down beside her. "Oh dear. You can't want me to leave now."

"Then I'm staying too," Lucien said, walking to the far side of the fireplace, where he leaned against the mantel.

Ada wasn't at all sure she wanted them as an audience for whatever Jonathan was here to say. But she also wasn't able to form words at the moment. She'd never thought to see him again.

"Show him in," Evie said, giving Ada's suddenly frigid hand a squeeze.

Jonathan entered, hat in his hands, his familiar face tugging at something deep inside Ada, something she'd thought forever buried. His brown eyes crinkled at the edges, his mouth splitting into his charming, boyish smile. "Ada, you look well."

Somehow, she managed to speak. "As do you. I'm shocked to see you, however."

His focus darted to Evie and then Lucien before settling on Ada once more. She answered his silent question. "Allow me to introduce my employers, Lord Lucien Westbrook and Mrs. Evangeline Renshaw."

Jonathan bowed. "I'm so pleased to meet the people who've given my Ada a haven."

Ada bristled. *His* Ada?

Smiling tightly, Jonathan continued, "I wonder if we might have a few minutes alone to speak privately. I've some news I wish to share with Ada."

Ada whispered to Evie, "I'll be fine. Would you mind waiting outside and taking Lucien with you?"

Evie squeezed her hand again before letting it go. "I'll be just outside if you need me." She stood and looked to Lucien, silently indicating he should go with her.

Lucien didn't seem to want to, but he went, his gaze fixed on Jonathan. "We'll be *right* outside."

The door closed, leaving Ada alone with the man she'd once loved. The man whose child she'd carried and who'd broken her heart. No, she'd served up her heart to be broken by engaging in such a foolish affair in the first place.

Ada hadn't meant to fall in love with Jonathan, even knowing his wife hadn't loved him herself. Their marriage had been arranged when they were children, and Letitia had made no secret about not even finding him attractive. Ada sometimes wondered if the things Letitia said had prompted Ada's tendre for him, that perhaps she'd felt bad for him to be trapped in a marriage in which neither he nor his wife were particularly happy. Like Ada, Jonathan deserved to be loved and appreciated. Though they'd tried to resist their mutual attraction—and had for over a year—their lonely hearts had latched on to each other, and Ada had convinced herself that it was all right, that what they shared was pure and true, even though he was already married to another. She hadn't thought past her own need for love and intimacy. In many ways, she felt as much guilt for her behavior with Jonathan as she did for her sister's death.

Jonathan came to perch beside her on the settee, pulling her from her reverie. He angled his body toward her and set his hat down behind him on the cushion. He gazed at her with an expression she'd seen many times—abject longing. Did he still harbor feelings for her? "You look so very well."

"Thank you. I am well. How did you find me?"

"I hired someone, actually. It took some time to locate you." He glanced around the office. "What sort of club is this? What is it you do here?"

There was a touch of alarm in his questions, and she wondered what he thought the Phoenix Club was. "It's a members' club—for men and women. It's unlike anything else in London. I am the bookkeeper." She cocked her head. "What did you think I was?"

Relief relaxed his features. "Honestly, I had no idea. But when I was told the other side was for women only and this side was for men, my imagination ran a bit wild."

"Did you think I'd become a prostitute?" She'd told him what she'd done that one time, when she'd been at her absolute lowest. "I said I'd never do that again."

"I know, but life can be difficult." He reached for her hand. "I would never judge you for it, my darling. I still love you so very much."

His feelings hadn't waned. She never expected this. "Why are you here?"

"Letitia died last year giving birth to our fourth child. She's a girl, which has delighted Rebecca."

Ada was sad that his wife had died, especially in childbirth. It was one of her greatest fears. Leaving a child motherless and vulnerable was perhaps the primary reason Ada had decided not to have the baby. "I'm so sorry about Letitia." She patted his hand and then drew hers away, which was awkward since his hand was in her lap.

He took the hint, however, and pulled it back. "It has been difficult, particularly on the children. Rebecca has tried to play mother, which shouldn't surprise you."

Rebecca was his eldest daughter, a commanding and inquisitive child whom Ada had adored. She would be ten by now. There were also two boys, daring and playful.

"No, that doesn't surprise me," Ada murmured. She did miss his children. And for a long time, she'd missed Jonathan.

"You can probably imagine why I've come." His eyes held an expectant glimmer.

"I can't, actually." Did he want to ask her to return as his governess so they could continue their affair? She'd never told him about the child. What would have been the point? She'd simply given her notice, saying she'd found another position.

"I want you to be my wife. To be the mother of my children. They adore you so. They can hardly wait for me to return with you."

She blinked at him. "You told them you were coming to see me?"

"To *fetch* you. Honestly, part of the reason I decided to look for you, aside from my own desires and the love I still have for you, was them, Rebecca in particular. Six months after her mother died, she came to see me and said it was time I found a new mother for them. She suggested you, but I must confess I never stopped thinking about you. Our months together were the happiest of my life. I'm ashamed to say that Letitia's death filled me with hope that we might have a future together. I'm so pleased to find you haven't wed someone else."

Ada couldn't help feeling a rush of happiness that Rebecca wanted to have her for a mother. But then she felt a surge of dread that Jonathan's feelings hadn't changed while hers had. She decided to ignore the latter in favor of the former. "I do miss the children. They're all well?"

"Very, including the babe. Her name is Constance."

All the air left Ada's lungs. "Not for me?" She practically squeaked the last word.

"Only I know that, but yes. As I said, you've never been far from my mind, Ada. Or my heart. I would have started to search for you sooner, but I thought I should observe a mourning period—for the children."

This was so strange and unexpected. Ada felt as though she were watching this encounter as a spectator, as if it were happening to someone else. She couldn't return his sentiments as much as she might want to. Did she want to? This was all she'd wanted for so long—a family to call her own, a place where she was wanted and needed. "I've, ah, been so fortunate here at the Phoenix Club. I am quite content."

"I'm relieved to hear it, but you can't want to stay here forever? I want you to come back to Cornwall with me. You'll be mistress of Tidwell and mother to four children who already love you—plus any others we will have together." His brown eyes shone with love and hope.

Ada couldn't ignore that it was tempting, especially the part about future children. She'd never even dared to dream that would be possible, that she and Jonathan could live happily as husband and wife with children of their own. To do so would mean she'd wished for his wife to die, and she'd never wanted that.

"This is such a shock," was all she could manage to say. She was more than happy at the Phoenix Club and with her current life.

A life that, at the moment anyway, included a certain viscount she was, unfortunately and unrequitedly, madly in love with.

"I can imagine," he said. "I'm sure you need time to think and to adjust to such a big change. You seem to have a good life here, and I presume leaving it might be difficult. I can only hope you'll want to." He gave her a warm, encouraging smile, reminding her of his kindness and concern, traits she'd adored, especially after the cold bitterness of her own family.

She would at least do him the courtesy of considering his proposal. It was the sensible thing to do, and if she'd learned to be nothing else, she was sensible. He was offering her a lifetime of security and love. A family. A permanent place. "I presume you're staying somewhere in town?"

"Yes, with an old friend from my school days—Reginald Huxton."

"I know Reggie. He and his wife are members here." Ada had no idea they knew Jonathan, but then why would she?

"I didn't realize. I wasn't specific about where I was going today." He lifted his hand as if he were going to touch her again but then changed his mind and set it back in his lap.

Ada gently exhaled with relief. She wasn't entirely sure how she felt about seeing Jonathan again, but she knew she wasn't ready to resume their relationship. She stood, eager to be alone with her thoughts. Or at least not with him.

Jonathan also got to his feet. "When can I see you next?"

"I'm not sure. You've given me a great deal to think about. I do have a good life here and I'm very happy."

"You look happy. There's an air of joyful calm about you, but then you always possessed such a positive energy."

"You used to say I was brighter than the sun." She felt a surge of nostalgia and perhaps a bit of sadness for what she'd lost. But she'd come to terms with that some time ago.

"You still are." He took her hand and kissed the back. "You know where to find me. Just know that I'll be back if I don't hear from you soon."

She followed him to the door, holding it as he left. Evie and Lucien stood just inside the members' den. They watched as Jonathan walked from the office, then hastened to join Ada.

"What did he want?" Evie asked.

Ada blinked as if she were coming out of a trance. "His wife died. He asked me to marry him."

Evie's eyes rounded, and Lucien wiped a hand over his face.

Evie looked at her expectantly. "What did you say?"

"That I had to think about it." Ada's insides roiled—this was so utterly unexpected.

"Are you truly considering it?" Evie sounded as if she were holding her breath.

"I don't know. I think I'd be foolish not to. There's a great deal of security in being a gentleman's wife." It was as if she were trying to convince herself, which she supposed she was.

"You have security here," Evie said, sounding irritated. "This is far greater than anything a *gentleman* can give you. Particularly one who took advantage of his station as your employer."

Ada wasn't surprised by Evie's reaction, nor did it bother her. "I was as much to blame as he was. He didn't take anything I didn't freely offer." She belatedly realized they were having this conversation in front of Lucien. Heat climbed her neck, and she cast a nervous glance toward him.

"I'm afraid I agree with Evie," he said. "He absolutely took advantage, even if you encouraged him. Gentlemen don't conduct liaisons with their governess or any of their other employees, for that matter."

Ada knew she'd been naïve and forlorn. She'd wanted a connection with anyone, and Jonathan had wanted that too. "But he's here now declaring his love and proposing marriage. Our behavior in the past was wrong, but I won't blame him for it when I was an eager participant."

"Do you still love him?" Evie asked softly. "When I first met you, I wondered if you'd ever get over leaving him. But you haven't mentioned him in a very long time. Indeed, I'm not sure you spoke of him after we left Cornwall."

Because Ada had promised herself that she would leave him and the love she'd felt for him there when she'd come to London with Evie. So, she'd never spoken of him.

Evie's question thundered in her mind: did she still love him?

"No, I don't love him anymore." The answer came fast and certain. "I am fond of him, and I always will be. He gave me solace and hope when I had none."

A shocking thought rose in her mind: perhaps she hadn't really loved Jonathan at all. Or perhaps it was that her love, or the way she loved, had changed. Because what she felt for

Max was wholly different. Max made her *feel* brighter than the sun.

But Max wasn't offering marriage nor would he ever.

"If you'll excuse me, I've work to do." Ada summoned a half-hearted smile and returned to the ladies' side of the club.

CHAPTER 19

The Duke of Evesham's butler showed Max up to the drawing room. In his youth, Max had been in this house several times before with Lucien. It looked much the same and still carried the austere elegance one would associate with the duke.

But Max wasn't here to see Lucien's father. He was calling on Lucien's aunt, Lady Peterborough. She was currently residing with her brother after leaving her husband's household. Prudence had told Max that once her existence was known, Lord Peterborough had tried to send his wife to a convent in Wales. Evesham had intervened and brought his sister here.

Lady Peterborough was not in the drawing room when Max went in. The butler left him to meander about the room. He removed his hat and did a circuit before realizing he was nervous. He took a position near a window and Lady Peterborough swept in, her dark-brown-and-gray hair intricately styled atop her head, a coral necklace at her throat, and a persimmon gown cloaking her round frame.

The countess didn't get very far, for as soon as she saw

Max, she stopped short, her gaze fixing on him. "Good heavens, you look even more like your father now." She blinked and moved toward him. "Except for those nasty scars, of course." She spoke matter-of-factly, without a hint of malice, and he assumed she was a woman who said what she wanted. He respected that. It also meant he would learn what he came to discover. He hoped that would be the case.

"You knew my father very well," he said, not certain how to begin.

She laughed softly as she sailed to a chair near the center of the room and sat down. "I think you know that since you are aware of your half sister, who is my daughter. Thank you for giving her a dowry, even if it was late." She wrinkled her nose slightly as she clasped her hands in her lap.

Max took a chair opposite her and rested his elbow on the arm. "I was quite shocked to learn about her," he said evenly. Hell, if she was going to speak plainly, so was he. "I keep saying that, but the truth was that I was hurt and furious to learn my father had been unfaithful to my mother."

"And not just with me." She pressed her lips together. "You may not have known that. I apologize."

"I did not," he said tightly, wondering if he'd ever known his father at all. "I suppose that means he didn't really love my mother, that he was unhappy with her."

"I don't think that's necessarily true." The countess tipped her head as she regarded him. "Honestly, he didn't talk about your mother, and I didn't ask."

"I believe you were otherwise occupied," he said sardonically and with a hint of enmity.

"Being lovers, you mean. It was more than that. I cared deeply for him. He was a wonderful man. His death saddened me greatly."

He didn't give a damn about her feelings regarding his

father. "Wonderful men aren't adulterous." Max hated him anew even as he missed him terribly. "His death devastated me, as did my mother's."

"Of course," she murmured. "Why have you come today?"

This was where he struggled to explain. "I suppose I wanted to know about your relationship with him, whether you loved each other."

"I have been trapped in an unhappy marriage, and your father was charming and complimentary. He made me feel... exceptional." There was a glimmer of something in her eye. She may not have loved his father, but he could see that she had indeed cared for him.

"Did my mother know about you or Prudence?"

"I don't think so, but I can't say for sure. Your father was very supportive when I told him I was carrying. I'd hoped Peterborough would just accept the child as his own since I'd already given him an heir and a spare."

"He refused?" Max knew the answer, but wanted to hear her tell what happened.

"Oh, yes. He was beyond furious. He sent me to a convent until I birthed Prudence. Your father had arranged for her care."

"My father did that?"

"Yes. He wanted to ensure our child was adopted by a family, that she would be raised in a good household. Prudence's adopted father was a teacher. She's well educated, if you don't know."

Max heard pride in her voice. "Was it difficult to give her away?"

"Nearly impossible. But I had no choice. Your father considered taking her, but it was a flight of fancy. He admitted he couldn't. I suppose based on that, it's likely your mother wasn't aware of me or Prudence."

Thinking back to his mother's death, Max recalled his father's grief. He'd certainly appeared to love her. "I'm struggling to understand my father's infidelity. I never would have guessed he loved anyone other than my mother."

"Perhaps he didn't. One does not need to be in love to engage in an affair. You haven't loved all the women you've… well, you know. Have you?"

Of course he hadn't. But it had been a long time. He'd loved Lucia desperately. And since her there had only been Ada. He was fairly certain he loved her too. The anguish that caused him nearly bent him in two.

"I have been in love," he said softly as he looked her dead in the eye. "And I would never be able to be with anyone but that woman." He suddenly wondered if he was somehow being unfaithful to Lucia. No, she would want him to carry on. Of that, he was certain.

"Your father would be proud of you. I understand things have been difficult for you since returning from the war. You were terribly wounded?"

He nodded. "I'm getting better, however."

"I'm so glad to hear it. I saw Prudence yesterday, and she said that you and she had a nice walk the other day. She also said she thought you might carry forward as siblings. Your father would be thrilled to know that. I hope that gives you solace."

He didn't want it to—because he was still angry with his father—but it did. And he supposed that was why he'd come today, for whatever insight into his father this woman could provide. Knowing that he'd arranged for his daughter's care and would be gladdened for her and Max to be siblings made him feel…lighter. It made him think the anger he felt would fade in time. Perhaps this was like his other wounds, and with time and care, he would overcome the pain and forgive his father. Ada would say that was a brilliantly sensible way to think about it.

Max stood. "Thank you for seeing me today."

"You even sound rather like him." A wistful smile curled her lips. "It was my pleasure to spend time with you, Warfield. I hope I'll see you again."

"I suppose we will since we appear to be family. Good day." He turned and left, making his way downstairs. As he stepped into the entry hall, he saw Lucien doing the same, coming from Max's right.

Sporting a bright yellow cravat, Lucien blinked in surprise. "I didn't realize you were here."

"I called on your aunt."

"I hope that went well."

The air between them felt stilted, but Max supposed that was appropriate since the last time they'd seen each other, they'd exchanged blows. Everything Ada had said to him about Lucien and their friendship rose in his mind—loudly.

"It did. I take it you just met with your father," Max said, nodding toward his cravat.

Lucien glanced down. "You remember?"

"That you wear ridiculously colored cravats to annoy him? Yes." Max couldn't help smiling, which was odd since until a fortnight or so ago, he could barely force himself to do so. "Does this mean your relationship with him is the same as ever?" The duke favored his eldest son and heir and his youngest child and daughter. Lucien had somehow always been lacking.

"It may be marginally improved, actually, likely due to his other two children being happily wed. That would never prevent me from taunting him, however," he added with a grin. "In any case, he'll soon realize I'm still a disappointment to him, and things will worsen once more."

"You sound resigned."

Lucien shrugged. "I have no expectations for improvement. Are you on your way back to the club?"

"I am. I walked."

"Do you want company?"

The old Max—the one who'd never met Ada Treadway—would have scowled and said no. But he began to think that Max might be gone, or at least greatly diminished. "I would, thank you."

They left the house and made their way from Grosvenor Square toward St. James's.

After a few moments, Max said what he needed to, "I want to apologize for last night."

"There's no need. The fireworks set you off."

"I thought we were back in Spain. Then those ruffians surrounded Ada. It was as if I finally had the chance to save Lucia."

"Christ." Lucien clapped his hand on Max's shoulder briefly.

Max winced and pulled away. "That's where I was stabbed."

"Shit. Sorry!" Lucien looked stricken.

Then they both laughed. For far too long. Max didn't remember laughter feeling *that* good.

Lucien glanced at him as they walked past Chesterfield House. "You're all right, though?"

"The shoulder's fine."

"And…the rest?"

"You mean my mind and my demeanor? I won't lie—it's difficult. I had a hard time leaving my bedchamber today."

"Is it often like that?" Lucien asked softly.

"It depends on what you think is often," Max said wryly. "Ada has a theory that I'm wounded on the inside and finally starting to heal. I think she must be right since I haven't laughed like that in years." Aside from laughing with Ada, Max didn't remember the last time.

"You and she seem to have formed a bond."

"I don't know about that, but we've become friends, I suppose. She managed to bring me out of my stupor, or whatever you want to call it."

"How?"

"Hell if I know. I found her thoroughly annoying. She's also persistent and so bloody cheerful."

Lucien grinned. "She wore you down."

"That's probably the best way to characterize it. But it was more than that. She showed me how I was neglecting the people at Stonehill. I may not care about the estate, but it's their livelihood, and I owe it to them to keep it up."

"She did what I was unable to do during my many visits." There was no anger in Lucien's statement. Indeed, he sounded almost wistful.

"It wasn't for your lack of trying. Unfortunately, I think you were doomed to fail—and that was entirely my fault. I was never going to let you save me again. Not the way my mind was working." Before Ada had brought the light into his darkness. Max met Lucien's eyes. "I know it doesn't make sense, but you were there. Surely you know—"

Lucien touched his sleeve. "I know. And I should have realized we were dealing with what happened in very different ways. I never should have expected you to respond as I have."

"And how is that?"

"Well, I'm not going to discuss it." Lucien smirked. "*That* is how I deal with it." He inhaled sharply and looked forward. "Since you are dedicating yourself to Stonehill, does this mean you've changed your mind about marrying and providing an heir?"

"Nothing has changed on that front."

"What about Ada?"

Max nearly stopped. Thinking of her and an heir in adjacent thoughts made him feel... He didn't know how it made him feel. He flexed his hands as they walked. "What about her?"

"There's no chance you could be more than friends? That perhaps there's a chance for a future at Stonehill?"

"You are as meddlesome as Ada."

Lucien grimaced. "I was only asking."

"There is nothing between me and Ada." Nothing that wasn't temporary anyway. "I'll return to Stonehill—probably tomorrow. I'm deeply grateful for her help, but she's quite happy at the Phoenix Club. She truly loves her position there, if you don't already know that."

"I do know that. She does an excellent job." Lucien frowned, and Max could practically see the wheels turning in his mind. That was another thing he had in common with Ada. They were both loud thinkers.

"Is there something else you feel the need to say?" Max suppressed the urge to roll his eyes.

Lucien hesitated before shaking his head. "No."

"I don't believe you."

Exhaling, Lucien pinched the bridge of his nose. "I'm actually trying not to be so meddlesome, especially in relationships. I stuck my nose in a few times recently and have been informed that I should mind my own business."

So he *was* trying to play matchmaker. Since Max didn't want that, he abandoned the topic.

"Speaking of meddling, I'm afraid I did interfere with something." Lucien cast a pained look toward Max.

"Hell, what did you do?"

"I bought Arrow."

Max did stop this time. "My horse?"

Lucien paused, turning toward him. "Yes. He's being delivered tomorrow. If you want him, he's yours."

Max faced him. "Why would you do that?"

"Honestly? It was Ada's idea. She said he was sold at Tattersall's and asked me to find him. When I did, his new owner offered to sell him. It sounds as if he's not happy."

Fuck. Max felt like someone had reached into his chest and was squeezing his bloody heart. "Please tell me you mean the owner and not my horse."

"I think you know what I meant." Lucien twitched his lips in sympathy. "Sorry."

"I'll take him." Max started walking again, his mind churning as they neared Piccadilly. Ada had inquired about Arrow? Old Max would have been furious at her interference. New Max, *improved* Max, wanted to kiss her.

"I'm so glad." Lucien whistled for a moment. "It's Tuesday, which means the ladies come into the men's side of the club tonight. It's the most entertaining night of the week. You should come downstairs. I'm sure Prudence will be there if you'd like to spend time with her. Dougal should be there too."

"Why not? I'm here, aren't I?"

"Should we try the Siren's Call again?" Lucien wondered. "I feel bad about how that ended."

Max recalled how his night had finished and had no such regret. He didn't say so. "I think we've graduated from the Siren's Call. Your club is just fine. Splendid, in fact."

"Good, because I honestly hate going to other places now." Lucien chuckled.

"You really should be proud of what you've built," Max said earnestly. "I'm not at all surprised. You've always been wonderful at bringing people together—and at coaxing out the best in people."

"Not always. You were a tough nut to crack, my friend."

Friend. Yes, they were friends, and Max had been foolish to ever think or say otherwise.

Max paused and turned to Lucien again, the busy traffic of Piccadilly going by despite the seriousness of this moment. "Thank you for saving my life."

Lucien had stopped too, his gaze meeting and holding Max's. "I would do it again."

"Even if it meant getting injured again?" Lucien hadn't been as badly wounded as Max, but he hadn't emerged unscathed.

"Even if it meant death."

"Well, damn. Now I feel *very* badly for my behavior."

"Good, that was my intent." Lucien said with a laugh, and Max joined him.

Perhaps he shouldn't leave tomorrow after all.

~

*B*y the time Ada walked into the library on the men's side of the club that evening, she felt as though she'd been stretched taut on a torture rack. She'd spent the day trying to work and mostly failing as she kept thinking of Jonathan's arrival and proposal. Memories of their time together, of the love they'd shared as well as the very sensible prospect of becoming Mrs. Hemmings, kept pressing to the front of her mind.

Ada went directly to the liquor, where a footman poured her a glass of Irish whiskey. "Thank you." She moved to the corner where she could drink—probably too quickly—in relative privacy. But she kept her eye on the door.

Her vigilance was soon rewarded as Max strolled in. Only, he looked different. She realized his blond hair had been trimmed, and he was wearing what looked to be new clothes. She'd never seen them before and they appeared to be the latest fashion, certainly more current than what he typically wore.

She moved toward him without thinking, as if pulled by an invisible thread. His gaze met hers and seemed to sizzle with heat. Suddenly, the stress that was bunched in Ada's shoulders dissipated. And she hadn't even touched her whiskey.

"Max, you look splendid." She couldn't help staring at him, her body thrumming with desire.

"You are beautiful, as always," he murmured.

"Have you seen the mezzanine?" she asked, overcome with the need to touch him, to kiss him, to somehow alleviate the desperate need pulsing within her.

His brow furrowed, and she took his hand, glad the library was virtually empty and didn't contain any of their friends or family. Keeping an eye out for those very people, she led him quickly to the mezzanine, which was completely empty, as it should be this evening. Then she took him through a pair of draperies into the area that overlooked the ballroom below, which would also be empty, where the orchestra played during the assemblies. The drapes were closed on the ballroom side, so they couldn't see the ballroom below.

She put her whiskey on a table where they kept refreshments for the orchestra. It was nearly dark with only the scant light filtering through the small break in the draperies they'd come through. "I'm afraid I can't resist you at the moment. You look far too delectable."

Ada launched herself against him, curling her hands around his neck. He clasped her tightly, lowering his head to kiss her. Their tongues met in a fierce dance as she thrust her fingers into his newly shorn hair. She stood on her toes, pressing her hips to his, desperate for relief against her sex.

He broke the kiss to feast upon her neck, cupping her nape as she arched backward in his embrace. "If I'd only known I just needed a new costume and a trim for my hair..." He gripped her backside and ground against her, giving her precisely what she wanted.

Moaning, she pulled his head back to hers and kissed him again, greedy for his taste and touch. "I need you, Max. Quickly."

She looked about, wondering how they could accomplish what she wanted, and groaned in frustration.

He cupped her jaw, dragging his thumb across her cheek. "Shhh. Tell me what you want."

"You. Inside me."

He arched a brow. "You're certain?"

She tugged at his hair. "*Please.*"

Reaching for the whisky, he lifted it to his lips and drained the contents. "Don't want it to spill." He smiled seductively before setting the empty glass back down. "Turn and put your elbows on the table."

She stared at him, knowing what he meant, but taking a moment to process it because she'd never done that before. Excitement pulsed between her legs. She turned and leaned over the table.

He pulled her gown up and settled it about her waist. She heard his sharp intake of breath just before his hand moved over her backside, gently caressing her flesh.

"Move your legs farther apart." His voice was low and harsh, and so provocative.

She could have listened to him give her commands all night and probably found her release from that alone. Opening herself up to him, she felt vulnerable, and that made her even more aroused. Her body screamed with want, every nerve on edge waiting for his touch where she wanted it most.

He squeezed and massaged her, attending to both globes of her backside. She was astonished at how his caresses heightened her desire and expectation. Then, at last, he stroked the folds of her sex, and she moaned over and over, her hips moving against his hand.

His touch was relentless, his fingers sliding into her, then rubbing her clitoris in a slow sequence of blissful torment. She gripped the other side of the table and pressed her cheek against the cool wood, closing her eyes as delicious pressure built in her sex. When he removed his hand, she cried out in distress. She'd been so close to her orgasm.

But his cock slid into her, and she cried out again, this time in relief. "Don't let go of the table, Ada. I'm not going to be gentle."

She nearly came right then.

Max seated himself fully inside her, then withdrew. He clasped her hips, holding her firmly as he drove into her hard. Ada held the table and kept her feet planted on the floor as he speared into her deep and fast, filling her with impossible ecstasy. She came like never before, her muscles clenching around him, his primal thrusts prolonging her pleasure.

He left her, and she somehow had the presence of mind to tell him to use her petticoat. He grunted, his legs still moving against the backs of her thighs as he spent himself.

Ada smiled against the table. "Thank you. That was lovely."

"I'm sorry about your petticoat." He smoothed her dress back down.

She straightened, and he held her arm as she turned. "It will be fine. I hope we didn't crumple your new clothing. Whenever did you find time to get that?"

"Lucien asked his tailor to work a miracle today, and his valet trimmed my hair."

"I noticed. You were exceedingly handsome before, but now you completely take my breath away."

"You flatter me." He kissed her again, softly this time, his lips teasing hers.

"And *you* drank my whiskey." She slid her tongue into his mouth and tasted it.

He pulled back, laughing. "I'll get you more. Shall we return?"

"Yes, I suppose we should before we're missed. Should we enter the library separately, I wonder?"

"Will anyone really think we were shagging in the orchestra alcove?"

Ada grinned. "I doubt it." She took his arm.

As they made their way back to the library, she asked how his interview with Lady Peterborough had gone.

"Better than I expected, actually. I thought I wouldn't be able to see past my anger for my father—and for her as the woman who'd lured my father away from my mother."

Ada struggled to take a breath. This was why she hadn't told him about Jonathan, that he'd been her employer *and* married. "I'm glad to hear it went well."

"I still can't make sense of it. Lady Peterborough cared for him, and he must have cared for her. However, he seemed genuinely sad when my mother died and said he'd loved her. I can't understand loving someone and seeking pleasure elsewhere."

That hadn't been the case with Jonathan. He hadn't loved Letitia, and she hadn't loved him. Still, Ada couldn't bring herself to tell Max the truth. Even if he tried to understand, he would never see her in the same way again.

That sentiment made it seem as though she expected a future with him. There wasn't one. He would return to

Stonehill, and she would…what? Continue here in the position she adored or become the mistress of her own house with a family and a man who loved her?

A man she no longer loved or wanted, and those things were important. No, they were vital. Max had reminded her of that just now, just by simply being.

She would visit Jonathan tomorrow and decline his proposal. Immediately, she felt lighter.

"Let's go to the members' den," Max said. "I haven't been in there."

She smiled up at him, grateful for every moment they had together. "Then we must."

This proved to be a very bad decision as the first people they encountered were Reginald Huxton and Jonathan Hemmings.

"Evening, Ada!" Reggie said with a hearty smile.

Ada's heart hammered against her ribs. Her head felt light, and her knees were like jelly. She clutched Max's arm more tightly. "Allow me to present the Viscount Warfield."

Reggie inclined his dark head. "Pleased to meet you, my lord."

Ada forced herself to continue even though she wanted to turn and drag Max to the library. Oh, why hadn't they gone there instead? "This is Mr. Reginald Huxton."

Reggie quickly spoke. "And my guest, Mr. Jonathan Hemmings. He's visiting from Cornwall, but then you know that already, Miss Treadway."

Jonathan's eyes glittered with joy. "I will be so happy when you address her as Mrs. Hemmings."

Beside her, Max stiffened. He turned his head toward her. "What is he talking about?"

Panic clawed at Ada's insides. She blurted, "He asked me to marry him. I haven't yet given him an answer." She sent Jonathan an irritated glance.

"How do you know each other?" Max asked in a rather stilted voice.

"Ada used to work for me," Jonathan said. "Though, that is just how things began." He smiled at Ada as if they shared a wonderful secret.

Max's gaze darkened. "This is the man you told me about?"

She swallowed. "Yes."

His eyes suddenly blazed hot. He looked to Jonathan. "You're just now getting around to marrying her? Not when she was carrying your child?"

Ada gasped, then slapped her palm over her mouth. Had he really just said that out loud?

Jonathan blanched. He stared at Ada. "What child?"

"Er, perhaps we should—" Whatever Reggie meant to say was cut off by Jonathan.

He stepped toward Ada, his expression full of love. "You didn't tell me because of Letitia, because we couldn't be together. Oh, my darling, I'm so sorry. But we can raise our child together now."

Max turned toward Ada, his arm going slack, so she had to remove her hand. "Who is Letitia?"

Jonathan answered. "My wife. She passed away last year."

Max stared at her, his voice and expression frigid, as if he were carved from granite.

Numbness overtook her. "I was their governess. I didn't tell you because I knew it would upset you."

"What a perfectly awful reason to lie. But then I suppose you saw me as too fragile to hear the truth." He spun on his heel and stalked from the members' den.

Ada fought to breathe. She felt as though she were being squeezed from all sides. She'd expected his anger, but not about that. Her fear had stemmed from Max learning she'd carried on an affair with a married man, not that she saw him as weak. That he thought that tore her apart.

Jonathan put his hand on her waist and guided her to the wall. "You look rather peaked, my darling. What can I do?"

She pulled away from him. "Nothing. I am not your darling, nor am I your concern. I should have told you earlier that I don't want to marry you."

His brow furrowed. "But what of our child?"

"There is no child. I chose not to have it."

"I don't understand."

Of course he didn't. "I was foolish to carry on with you, to love you. I was young and vulnerable, desperate for any sort of connection, especially for love. If that's what it even was. I honestly don't know anymore." She knew she was always more concerned for others than for herself. Her family and their treatment of her had taught her that she was of lesser value, that she needed to work hard to care for others and to never let them down.

"Of course it was love," he insisted. "I still love you. So much."

"I'm sorry, but I don't love you." Ada was desperate to go after Max, to beg him to listen. That he thought she judged him too weak to hear the truth nearly drove her to her knees. She put her hand on the wall. "I should have told you when you called earlier, but I was so shocked to see you. Our time together was a lifetime ago. I have a new life now." And she desperately loved someone else.

"It feels like yesterday to me," he said with a touch of defiance.

"Go home, Jonathan." She agonized over the heartbreak in his eyes, but she couldn't change that for him.

Belatedly, she wondered how many people had overheard their conversation. They'd kept their voices low, but whatever damage had been done was unchangeable.

She could only try to repair what really mattered. Spinning about, she rushed out of the members' den and upstairs to Max's room, thinking that was where he must have gone.

Before knocking, she tried to take a deep breath and failed. She'd been an utter fool.

CHAPTER 20

*A*s angry and hurt as he felt learning Ada hadn't told him the truth, Max had to wonder if she'd been right. Perhaps he *was* too fragile. Just look at him, hands shaking, breathing shallow, pulse racing.

It was more than that. She'd kept something from him. Something vital and intrinsic to who she was, while he'd revealed everything. He thought they'd shared a singular connection.

The knock on the door didn't surprise him. He stood there, silently, pondering what to do.

"Max, are you in there? Can I please talk to you?" Ada's voice was dark and anguished.

Without thinking, he went and opened the door.

She was pale, her eyes wide. "May I come in?"

He stepped aside without a word and closed the door behind her. Had it just been a short while ago that they'd shared such fierce, wonderful passion?

Turning toward him, she clutched her hands together anxiously. "I'm so sorry I didn't tell you the truth about Jonathan. It wasn't because I thought you couldn't manage it." She looked away, her cheeks coloring with shame. "I didn't tell you because I knew you'd think less of me given what your father had done. Just earlier, you were telling me about the anger you felt toward Lady Peterborough. *I* am Lady Peterborough—or I was anyway. I couldn't bear your disdain."

This hadn't been about protecting him. She'd wanted to protect herself. He couldn't think of what to say.

He wanted to say that he wouldn't have been angry with her for carrying on with her married employer, but fidelity was important to him. Whether that was because of the strong love he'd felt for Lucia and that he now felt for Ada or due to his father's unfaithfulness, he didn't know. It was likely all of that.

One thing he did know—he wanted to understand. If he could. "You were his governess?"

"Yes. He and his wife had an unhappy marriage. They didn't love one another."

"He took advantage of you." Max despised men who used their positions of power to corrupt, especially when they used it to manipulate women.

She turned from him and went to stand in front of the hearth, her head cast down. "I hadn't thought of him taking advantage of me, but Evie said he did and then Lucien did and now you are. I just wanted someone to care for and someone to care for me. I think in some ways, he felt the same."

The wounded man inside him felt compassion for that young woman, but not for her employer. "No man should engage in an affair with his employee, no matter how he feels about her." He realized he could never have hired Ada to be his steward. There would be no greater torture than having her near and maintaining his distance.

He stared at her back, his insides blistering. "Lucien and

Evie knew all about this. You insisted I bare all to you, that you wouldn't judge me, yet you wouldn't give me the same courtesy?" He felt as though he'd been gut punched.

She faced him, pain etching her features. "I didn't think of it like that. I'm so sorry." She sniffed. "You are such an honorable man. I've let you down, and I'm so ashamed."

Why would she have thought of it like that? They'd made no promises or commitment to one another. She wasn't in love with him, not like he was with her. Nor had he even told her.

"Don't be ashamed. You know I'm nowhere near honorable." In fact, he'd all but announced to the entire club that she'd been unwed and carrying that man's child. "I hope I didn't ruin things for you downstairs. I shouldn't have said what I did."

She shook her head. "Please don't concern yourself with that. I'm sorry you were so shocked—that's entirely my fault, not yours."

"You don't owe me your darkest secrets. You don't owe me anything." He wasn't angry anymore, but the hurt remained. He was such a bloody disaster. *Still.* And he had to expect he always would be. She ought to marry someone like Hemmings. He could offer her a real future, stability. Even if she didn't love him.

"I'm not marrying him. I don't love him."

Had she heard his thoughts? "I'm going to return home tomorrow," he said. "I want to thank you for all you've done for Stonehill. And for me." Parting in this manner was for the best. Anything else would have been difficult and messy.

She nodded. "I will always be here for you if you need me. I hope you'll let me know if I can help with Stonehill."

He wouldn't. "Certainly."

He could see she was upset. But he didn't want to say anything to change that. This was easier—for both of them.

Going to the door, Max opened it. "Good night, Ada."

She walked toward him, pausing at the threshold. "Good night." Outside the door, she looked back over her shoulder. "And goodbye."

Max closed the door and rested his forehead against the wood. The joy he'd felt earlier seemed a distant memory. He wondered if he'd ever feel it again—how familiar that fear was to him.

Pushing away from the door, he went in search of the Irish whiskey he'd had the forethought to ask a footman to bring to his room the day before. Tonight, he would banish his emotions, and tomorrow, he'd return to Stonehill, where he was quite adept at keeping himself stoic.

He just hoped he discovered how to get through the pain of loss—again—without falling into despair.

～

*A*fter sending his cases downstairs, Max made his way to Lucien's office. He'd spent a perfectly horrid night not sleeping. He wasn't sure what was worse—the nightmares or not being able to sleep because he was plagued by doubt and uncertainty.

Leaving was the right course of action. There was no reason for him to stay in London.

Lucien stood from his desk as Max stepped into the doorway. "Morning! What happened last night? I heard you were in the club, but I didn't see you."

"My shoulder was aching," he lied. "I turned in early. I wanted to be fresh for today. I thought I might try riding Arrow for at least part of the trip."

Lucien's brows jumped. "Wonderful! He should be here shortly. I imagine you're looking forward to seeing him."

"I am, actually." More than Max would have thought. He'd

missed his horse. It was just one of the emotions he'd quashed since returning to England.

This reunion with Arrow felt right. He wished he'd been the one to realize he wanted it. But as with everything else in his life since Spain, he'd needed others to give him the push, to make him realize what he ought to do.

"Have you said all your goodbyes?" Lucien asked. "I imagine it will be a while until you return to town."

Max ignored his question. "I suppose I'll come back when Parliament reconvenes."

Lucien grimaced. "I'm afraid you may be an earl by then. I did put it out that you didn't think the elevation was necessary, but the general consensus is that you deserve it and changing the title from viscount to earl is easier than awarding you a new title."

"Is it?" As a second son, Max had never paid any attention to that nonsense.

"How should I know? I know as much as you about such things." Lucien started toward him. "Come, let's go down to the dining room so we can see when Arrow arrives."

Max turned and accompanied Lucien downstairs, where they immediately encountered Glastonbury.

"Morning, Warfield, Lucien." Glastonbury looked to Max. "I brought Prudence to meet Miss Treadway and thought I'd come see if you'd left."

Damn. Max glanced toward the ladies' side of the club. He really ought to say goodbye to Prudence before he left since he hadn't seen her last night. He had, however, sent her a note that morning. Besides, he couldn't just wander into their side of the club, and that had nothing to do with the paralyzing certainty that he'd encounter Ada.

"You seem a bit pained, Max," Lucien noted. "Everything all right?"

"I was just thinking I could say goodbye to Prudence in person since she's here."

"Actually, I think they just left," Glastonbury said. "They're taking an excursion on the Thames."

They were? Damn *and* blast. Max had wanted to take Ada onto the water, to help her conquer her fear. She'd done so much for him. Despite that, she'd said she'd let him down. She could never do that.

He'd let *her* down. He'd turned away from her last night. He'd done the absolute wrong thing, which was to retreat into himself when things became too difficult.

Bollocks. What was he doing?

"You're sure that's all?" Lucien asked.

"No," Max whispered. He wasn't sure of anything. Except one thing—he loved Ada. "I'm afraid I'm broken. That I'm not a whole person."

Lucien stepped closer. "You aren't broken, and you *are* a whole person. You've come so far. Don't lose hope."

"I'd echo that sentiment, if I may," Glastonbury said quietly. "I feared I was broken for a very long time—most of my life, really. My, ah, family has a mental affliction that occurs in many of us, and I was certain I would be affected."

Lucien blinked at him. "I didn't realize that."

"I worked very hard to keep it hidden. My father was terribly afflicted. It is the reason he nearly bankrupted the viscountcy." Glastonbury smiled weakly. "I loved him, but he was exhausting. And terrifying. I never knew what kind of day it would be, whether he'd be happy and more like himself or disconsolate and difficult."

Max's blood went cold. Glastonbury could have been describing him. He'd been that person, and anyone at Stonehill could attest to that. Hell, even Lucien could. Max darted a glance toward Lucien and flinched inwardly to see that he was watching him.

"You are *not* like that," Lucien said, accurately assuming what was racing through Max's mind.

"The hell I'm not." Max's shoulders tensed, and pain shot from his wound. "I've made a horrible mistake."

"You're getting better," Lucien argued. "And it started when she came to visit."

He didn't have to say who "she" was.

Glastonbury looked from Max to Lucien and back again. "Are we talking about Ada? Prudence thinks there's something between her and you."

"There is." That came from Lucien, not Max.

Max curled his hands into fists and held his breath, neither of which he did on purpose. His body had simply tightened up.

Lucien's dark brows pitched into a V. "Dammit, don't make me meddle." He exhaled. "You're going to make me meddle. Don't try to deny there's anything between you and Ada. I know all about the scene in the members' den last night. I didn't realize Huxton's guest would be that dolt who'd come to see Ada earlier in the day."

Max stared at Lucien. "*That's* what you were referring to yesterday when we walked back from Evesham House. You bloody well should have meddled *then*."

Lucien put a hand on his hip. "Indeed? What would you have done? Would anything be different this morning?"

No, because *Max* was the dolt. And he was paralyzed by fear. "I can't lose her like I lost Lucia." His voice was barely audible.

"So it's better to leave her?" Lucien shook his head. "That makes no sense."

Glastonbury grinned. "It makes perfect sense. Fear makes us do incredibly stupid things—I should know. And fear when we're in love? Well, that makes us complete idiots." He pinned Max with a serious stare. "Do you want her?"

"I do. But I don't think she wants me. Not…forever."

"Why wouldn't she?"

"I told you. I'm broken."

Lucien snorted. "That wouldn't deter Ada. She'd spend her life fixing you and be happy to do it."

Max glowered at him and realized he hadn't glowered at anyone in a while now. The muscles felt a bit tired. "I don't want to be her project." He wanted to be her equal. Someone she trusted and shared herself with—and he would show her he could be that person. That he *was* that person.

"I daresay she doesn't see you that way, not if she loves you in return."

"I don't know how she could. I'm a total disaster. Furthermore, she has a life she loves here in London. There's nothing I could offer her at Stonehill that she could want."

Glastonbury shook his head. "Except *you*. Perhaps you are a dolt. I jest." He gave Max a plaintive look. "Can I give you some advice? Well, I'm going to anyway. Don't think that you can't possibly deserve her—that's not up to you. That's her decision, and she will likely surprise you."

Max was always going to be afraid of losing her—he was fairly certain that was part of him now after Lucia. But letting Ada go was worse. He had to stop *letting* things happen. He wanted her. He loved her. And he damn well needed to tell her so.

He turned to Lucien, who shrugged. "I don't know that she'd leave the Phoenix Club. But if you don't tell her how you feel, you'll never know." His gaze moved to the window. "I think your coach just arrived."

"Good." Max pivoted toward Glastonbury. "Where on the Thames did they go?"

"To the Horse Ferry to take a wherry. They are going to Somerset House, where a coach will meet them."

Max didn't have gloves or a hat, but he didn't care. "Lucien, keep Arrow for me until I return."

"Don't hold anything back, Warfield!" Glastonbury called after him.

Waving his hand in response, Max dashed out the door and ran to the coach. "Og, to the Horse Ferry with the utmost haste."

"What the devil?"

"Hurry!" Max climbed into the coach and slammed the door. A moment later, they were on their way.

Instead of fear, he felt hope. Whatever happened, this was right. It was what he needed to do.

He'd certainly been an idiot last night. She'd been so distraught. And that had been due to her own fear that he would reject her if he knew the truth about her affair with her married employer.

She'd been right to be afraid. He *had* rejected her. He'd used it as an excuse to assuage his own fear.

He hated that he'd hurt her. After everything she'd done for him, all the ways in which she'd guided him from the dark, he'd pushed her aside. She deserved far better. She deserved everything.

Ada was a light, and whenever he was with her, he felt hope. What had started as a glimmer as she'd worn down his defenses had become a shining beacon. He didn't want to carry on without her. He didn't want to return to the wilderness without her by his side.

She was the star he was meant to follow.

CHAPTER 21

*A*fter a mostly sleepless night, Ada contemplated whether she ought to postpone her wherry adventure. Perhaps today was not the day to conquer her fears. Indeed, today seemed perfect for burying her head beneath the bedclothes and ignoring the world.

Particularly due to the fact that Max was leaving.

But then she'd decided it would be good if she were gone from the club when he left. Then she wouldn't be tempted to run after him and beg him to stay.

Ada went downstairs just before their appointed time of departure for Horse Ferry. Prudence had just arrived and was standing in the entry hall with Evie, their heads bent together, whispering.

"Ready?" Evie asked brightly.

"Yes." Ada followed them outside into the warm summer morning. They were taking Evie's coach, which would then meet them at Somerset House.

Once they were situated—Ada in the rear-facing seat and the others opposite her—Prudence frowned. "Ada, I'm sorry, but you look terrible. And given what we heard last night about the scene in the members' den, I can guess why."

Tears threatened, but Ada didn't think she had any left to shed. "Was the entire club abuzz?" Ada wondered if she'd have to find new employment. Max had made it plain that she had engaged in an affair and gotten with child. Oh, how she'd hoped no one had heard.

Evie looked at her in sympathy. "Not the entire club. It was clear there was a…situation, but the circumstances are not known. *I* can guess, however, because I know all the players."

Prudence knew them too, and Ada could only assume Evie had told her about Jonathan's proposal.

"And now I've heard that Warfield is leaving today," Evie said. "Alone?"

"Whom would he be leaving with?"

"Don't pretend there's nothing between you and him," Prudence said. "We're your closest friends. We know you. We're also quite capable of seeing the both of you and how you interact. It was abundantly clear at Vauxhall that you care for each other. The question I have is how much."

"I love him." Ada turned her head, unable to bear their sympathy another moment. "But you know me, I crave love like a bee needs honey."

"So? That doesn't mean it isn't real."

Ada glanced toward Evie who'd spoken. "I'm doomed to love people I shouldn't or who can't love me in return. Time and time again, I'm reminded I should be alone."

Evie sniffed. "Well, that sounds rather pitiful."

Indeed it did. "I lied to Max about my affair with Jonathan. I left out the part about him being married. I didn't think Max would understand." That was what agonized her the most. Why would she think that? He'd revealed himself to her completely, and she ought to have done the same.

"You mustn't continue to torture yourself," Prudence said softly.

The counsel Ada had given Max on more than one occasion came back to haunt her—guilt was a terrible thing. This was fresh guilt, however. She should have been honest with him as he'd been with her. Now she had to deal with the consequences.

"Did you tell Max the truth?" Evie asked. "Is that why he's leaving today? If so, good riddance. If he loved you, he would understand why you were afraid to tell him."

Ada took a deep breath and pressed her spine against the back of the seat. "This isn't a novel, Evie." She closed her eyes briefly and exhaled. Then she looked at her friends and summoned a smile. "I would like to forget about last night and Max for a while if I can. Today is a monumental day for me, and I would like to focus on overcoming my fear."

Evie and Prudence exchanged a glance, then looked back to her and nodded.

Prudence smiled. "Of course. We only want what's best for you. I would hate to see you hurting."

"I will recover from a slightly broken heart." What an understatement that was. "Anyway, there is no future for Max and me. He is a reluctant viscount with no desire to wed who lives a long day's travel from London. I am a successful, independent woman with a thriving life *in* London. We are completely mismatched."

That made her feel better. Even if she hadn't been a fool to keep the truth from him, he would have left all the same. Perhaps not today, but soon. The circumstances of that parting would actually have been much more painful. This was like removing the thorn at once instead of having to work it from one's flesh.

They arrived at the Horse Ferry and the coachman negotiated their wherry ride. Evie had arranged this because the watermen could be rather aggressive, particularly if there were multiple men vying for their business.

Their waterman was called Gradon. Thick, with muscular arms from rowing, he had a broad smile that showed a missing tooth on the lower right side. "Who's gettin' in first?"

"I will," Evie said, taking his hand as she climbed into the boat from where the stairs met the water.

Prudence went next, and then it was Ada's turn. The boat bobbed in the river, and sweat broke out across Ada's back and beneath her breasts. Perhaps this was a bad idea.

"Come on, Ada. You can do it," Evie encouraged warmly.

"I'm afraid," she blurted to Gradon.

"Oi, there's no need to be afraid," he said cheerfully. "I'm quite good at rowing. Have ye never been on a boat before?"

She could row his boat, but absolutely did *not* want to. "My father was a fisherman."

"Then ye should be an expert! Come on, then." He grabbed her hand and pulled her forward so that she had to step onto the boat.

Ada yelped, clutching him as if her life depended on him. And she supposed it did.

Gradon laughed. "Ye've quite a grip there. I bet ye could row."

"Yes, actually," she murmured, willing herself to breathe.

Evie and Prudence were seated at the back of the small wherry. They held up their hands for Ada.

"Get yerself seated," Gradon said, peeling Ada away from himself.

Ada took two steps and grabbed her friends, who settled her between them. They kept hold of her, each clasping one of her hands.

Prudence smiled encouragingly. "There now, this is fine, isn't it?"

"Just fine." Ada still couldn't take a substantial breath.

Gradon pushed them away from the stairs and, standing at the bow, rowed toward Westminster. The wherry bobbed along the water, and Ada squeezed her friends' hands.

"How long will this take?" she asked tightly.

"Not long," Evie said merrily. "Just enjoy the lovely summer day." She tipped her face up to the sky, smiling in the sunlight.

Ada clenched her teeth. She didn't want to watch Gradon rowing. He looked too precarious standing there as the boat rose and dipped on the water. He could so easily topple into the Thames.

She squeezed her eyes shut as if she could block out the terrible thoughts of what her father might have suffered when his boat went down. No, she wouldn't think about that. Imagining him cold and afraid and...dying never failed to fill her with unparalleled anguish. She felt as if she were the one drowning.

"Don't think about it, don't think about it, don't think about it." She whispered the words over and over.

"Should we have him take us to the nearest water stairs?" Prudence asked softly, her voice thick with concern.

Ada opened her eyes. She refused to be cowed any longer. She could do this.

Looking about, she saw that they were quite a way into the river—not in the center, but much too far away from safety. Other boats moved around them, not too close, but Ada stared, horrified, at the people laughing and chattering. How could they be enjoying themselves?

She swore under her breath. The point was to enjoy the ride. And that didn't just mean this wherry trip. Life was a journey, and if you couldn't seek and find joy, what was the point?

"Stop!" she called out.

"What's that?" Gradon turned his head, pausing his strokes.

"Would you stop for a moment?" She wanted to see if she could just sit in the wherry and become accustomed to the motion of the water. Perhaps she could start to relax a little.

The waterman frowned. "I shouldn't."

"Would it help?" Prudence asked her.

"I think it might and I'd like to try."

"I'll double your fee," Evie said to Gradon. "Just stop for a few minutes so Miss Treadway can acclimate herself. It's terribly important." She flashed him a coquette's smile, her lashes fluttering, and Ada thought Gradon would probably refund their money rather than take twice what they'd already paid.

The waterman smiled dizzily, and for a moment, Ada feared he actually would careen into the river. "For a few minutes." He sat down abruptly, setting the long oar across his lap.

"Ada!"

"Did you hear that?" Prudence asked, looking off into the distance.

"Ada, wait!"

Yes, Ada had heard that. She squinted and saw another boat coming at them. A moment later, she recognized Max. He wasn't wearing a hat.

"Ada, thank goodness I found you."

Now it was Prudence and Evie who gripped Ada tightly.

"Move closer," Max said loudly to his waterman.

The man shook his head, but Ada couldn't hear what he said.

"What the devil is he doing?" Gradon asked, tipping his hat back on his head. "Does he know ye?"

"Yes," Ada answered, her heart swelling. He'd come looking for her. On the river.

"He won't let me come closer!" Max shouted. "Says he'll be fined or something." He sent a glower toward the waterman, and Ada could practically hear him growl. She covered her mouth as she giggled. That was the beast she'd met.

"It's too dangerous for him to come closer," Gradon warned. "He might capsize or take us down with him."

Panic seized Ada's lungs. "Don't come any closer!" she cried.

Even from this distance—which was at least twenty yards—she could see his face fall.

"I love you, Ada," he shouted. "I know you probably don't want to hear that. It certainly wasn't in my plans, but I love you most desperately."

Between her trepidation about being in the wherry and the sudden appearance of the man she'd thought she couldn't have, Ada's heart was racing. He loved her?

He went on, his voice loud and clear across the water. "I was a rotter last night. I don't care what you've done. I won't judge you, just as you haven't judged me." He wiped his hand over his face. "I don't know what I did to deserve that kindness from you, but it saved me completely. I owe everything to you."

Ada raised her voice. "No, you don't. You are so much more than what you've suffered."

"Only because you showed me. You've shone your light and given me the path from the darkness. I know who I want to be. Your husband, if you'll allow it." He knelt in the wherry. "Ada, will you marry me?"

Other boats had gathered—as close as was safe apparently—and the occupants were watching. An eerie silence had fallen.

"This is the most romantic thing I've ever witnessed," Evie murmured.

Prudence beamed. "It's absolutely fitting for Ada."

"But—" Ada struggled to find words.

"I know you have a life here and that you love your position at the club. Perhaps you can remain employed there. I'm sure Lucien will work it out for you. They'd hate to lose you. In fact, you can stay in London, and I'll be with you as much as I can. Once Mrs. Tallent is up to speed at Stonehill—"

Ada cut him off. "Just stop! Yes, I'll marry you." Her stomach flipped, and it had nothing to do with the wherry.

Max suddenly pitched forward into the river. Ada screamed. She launched from her seat to the edge of the wherry, tipping them toward the water.

"Ye daft chit!" Gradon hollered. "Get away from there. Ye're going to send us over."

Ada sprawled backward. "Save him, please!"

"He don't need saving. He's swimming."

Evie helped Ada up before retaking her seat.

Then Max's hand appeared on the side of the boat.

"Bloody hell," Gradon muttered. He gestured Ada and the others. "Get to that side so we don't tip over."

They scrambled to do what he said as Gradon moved to pull Max into the boat. "Ye're an idiot."

Max grinned. "Yes, I am."

Gradon rolled his eyes. "Sit in the middle there and don't move or ye'll unsettle the boat. Ye ladies get to the back."

"Can I sit in the middle with him?" Ada asked, desperate to touch him.

"Be quick about it," Gradon grumbled.

Ada joined Max and immediately put her arms around him—carefully, lest she rock the wherry too much. He embraced her in return, and she became thoroughly damp.

She pulled back in alarm. "How is your shoulder? You should not have done that."

He grimaced. "Probably not. But I'd do it again." He smiled at her and kissed her.

Around them there were shouts and applause.

"You've an enthusiastic audience," Evie said with a laugh.

"I can't believe you followed me here," Ada said.

"I couldn't leave without telling you how I felt and begging you to be my wife. Did you really say yes?"

She nodded. "I love you too. I have for some time. I never imagined you could feel the same about me."

He stared into her eyes, truly perplexed. "Why?"

"I don't know." She shrugged. "I suppose I thought I was destined to be alone, that I wasn't worthy of love or family."

"That could never be true. You make everyone around you feel so special and valued—like family."

She'd never thought of herself like that. She was cheerful and kind, but Max made her sound like someone who was... worthy. "I thought I was meant to be alone, that I deserved to be after all I've done." Apparently, she wasn't as adept at dismissing guilt as she wanted to believe.

"No more than I deserved to live a life of darkness and despair. You showed me that wasn't true, that I could have and be so much more. I just have to work for it instead of hiding away." He caressed her cheek. "Will you let me try to do the same for you? I don't know if I can give you even a fraction of what you've given me—"

She put her finger over his gorgeous lips. "You've already given me more than I dreamed. You've given me the impossible."

She kissed him, heedless of their audience or the wherry or the fact that they were now both quite wet. She didn't care about anything but him and their future together.

~

*M*rs. Renshaw's drawing room was an extremely feminine space, with floral wallpaper and a combination of bold and soft hues. It made Max feel more beastly than usual, or perhaps he was still trying to find his comfort in a group. By the time he and Ada had returned to the Phoenix Club with Prudence and Mrs. Renshaw, the latter had planned a dinner for that evening to celebrate his and Ada's betrothal. Max would have preferred to be alone, but he could see how happy Ada's friends were and wouldn't deny them this occasion. It wasn't even a large group—just Mrs. Renshaw, Prudence, Glastonbury. Lucien and Dougal hadn't yet arrived.

Perhaps his slight anxiety was due to the massive change he'd made today. He was getting married. His gaze found Ada. She stood with Mrs. Renshaw and Prudence, glowing as she'd been since he'd met her in the middle of the Thames.

There was a small voice in the back of his mind that questioned his decision, but Max kept telling it to be quiet. This wasn't what he'd planned, but it was, without debate, what he wanted. He knew better than to expect a quiet mind. He wasn't even sure what that felt like anymore.

"Lord Lucien," the butler intoned as Lucien strolled into the drawing room.

Max frowned. Lucien looked distraught. He was not wearing his usual affable expression, and Max would have expected that given the news of the day. Both Lucien and Glastonbury had been at the club when they'd arrived and had tried to insist on drinking a toast to the betrothal. Max had managed to put them off since both he and Ada were soaking wet and in need of a bath. They'd shared that bath in her chamber.

"Good evening," Lucien said. "I regret to inform you that

Dougal won't be joining us. He's left for Scotland. He received bad news about his brother."

Max approached him and quietly asked, "How bad?" He almost didn't want to know. It reminded him of when he'd learned his father and then his brother had died.

"As bad as you can imagine," Lucien whispered. "There was some kind of accident. Dougal is now the heir."

Struggling to breathe, Max felt as though he'd been hit in the gut. "I'm so sorry for him," he murmured, the pain of his own loss rising to the surface.

Lucien clapped him on the shoulder. "I'm sorry for him and for you."

Ada came to Max's side and put her arm around his waist. "What's wrong? You look distressed."

"Lucien says Dougal's brother has died." At least Dougal still had his father. Max looked to Lucien. "I imagine Dougal will spend some time in Scotland with the earl."

"I would expect that, especially given how close they are."

"I'm so sorry to dampen your evening," Lucien said.

"Not at all," Ada said warmly. "We will keep Dougal in our thoughts."

"He would appreciate that." Lucien looked from her to Max and back to her again. "We should discuss what you proposed earlier."

In the brief time they'd spoken to Lucien before hurrying upstairs to remove their sodden clothing, Ada had expressed her desire to maintain her position at the club. She pivoted toward Lucien, eager to make her case. "I know it will be difficult if I'm not here all the time, but you managed all right for the fortnight I was at Stonehill. I'd be in London during the Season and at least one week a month the rest of the year."

"You've given this a great deal of thought." Lucien sounded pensive.

She nodded. "I love my job, and I'd be very sorry to leave it."

"Does that mean you *would* leave it?" Lucien kept his voice neutral, but Max saw the slight crease in his brow.

"If you're asking whether I'd chose to stay at the Phoenix Club instead of marrying Max, the answer is no. As much as I love working there, I love Max more." She pressed against his side, and he felt as though he might burst with joy.

"Her plan could work," Max said. "What if she hired an assistant to help while she's gone? Surely you know someone, or several someones, in need of employment?"

Ada looked up at Max in adoration. "That's an excellent idea."

Lucien grinned. "Either you two fell hopelessly in love today or you were both incredibly adept at cloaking the depth of your feelings. I suspected you might have a tendre for each other, but it's now painfully obvious you can't seem to draw breath without the other."

"Er, I might have been hiding how I felt," Ada said sheepishly.

Max put his arm around her. "I don't think I fully grasped my emotions. That will happen when you've been avoiding them as long as I have."

"I couldn't be happier for you both. Let me think on the specifics of the club, but you have my support—we'll find a way to keep you entangled. You are far too valuable to let go. Truly, I don't know what we would do without you, Ada." Lucien gave her a proud nod and took himself off.

"Are you relieved?" Max asked.

"Yes. And flattered." Her smile was so bright. "It's nice to feel so wanted."

"You're wanted *and* needed. None of us can function without you."

She narrowed one eye at him. "This is why you're marrying me, isn't it?"

He turned toward her and put his hands on her waist, not caring about the others on the other side of the room. "I'm marrying you because I love you completely—as completely as a fraction of a man can."

She put her hands flat against his chest. "You are not a fraction of a man. Indeed, I sometimes think you are more man than I can manage."

Laughter bubbled from his chest, and it was the loveliest sensation. "There is nothing you can't manage."

"If you say so." She smiled up at him, probably not meaning to be seductive but provoking lustful thoughts just the same.

"I do. I have not yet thanked you for finding Arrow. I took a short ride late this afternoon and it was as if we'd never been parted. I don't know why I let him go. I suppose I thought it would be less painful."

"That sounds familiar," she murmured. "It seems we were both ready to let the other go rather than risk our hearts."

He looked into her eyes and saw the reflection of his immense love for her. "I'm still afraid I'll lose you. Perhaps I always will be. But I will do everything in my power to keep you safe."

"I know. And I'll do the same for you. For the first time in so long, I feel truly connected to someone. I know you won't leave me."

He squeezed her waist and brushed his lips across hers. "Never."

The butler came in to announce dinner, and they reluctantly parted. Max offered her his arm, and they walked downstairs to the dining room.

"I wonder if you might teach me to ride?" Ada asked.

"I should love that. I'll visit Tattersall's to purchase you a mount."

"I suppose you must, given the dearth of livestock in your stables at Stonehill."

"Perhaps I should buy a few horses. Can I afford that? I reviewed the books before I came to London—your work astonishes me—but you know them better than I do."

She laughed softly. "Yes, you can afford them."

"Even after I buy you an enormous and outrageously expensive betrothal ring tomorrow?"

"Well, perhaps it needn't be *outrageously* expensive. Unless you insist." She looked up at him, smiling. "I truly don't need anything grand. All I need is you."

When they were seated, Lucien lifted his glass of wine. "A toast to my very dear friends, Max and Ada. May they always be as happy as they are today—happier even."

A chorus of "Hear, hear," went round the table as everyone raised their glasses.

Joy expanded within Max, and he realized he *was* a whole man, and that Ada had made him that way.

EPILOGUE

Stonehill, October 1815

"*L*ady Warfield!" Mrs. Bundle called as Ada stepped outside to cut a bouquet of what could be the last of their autumn flowers from the garden.

After nearly three months of marriage, she was finally becoming used to her new honorific. Turning with a smile, she greeted the housekeeper, who was thrilled, but harried, to be overseeing the first house party at Stonehill in years. She was also trying to settle the new butler in. Wick had started last month.

"Is aught amiss?" Ada hoped not, but if so, they'd manage. The guests would arrive that afternoon.

"There is a change to the dinner menu. The turbot was bad."

"I trust whatever alteration you need to make." Ada saw the concern in the woman's gaze. "You are doing a marvelous job. Truly."

Mrs. Bundle seemed to relax, her forehead uncreasing. "I don't want you to think I can't manage this sort of event."

"I would never think that. This is the first time Stonehill has supported so many people, and there are a good number of new retainers. None of our friends or family will have any complaints. Nor will his lordship or I."

"Thank you for saying so." Mrs. Bundle glanced toward the basket hanging from Ada's forearm. "Are you gathering flowers? I could have had one of the maids do that. Or, better still, one of the gardeners. I am still getting used to having so many people." She added the last in a wry murmur.

"Aren't we all?" Ada responded with a smile. "I don't mind cutting the flowers myself."

"No, I don't suppose you do." Mrs. Bundle grinned before going back into the house.

Ada turned to the reinvigorated gardens and couldn't help letting out an exhalation of pleasure. There was still much work to be done, but the gardener they'd hired in July had worked wonders in a very short time. He'd had plenty of help with a handful of young men and boys working along-side him. Plus, Ada and Max hadn't been able to keep their hands out of it.

The return of flowers to Stonehill was one of the things Ada was most proud of.

As she strolled to the garden with the late-blooming flowers, she saw Max standing amongst them. He was perhaps the only person more pleased than she by the reha-bilitated gardens.

He looked up as she approached, his gaze raking her from head to toe. His perusal never failed to ignite a heat inside her. She knew it wouldn't cool until he put his hands on her.

"Is that a new gown?" he asked. "It's beautiful on you, but I think it will look even better on the floor of our bedchamber later."

The heat flamed into a conflagration. "If you don't moderate your compliments, later is going to be in five minutes, and we have things to do before the guests arrive." She glided toward him and touched his chest. "Your valet has mastered a new knot, I see."

She'd taken her time to find the right person for Max and had ended up hiring a former batman from the army. He was a few years older than Max, and after two months together, there was no question they were a perfect match.

Mrs. Tallent walked toward them, coming from the direction of her house, which she'd moved into in August when they'd found a tenant for her farm. The new residents were a lovely young couple, newly wed, and eager for the chance to start their life.

"Good morning," the steward said, eyeing the flowers. "These are so stunning. I do love walking past them every day."

"You should have a bouquet for your home," Ada said. "Any time you'd like to take some cuttings, you must."

"Thank you. I shall keep that in mind." She looked to Max. "Do you still have time to discuss the repairs to the mill?"

"I would make time, even if I didn't. I'll be in shortly."

Mrs. Tallent nodded, then took herself toward the house. She often worked in Max's study, which had shocked Ada at first. That had been such a sacrosanct place when she'd first arrived at Stonehill. Max had come so very far, though he still had a great distance to go.

"I suppose you must go," Ada said, effecting a faux pout.

"Yes, but my offer to decorate the floor of our bedchamber with your garments still stands. Meet me in an hour?" He gave her such a charming, seductive stare that Ada couldn't have said no even if she'd wanted to.

And she really should.

But she absolutely would not.

"I shall count the minutes." She stood on her toes and brushed her lips against his cheek.

He captured her waist and claimed her lips, kissing her soundly and driving her to complete breathlessness. "I must be off, but I won't be long—we could probably say thirty minutes. Mrs. Tallent is highly capable. She hardly needs my help." Releasing Ada, he started toward the path. "Hiring her may have been the best decision you've ever made."

Ada disagreed. "Better than marrying you?" she asked coyly.

"Most definitely." He waggled his brows in a playful manner that was so unlike the cranky ogre she'd first met. "You may still live to regret that."

She laughed gaily, her heart overflowing with love. "Impossible."

Now that Dougal MacNair is heir to the Earl of Stirling, he has less time to serve his country as a spy. However, he has at least one more mission: to train a new operative, an intellectual lady with a fiercely independent streak. Find out what happens when they have to pretend to be married in IRRESISTIBLE, the next book in the Phoenix Club series!

Would you like to know when my next book is available and to hear about sales and deals? **Sign up for my VIP newsletter** which is the only place you can get bonus books and material such as the short prequel to the Phoenix Club series, INVITATION, and the exciting prequel to Legendary Rogues, THE LEGEND OF A ROGUE.

Join me on social media!

Facebook: https://facebook.com/DarcyBurkeFans
Twitter at @darcyburke
Instagram at darcyburkeauthor
Pinterest at darcyburkewrite

And follow me on Bookbub to receive updates on pre-orders, new releases, and deals!

Need more Regency romance? Check out my other historical series:

The Untouchables
Swoon over twelve of Society's most eligible and elusive bachelor peers and the bluestockings, wallflowers, and outcasts who bring them to their knees!

The Untouchables: The Spitfire Society
Meet the smart, independent women who've decided they don't need Society's rules, their families' expectations, or, most importantly, a husband. But just because they don't need a man doesn't mean they might not *want* one...

The Untouchables: The Pretenders
Set in the captivating world of The Untouchables, follow the saga of a trio of siblings who excel at being something they're not. Can a dauntless Bow Street Runner, a devastated viscount, and a disillusioned Society miss unravel their secrets?

Matchmaking Chronicles
The course of true love never runs smooth. Sometimes a little matchmaking is required. When couples meet at a house party, what could go wrong?

Wicked Dukes Club

Six books written by me and my BFF, NYT Bestselling Author Erica Ridley. Meet the unforgettable men of London's most notorious tavern, The Wicked Duke. Seductively handsome, with charm and wit to spare, one night with these rakes and rogues will never be enough...

Love is All Around

Heartwarming Regency-set retellings of classic Christmas stories (written after the Regency!) featuring a cozy village, three siblings, and the best gift of all: love.

Secrets and Scandals

Six epic stories set in London's glittering ballrooms and England's lush countryside.

Legendary Rogues

Five intrepid heroines and adventurous heroes embark on exciting quests across the Georgian Highlands and Regency England and Wales!

If you like contemporary romance, I hope you'll check out my **Ribbon Ridge** series available from Avon Impulse, and the continuation of Ribbon Ridge in **So Hot**.

I hope you'll consider leaving a review at your favorite online vendor or networking site!

I appreciate my readers so much. Thank you, thank you, *thank you*.

ALSO BY DARCY BURKE

Historical Romance

The Phoenix Club

Improper

Impassioned

Intolerable

Indecent

Impossible

Irresistible

Impeccable

Insatiable

The Matchmaking Chronicles

The Rigid Duke

The Bachelor Earl (also prequel to *The Untouchables*)

The Runaway Viscount

The Untouchables

The Bachelor Earl (prequel)

The Forbidden Duke

The Duke of Daring

The Duke of Deception

The Duke of Desire

The Duke of Defiance

The Duke of Danger

The Duke of Ice

The Duke of Ruin

The Duke of Lies

The Duke of Seduction

The Duke of Kisses

The Duke of Distraction

The Untouchables: The Spitfire Society

Never Have I Ever with a Duke

A Duke is Never Enough

A Duke Will Never Do

The Untouchables: The Pretenders

A Secret Surrender

A Scandalous Bargain

A Rogue to Ruin

Love is All Around

(A Regency Holiday Trilogy)

The Red Hot Earl

The Gift of the Marquess

Joy to the Duke

Wicked Dukes Club

One Night for Seduction by Erica Ridley

One Night of Surrender by Darcy Burke

One Night of Passion by Erica Ridley

One Night of Scandal by Darcy Burke

One Night to Remember by Erica Ridley

One Night of Temptation by Darcy Burke

Secrets and Scandals

Her Wicked Ways

His Wicked Heart

To Seduce a Scoundrel

To Love a Thief (a novella)

Never Love a Scoundrel

Scoundrel Ever After

Legendary Rogues

Lady of Desire

Romancing the Earl

Lord of Fortune

Captivating the Scoundrel

Contemporary Romance

Ribbon Ridge

Where the Heart Is (a prequel novella)

Only in My Dreams

Yours to Hold

When Love Happens

The Idea of You

When We Kiss

You're Still the One

Ribbon Ridge: So Hot

So Good

So Right

So Wrong

ABOUT THE AUTHOR

Darcy Burke is the USA Today Bestselling Author of sexy, emotional historical and contemporary romance. Darcy wrote her first book at age 11, a happily ever after about a swan addicted to magic and the female swan who loved him, with exceedingly poor illustrations. Join her Reader Club newsletter for the latest updates from Darcy.

A native Oregonian, Darcy lives on the edge of wine country with her guitar-strumming husband, incredibly talented artist daughter, and imaginative son who will almost certainly out-write her one day (that may be tomorrow). They're a crazy cat family with two Bengal cats, a small, fame-seeking cat named after a fruit, an older rescue Maine Coon with attitude to spare, and a collection of neighbor cats who hang out on the deck and occasionally venture inside. You can find Darcy at a winery, in her comfy writing chair balancing her laptop and a cat or three, folding laundry (which she loves), or binge-watching TV with the family. Her happy places are Disneyland, Labor Day weekend at the Gorge, Denmark, and anywhere in the UK—so long as her family is there too. Visit Darcy online at www.darcyburke.com and follow her on social media.

facebook.com/DarcyBurkeFans

twitter.com/darcyburke

instagram.com/darcyburkeauthor

pinterest.com/darcyburkewrites

goodreads.com/darcyburke

bookbub.com/authors/darcy-burke

amazon.com/author/darcyburke

Made in the USA
Monee, IL
27 February 2023